A NEW LOVE

"A man only has to look at you to know there's no other place he would rather be," Bren whispered, moments before his forefinger dropped to Latisha's lower lip and began to rub the soft flesh persuasively.

"Bren . . ." Her mouth quivered beneath his touch. She wanted to protest, but her heart was pounding so madly, Latisha feared she would faint.

"Don't say anything," he drawled softly. His forefinger now on her chin, he tilted her face upward. "Don't think anything. Just let me kiss those tears away."

Transfixed, Latisha met his gaze and positively felt herself swoon as her eyes closed. Bren grasped her lips and in one swift movement, took sensual control. His kiss was sweetly bruising and deeply provocative, enlivening something deep inside Latisha that had once felt wounded, but was now shaking with emotional healing. Bren's tempting, pulsing lips skimmed over every inch of soft, wet tissue, transferring something inexplicably tender, until they met with the tip of Latisha's tongue. His eyes closed. He savored the electric breath that passed between them, then stopped. Latisha gasped. The sudden loss of warmth, of intimacy, of closeness, left her equally as moved as it did Bren Hunter.

One More Chance

Sonia Icilyn

ARABESQUE
BET
BOOKS

BET Publications, LLC
http://www.bet.com
http://www.arabesquebooks.com

ARABESQUE BOOKS are published by

BET Publications, LLC
c/o BET BOOKS
One BET Plaza
1900 W Place NE
Washington, D.C. 20018-1211

All Kensington Titles, Imprints, and Distributed Lines are available at special quantity discounts for bulk purchases for sales promotion, premiums, fund-raising, and educational or institutional use. Special book excerpts or customized printings can also be created to fit specific needs. For details, write or phone the office of the Kensington special sales manager: Kensington Publishing Corp., 850 Third Avenue, New York, NY 10022, attn: Special Sales Department, Phone: 1-800-221-2647.

First Printing: October 2004
10 9 8 7 6 5 4 3 2 1

Printed in the United States of America

For Parissa, my pride and joy

One More Chance

Chapter One

"Latisha, what's going on?" the voice on the other end of the cell phone pleaded, sounding worried and concerned.

"Chaos," Latisha Fenshaw spat angrily into the mouthpiece. She sat on a deck chair in the garden that overlooked Long Island Sound along the Westchester County shoreline in New York. But the sky was overcast and there was a slight chill in the April air. Both were a clear reflection of her mood. "I found out yesterday," she continued to explain. "In the car. We were driving along and then he came out with it. *He's married.*" Her last two words were uttered in an escalating crescendo.

"Oh, Latisha," her sister groaned, the shock resonating in her voice, despite the long distance between them. Josette was in the Bahamas, enjoying two weeks of sun, sand, and sea with her boyfriend of two years. She hardly expected to hear such news about her older sister, which put a damper on her fun. "Where are you now?"

"At the house in the States," Latisha confided, staring forlornly at a small boat in the distance. "He said I could keep it . . . a sort of compensation. He's decided to go back to his wife." It was only then—when she heard herself say it—that the first tear of the day threatened to fall. "Josette, what am I going to do? I'm really hurt."

"Who wouldn't be?" Josette sympathized. "The man lied, cheated, and committed adultery to wiggle his way into your life."

"I feel so humiliated," Latisha added.

"It wasn't your fault," Josette quickly told her in an angry tone, offering another perspective on such awful situation. "You didn't know."

"Right, I didn't," Latisha agreed, as a fresh bout of tears glazed her coppery brown eyes. "I gave him my loyalty and trust . . . and he hadn't earned it."

"Don't beat yourself up," Josette quickly advised. "You didn't do anything wrong. Graham Jefferson is a gutless swine and he'll just end up cheating again on his wife with someone else."

"I shared a bed with this man," Latisha moaned, as a quick flash of the torrid memory tormented her. "Eleven months," she mused aloud. "Nearly a year, and for what?"

"At least he gave you the house in Rye," Josette reminded her, as a bolt of static coursed through the phone. "Are you still there?"

"I'm here," Latisha answered.

"He gave you the deed, right?"

"Yes." Latisha nodded to herself, aware that the nineteenth-century farmhouse that she had shared with Graham, which epitomized the architecture of rural New England, was worth somewhere in the region of half a million. "That's what I can't understand," she related to her sister. "It's the way he gave it to me. He had the deed right there in his briefcase and just handed it over . . . like it didn't mean anything."

"Oh?"

"And then he apologized for the pain he'd caused. He said it wasn't intentional and that in time I would find someone else."

"And he's right," Josette added reassuringly. "At least he cared enough to make sure you had someplace to live."

"Josette, I'm so confused," Latisha admitted finally, her brain so numb it still refused to make the right connections. "Did that man ever like me or was our eleven months together all a lie?"

"Latisha—"

"I mean, he knew all the facts," Latisha broke in. "He was in control all along. He knew exactly what he was doing. I'm not easily fooled, not by anyone," she insisted, as though she needed to hear herself say it—especially since for the last two years she had been on a mission of self-discovery that had helped her reconstruct a new sense of direction in her work and personal life.

"Of course you're not easily fooled," Josette agreed. "You're a woman of vision and focus."

"He's given me an education on men that I'll never forget," Latisha seethed. "I have always pursued my goals and have rarely been led astray. So how did I come to be with someone who was so deceitful?"

"He was a dirty rat," Josette spat out, more than aware of her sister's distress. "Why don't you come out to the Bahamas and stay with me and Steadman?" she offered. "There's nothing like a bit of sun to help you get over a broken heart."

Latisha briefly thought about it. "No," she said

finally. "You enjoy your holiday. I need time alone to get through this. I'll tell you everything when I see you, okay?"

"Don't do anything I wouldn't do," Josette warned.

"Like cutting something up?" Latisha seethed, as she felt a salty tear curl her upper lip. "It's not the leather in Graham's new Bentley that I want to get my scissors on. Rather it's a certain part of his anatomy that he keeps in his underpants."

"Ouch." Josette winced, as more static made her voice crackle into Latisha's ear. "Can you still hear me?"

"You're breaking up," Latisha answered. The battery on her own mobile was low and her sister was beginning to sound far away. "I have to go," she said bitterly. "I'll call you tomorrow."

The phone clicked off and Latisha found herself alone once more, staring at the waters of the sound and the sailor who was steering his small boat farther away from the bay. She gave a faint sigh. No matter how often she tried, she just could not get out of her head the events that had unfolded in the last twenty-four hours. *Graham Jefferson married!* she thought. The revelation was still with her, shaking her to the very core.

Her first reaction had been to burst into tears. Her second was that it was damn lucky that Graham was driving the car. If he hadn't been, there was no telling what she would have done to him. The thought of stabbing him came to mind—right through the heart. After all, Latisha told herself, Graham couldn't possibly have one. But tears were all she could manage.

She could still recall Graham's face. His cowardly expression, his milksop green eyes, the poltroon gaping of his mouth, and the lame excuses he had tried to give her were a testament to his yellow-bellied character.

She had thought dating a professional Caribbean man would have been different from the laid-back, unambitious men she had grown to know in her twenty-seven years, but he was no different. No different at all. Men were men.

It was only seven months ago, at a family wedding, that her own cousin Bertram had boasted that the male genes were set to mate at the first opportunity. It was not a question of culture, he had explained, but that all men were considered the weaker sex, not as evolved as their female counterpart. And in these modern times, women were winning. Latisha was appalled when Bertram suggested that the only thing a woman should expect to get was perhaps ten years before a man's animal nature, natural instinct, and attraction to other women would make him move on.

In her case, Graham had lasted only eleven months. She wondered what Bertram would make of that. Latisha could almost hear his voice now. "Graham wasn't programmed for the long haul, plus he's already married." There was that awful word again. *Married!*

Latisha was so shaken by it she rose from the deck chair and began to pace the lawn. Anger made her cold cheeks flush with color as she once again recalled the humiliating scene in the car. The grass was nicely trimmed, but chilly beneath her bare feet. She suddenly realized that she was still dressed in her nightgown and was thankful that the brushed cotton against her skin felt warm and soothing.

She wanted to cry again, but something inside refused to allow the tears to fall. *He doesn't deserve one teardrop,* Latisha told herself. Not anymore. Then she felt her anger well up and she began furiously pacing the lawn, recalling in her mind how she had argued with Graham. They had driven back to the house. Though this tranquil place did not seem nearly so tranquil the night before when she had stormed inside, venting like a woman scorned.

Tears had fallen then, as she screamed and hollered. "I asked you if you were married when we met," she had reminded him. "Three times—especially since you're thirty-five—and you told me no!"

"I didn't want to lose you," he responded.

"But you must have known I would find out eventually?"

"Not necessarily."

Then it suddenly dawned on her. "I met your family." And she had. They lived in Boston and were delighted that Graham had found such a gorgeous British beauty. She had stayed for dinner and listened to them prattle on about her accent, her slim figure, her good looks, and that they had never met a woman like her before. She had promised to visit again. "I met your sisters. Your mother made me tea!" She spat out the words with incredulous anger.

"Ma was being polite, for me," Graham divulged in a sheepish tone.

"She collaborated in your deceit?" Latisha said, choked with rage.

"She knew I was having problems with Amelika."

"Ameli . . . who?"

"Amelika . . . my wife."

"Oh God." Her voice was so muffled Latisha sat down.

She then learned that his wife worked in Montserrat at an orphanage after a volcanic eruption that destroyed many homes and lives on the island. They had been married eight years and had argued about having children of their own. His wife did not care to have any, having seen so much suffering in her life. But he did. And in a fit of determination, she had chosen to work in the Caribbean in an attempt to save what they had. The distance did not separate their love. He would fly out to see her and she, in turn, would fly to see him. It was a long-distance marriage that was working quite well until Graham met her.

"So you see," he had added for effect, "I couldn't lie to you anymore. I like to be honest."

"Honest!" It was hard for Latisha to calm down. "You're eleven months and three days too late to be honest. Do you even know what the word means?" Then curious bits of information began to take shape. "That explains the timing of gaps in our relationship when you were away on 'business trips,' " she acknowledged, as the jigsaw began to fit together. "You were with your wife."

Wife! Latisha blinked and dismissed the thought. She did not want to recall another moment, at least not now. Her watch dial read 10:44 A.M. and she still hadn't eaten breakfast. In fact, she had not eaten since hearing Graham's confession, after which just getting out of bed that morning had seemed almost impossible. Latisha knew she was still struggling with the idea. She was still in some sort of emotional time warp and was finding it very hard to think straight at all.

But there had been an upside to all of it. In his profound guilt, Graham had given her the 1834 converted horse stable and barn in Rye, surrounded by two acres of rugged countryside that was now the eight-bedroom house of her dreams. Latisha briefly glanced at it before deciding to head inside. She went straight to the living room and busied herself building a log fire. The three-story stone fireplace was the main feature of the room, as were the huge andirons that dated back to the 1850s. Latisha loved this room. She loved the house. The first things she had noticed on her initial visit were the copper and glass awnings over the front door before a look inside made her fall in love with the house's other nineteenth-century charms.

The fire was roaring nicely when she finally sat on the Navajo rug in front and hugged her knees. The room's original wide-plank wood floors felt hard beneath her bottom, even with the rug as a buffer, but Latisha did not care. It was Saturday, a quiet day, and she was in her favorite place, in front of the fireplace, warm and safe. It was here she hoped to find the right frame of mind to reflect. Looking back on how she had been misled and tricked in an eleven-month affair by a phony who actually believed he was good enough for her, Latisha felt the shame of having ever cared for Graham.

She saw her faults, saw her flaws, and wished

she had not been so transparent. She should never have believed everything he had told her. She should never have jumped into a relationship with him so quickly. She now realized Graham was the kind of guy who believed that a woman should be told only what she needed to know. That she should not worry about what she did not know. That she should only concern herself with what was being done for her and concentrate less on what was not being done.

Only a fool would have involved his own mother. The eighty-seven-year-old woman of mixed heritage, originally from Guadeloupe, who did not look a shade over sixty. With her smiling gray eyes and blue-rinsed hair, she had been overly polite in her soft French-accented voice, just like Graham. *Call me Constance*, Latisha thought, her mind tormented. His mother had been complicit in the elaborate, underhanded trickery of her son's seduction. Was this really how the rich acted? Latisha was now convinced it was. Graham would soon inherit his father's company on the small Caribbean island where he had been born, and then there would be no time for sincerity with anyone.

Latisha's face creased and frowned, and she hugged her knees more tightly, trying to comfort herself with the one truth she now knew: she had been naive, a mere simpleton in a master game that was full of hidden agendas and lies. She knew this now, having met a handful of Graham's friends. They had not bothered to inform her of Graham's marital status. Not one person seemed concerned about what Amelika Jefferson would think either. His wife was the woman, after all, who was really being cheated on and hurt.

I have to forgive myself for this, Latisha resolved silently. *If I don't, I'll surely go mad.* Even so, she wondered how she could possibly reassemble her life, having built her dreams around one unworthy man. He had been her hero. She had even imagined their future together—a lifetime of love, children, and financial security. But it was not to be. Because her Graham, the man with the adoring green eyes, beige complexion, dark brown hair speckled with gray, and the most kissable lips she had so far encountered, was *married*.

That one word was still bouncing around in her head when Latisha felt a sensation run down her spine. It happened the moment she heard a noise at the front door. It sounded like someone putting a key in the lock and she quickly rose to her feet, anticipating Graham's arrival.

Latisha looked at her watch, alarmed that it was now 8:30 in the evening. She had spent the whole day in front of the fire, recalling everything that had happened in her mind. A quick glance through the window and she realized it had grown dark. Now her heart skipped a beat as the sound of the lock being turned echoed around the room. Her pulse raced when she heard the front door open and someone enter.

Latisha was rooted to the spot. Her pride forbade her to rush into the hallway and into Graham's arms. He was the only other person who had a key to the house. It hadn't occurred to Latisha that Graham might possibly want a reconciliation. Or did he? She inhaled deeply in a desperate attempt to calm herself. She would not

make things easy for him. After all, he had betrayed her. It would not be so easy for him to turn
on the charm again. She would not fall for his
puppy-dog gaze, or that little sparkle that lit up
in his eyes whenever he looked at her. And she
would not jump into bed with him either.

If anything, their affair had hardened her in
that department. It was true that whatever they
had shared between the sheets was also a lie. The
intimacy had not been real. There was never any
genuine love there. She had hugged and kissed a
man who simply abused her trust. When Latisha
heard the slow footsteps make their way toward
the living room where she was standing in front
of the fire, shaking with emotion, she was determined that Graham Jefferson would never worm
his way back into her life again.

To her astonishment, the man who turned the
corner around the hallway and stood before her
in the living room was not Graham. Latisha had
never set eyes on him before. She knew it even
before the stranger raised his eyes and looked at
her. A thick black Afro, cut close to his scalp.
Cool pewter-colored eyes stared straight at her in
curiosity with a somewhat pensive look as if
poised for attack.

"Who are you?" he demanded, pausing to cast
a piercing look at her.

His voice was deep, smooth as silk, but with an
edge that rubbed against her frazzled nerves. He
had a haughty, square-jawed face, skin as brown
as nutmeg, with high, angularly shaped cheekbones and a long, straight patrician nose. He was
handsome, in a plain sort of way, though the
overriding impression was of strength and deter-

mination and an incredible will to succeed. Her hand automatically went to her chest where she clutched her nightgown, grabbing the soft brushed cotton fabric between her fingers in the protective fashion of a woman who felt undressed.

"I was about to ask you the same question," she said flatly. He must be someone sent by Graham, she thought. Probably one of his informal group of friends, she thought, who was gently persuaded to check in on her to see if she was all right. But Graham had nerve giving the man a key. What did he take her for exactly—a woman on the verge of suicide?

"Did Graham send you?"

The man kept his eyes on her. "Who?"

Latisha sighed, noticing that beneath the expensive fine navy-colored wool of his tailored suit, extremely powerful muscles seemed ready to burst forth. "Graham Jefferson," she told her intruder, realizing that something seemed to have happened to her voice. Her vocal cords sounded as though someone had grated chalk against a blackboard. "I assume that's why you're here."

"Look, lady." His dark brows knitted in polite annoyance, while he took note of the young, nubile woman in front of him, who could easily distract any man. "I don't know a Graham Jefferson. Never met the guy. All I know is that this is my house and you're trespassing."

"*Your* house!" Latisha gulped.

"Yes, *my* house." He nodded. And with that, he placed a slim titanium briefcase on the woodplank floor by his feet.

"I think there's been some sort of mistake," Latisha informed him immediately, clasping her nightgown even tighter as she caught the full heat of the stranger's expression. "You see, I live here."

He raised his hands slightly. "No, ma'am, you don't," came his quick reply, his eyes mocking her subtly. "And if you don't leave now, I'm going to call the police."

Latisha eyed him warily. "The *police!*"

"To escort you off my property."

"Now look here," Latisha said firmly, aware that there was a peculiar tingling feeling in the pit of her stomach, half fascination and half fear. "I don't know who you are or how you came by a key to get in here, but—"

"Lady," the man continued in a much firmer tone, "I'm gonna count to three, then—"

"What?" Latisha challenged, deciding that the stranger must be insane. Her nerves were twitching like a squirrel when he inched toward her. Though she was alarmed, Latisha was aware he held no weapon. Still, it did not stop her from quickly reaching for the poker by the fireplace and brandishing it defensively in front of him. "Don't move," she warned.

He took a step forward and held up both hands in surrender. "I'm not going to hurt you," he said calmly.

He looked directly into her eyes and something in his expression—something fleeting, something dark and intriguing—made Latisha's pulse flicker, half in trust and half in sheer exhilaration. "I'll use it," she threatened.

He took another step forward. "Put the poker down and let's see if we can straighten this out."

"No," Latisha said, tightening her grip on the poker, the vestiges of that strange sensation shimmering through her like the effects of a heat wave. "I'm ordering you to leave."

"Look," he snapped, annoyed. "I'm calling the police."

And as quick as a flash, he was taking large strides toward the telephone that was situated out of view on a table by the window. There was something familiar about the way he picked up the handset that made Latisha take note immediately. This man knew where the phone was located and he did not seem nervous about punching in the relevant numbers for the police.

"Wait a minute," she said, slowly. "You've been here before."

"Of course I have," he said, blithely.

Latisha slowly lowered the poker. Her stomach gave way to an unpleasant realization.

"Who are you?"

He replaced the handset in the cradle and faced her. "The name's Bren Hunter. I live here. And before you ask how I can prove it . . ." He looked up. "Those ceiling beams with the tree bark are made of tree trunks from the backyard. The kitchen used to be a chicken coop. Now it has a heated terra-cotta floor above a wine cellar that's storing 150 bottles of French vintage red. The work surfaces have been crafted from excavated Stoney Creek granite, and the kitchen table was made locally from two-hundred-year-old wood."

Latisha was sharp enough to know that Bren

Hunter had described everything to perfection. "I . . . I don't understand," she said, feeling totally lost. "You see, my ex-lover gave me this house as a gift."

Bren managed a careless laugh. "Graham Jefferson?"

"Yes." Latisha nodded, knowing in her heart something was most definitely wrong.

"Where did you meet this man?"

"At the Caribbean Expo last year, here in New York," Latisha explained. "He gave me the deed to this house to prove transfer of ownership."

"The deed!" Now Bren Hunter seemed completely shocked. He began to make his way toward her. "Lady, I'm sorry," he began, not looking the least bit sorrowful. "You've been had. My name is on the mortgage to this house at Chase Manhattan bank. I've got ten years left to pay on it. And as far as I know, the bank still has my deed."

"But . . ." The breath was knocked out of her. Latisha immediately took refuge in one of the hand carved wooden chairs situated close to the fire. She needed to think, and quickly. "I . . . I'm not clear what has happened."

"Do you have a photograph or anything to identify this man?" Bren inquired curiously.

"Yes, I do." Latisha rose abruptly to her feet. "In my handbag upstairs."

"Can I see?"

"Sure. I'll be right back."

Latisha could not get up the stairs fast enough. Rushing into the master bedroom that was formerly a hayloft and that was now cleverly partitioned using windows, she reached for her blue leather handbag by the ottoman, then plucked the only picture she had of Graham from it. Reaching for her cotton robe, she hurriedly put it on, catching sight of her reflection in the bedroom mirror.

It revealed a woman whose hazelnut-brown complexion seemed pale and ashen. Damp strands of glossy black hair hung limply around her shoulders, making her oval face seem older and her tired, tearstained, copper-colored eyes more drawn than usual. Her slender, almost fragile body beneath her bedclothes could not be seen, but the drooping of her shoulders was evident, as was the forlorn expression on her face. In all honesty, Latisha had never seen herself look so bad, such was the effect of Graham's devastating news. Now, as she made her way back downstairs, her stomach was churning in anticipation of what would happen next.

Bren Hunter was seated in one of the cream-colored armchairs with one leg bent at the knee and propped over the other when Latisha arrived in the living room. Lounging back in the chair, he had removed his jacket and shoes and had a drink in his hand, sipping it slowly. He looked at home— the master of his domain. He turned as Latisha came back into the room. With the crook of his finger, he loosened his very expensive-looking tie before he grabbed the small color snapshot from her.

"I've mixed you a drink," Bren told her, taking the picture and indicating with a nod of his head.

Latisha leaned forward and picked up a glass from the nearby table, noting again Bren Hunter's voice—silky smooth with a faint rasp just beneath the surface. "Thank you." Her own voice sounded suddenly raspy. No doubt, sprinting down all those stairs, she told herself.

Then Bren Hunter was out of his seat. "Clayton!"

Latisha almost dropped her glass. "Who?"

"Alan Clayton!" Bren raged.

"No." Latisha shook her head incredulously, as a strange sense of foreboding shot through her system. "That's Graham Jefferson."

"That's the name he gave you?" Bren probed hotly.

Latisha was weakened. "Yes."

Bren was furious. "This is the man who——" He saw Latisha's tears and became aware of her shaking body and quickly chose to remove the glass from her trembling fingers. "You'd better sit down." Urging her to where he had been seated, Bren glanced at her closely. "Are you all right?"

"No," Latisha admitted, her fingers plucking at a loose strand of hair near her left ear. She sucked in a hollow breath, as though a clenched fist had been rammed into her midriff. Her voice was choked with emotion. "He *lied* about his name?"

Bren gulped down his drink and slammed the glass hard onto the table. Still holding the one he had mixed for Latisha, he began to pace the room like a restless animal. "How long has he been in my house?" he demanded.

Latisha was dazed. "What?"

"How long?"

"I don't know." She sounded muffled.

"Well, how long has he been bringing you here?" he questioned harshly.

"A few months."

"Months?"

"My first visit, the fifth of July," she mumbled, "last year."

"Not the Fourth, Independence Day?" he asked.

"No," Latisha said, her voice almost a whisper. "Then again on Halloween. We roasted marshmallows and chestnuts in front of the fire."

"Bastard!"

Latisha's lips began to tremble. "Mr. Hunter . . . you're scaring me."

"And what else?" he demanded, his pacing growing in speed.

"The second of January. I flew over from England to be with him."

Bren's footsteps paused momentarily. "Flew over?"

"He wanted us to visit Times Square," Latisha said, weakened.

"And you were stupid enough to undertake, at your own personal expense, the journey across the Atlantic?" Bren snapped, amazed.

"I planned on using the trip to also visit my sister," Latisha replied tearfully.

"And you came the second of January, not on New Year's Eve?"

"No."

"And what else?" Bren insisted.

"The day after Valentine's. I was doing a talk in New York and—"

"A talk?"

"I support a charity there for—"

"So where was he on Valentine's Day?" Bren interrupted.

Latisha felt the eruption of tears brewing. "He must've been with—"

"What else?" Bren pursued.

"He's married," she concluded, on a throaty sob.

The pacing stopped.

Latisha nodded and collapsed in a flurry of tears. "He told me yesterday . . . in the early evening . . . then he gave me the deed and left."

"You didn't know he had a wife?" Bren raged.

"No," Latisha muttered.

"And you didn't check this out before you started seeing him?" Bren asked incredulously.

"Of course I did," Latisha cried, amassing a little pride. "I asked him three times on three separate occasions and he lied."

"But you believed him?"

"There was no reason why I shouldn't." Latisha hiccupped. "I looked his mother right in the eye . . . I met people who knew him. No one clued me in." She paused between tears. "I was dumbstruck when I found out the truth. He deceived me, and everyone around him collaborated on his deceit."

"I guess there's some truth in the saying that a man is measured by the company that he keeps," Bren said, noting Latisha's distress. "And Alan Clayton has some slippery ones at that. Didn't you have an inkling?"

"The relationship was beginning to feel complicated," Latisha confessed between more tears. "It was a long-distance relationship and that was difficult enough, but he always had an excuse when he could not see me."

"An excuse?"

"He'd speak in riddles," she expanded with more hiccups. "He'd phone and say something one day, then deny it the next with an e-mail or a text message. That sort of thing."

"You felt confused?"

"All the time," Latisha strained to explain. "He was always traveling, but he never visited me and if we did rendezvous, it was I who had to visit him. Normally, it would coincide with my work so there were no interruptions in my own schedule."

"Didn't your mother ever tell you that when you're in a relationship and you feel confused, it's very likely the man isn't being straight with you?" Bren asked.

"I have a good mother," Latisha said, weeping, "so don't bring her into this. She isn't responsible for the corrupt way Graham Jefferson . . . I mean Alan . . . Clayton chooses to live his life."

Suddenly, Bren Hunter was in the seat next to her. He handed over the glass. "Drink this." He took a hold of her free hand and held on to it while a faint smile withered on his lips. "You met one of the creepiest animals in the jungle—a heartless one."

"I'm finding this very hard to take in," Latisha said dazedly, swallowing a mouthful of scotch whiskey.

"I don't blame you," Bren revealed, annoyed that he had not found out about Latisha's presence in Alan's life sooner. "He's a cruelly selfish man, and I promise, by the time I'm done, Alan will be paying very dearly for everything he ever did to you."

"Why would you—"

"Let's just say Alan Clayton and I have unfinished business," Bren said sternly. He looked down at her, his lips curving slightly into a thin smile that came nowhere near the hardened steel in his dark pewter-gray eyes. "And I want you to promise me something."

Latisha could hardly speak. "What?"

"Please believe that not all men are like him," he told her in earnest. "There are men in this world who say what they mean and act on what they say. He is *not* one of them. He's no longer of any use to you."

"His time is over." Latisha nodded. "You've been very . . . tolerant and kind. . . ." Such was her grief, she could hardly speak.

"Look," Bren advised, sensitive to Latisha's predicament. "I don't want you to worry. I'm not going to throw you out."

"I have a sister in Florida," Latisha told him, sadly realizing she had no place to stay for now. "Maybe—"

"What you need is rest," Bren said, noting the fast flurry of fresh tears. "Are you in the master bedroom?"

She nodded.

"Okay," Bren acknowledged, seeing the play of emotions on her face. "When I turn in, I'll take one of the spare rooms. We can talk more in the morning."

Latisha was choked. "Thank you." She tried to smile. "You should at least ask a woman her name before she sleeps in your bed."

He tried to smile, too. "So what is the name of the woman who's been sleeping in my bed?"

"Latisha." Her voice was strained with more tears. "Latisha Fenshaw."

"Latisha," he stated sweetly, his voice affirming a soft, sexual appeal. "Finish your drink. It'll help you sleep."

As she pulled the sheets around her body that night, Latisha did not feel so lucky to have received Bren Hunter's generosity. Without knowing it, she had trespassed on his property, invaded his house, taken advantage of his private library, admired his works of art, taken bottles from his wine cellar, wandered up to his attic where she had looked through his telescope across the Long Island Sound, and now she was sleeping . . . in his bed.

She could not understand why he had remained so calm when she had clearly violated his privacy and much of his private property without his consent. But Latisha did not have the energy to contemplate the answers. The trespassing seemed to take second place to the heartbroken way that she was feeling. Alan Clayton had not only infringed upon her affections, he had taken Bren Hunter for a fool, too.

Before closing her eyes, the last thought to torment her mind was an image of the man whom she had known as Graham Jefferson. Latisha wanted the truth—the entire truth. That meant she needed to know everything Bren Hunter knew. And the sooner the better.

Chapter Two

It was another struggle, but Latisha finally made it downstairs. The first thing she saw was a locksmith at the front door, changing the locks. She offered him a nonchalant good morning, then made her way into the kitchen, where she found Bren Hunter making himself a cup of coffee while talking with someone on the telephone. On hearing her footsteps, he swung around.

"Just a minute, Chico," Bren said into the mouthpiece, breaking his concentration to smile at Latisha, his brows raised in surprise. "You're awake." Returning his attention to the phone, he ended the call. Latisha realized that it was 7:30 in the morning, and that Bren had obviously expected her to sleep for much longer, given the circumstances.

"I couldn't sleep," she admitted, taking refuge on a stool, her senses now fully aware of how appealing Bren was. His only clothing was a simple blue cotton towel around his waist. His pectoral muscles and toned abs exuded ultramasculinity.

Bren handed her a cup of coffee, telling himself that she had probably tossed and turned the entire night. It was no different than what he himself had gone through. He had been unable to sleep, too. However, Bren's tormented sleep had more to do with finding such a beautiful woman in his home than anything else. Even now, it felt unreal to him to find her seated in his kitchen. Then he had been ravaged with a mixture of rage and loathing that such a wonderful, decent woman had been toyed with and hurt.

He had no idea what he could say to Latisha to alleviate the pain of what she must be going through. How could any woman bounce back after what she had learned about the man she had trusted her heart to? It was a question that troubled him. More so because in a faithful sort of way he felt he wanted to get to know her. Touch her. Taste her. Lose himself in her. He also understood the impossibility of it, too.

She could never trust a man again. And he did not blame her. Yet, as a man who had made his own mistakes with women and had come to understand the demands required, he felt a certain obligation toward Latisha Fenshaw. With him, he wanted her to feel secure. He doubted very much she would let her guard down, but he felt he should try to make her feel comfortable.

"It's fresh-ground coffee," he informed her, pulling up an adjacent stool and planting himself firmly on it. "You'll feel better if you drink it while it's hot."

Latisha took a sip and immediately felt the invigorating aroma of Colombia's finest, mingled with the pungent scent of Bren's musky aftershave. She felt a sexual response, but was confused. Instead, she kept her mind on the coffee, remembering that Graham, or Alan, also used to make it, no doubt from Bren's stock. She felt a tremor of panic run along her spine at how easily things could change, and so quickly.

"That's a shrewd move," she muttered softly, taking her mind elsewhere for fear of finding herself crying once again. Bren's curious gaze settled on her. "Changing the locks," she added, dipping her head.

"Yeah," Bren agreed, eyeing her closely. "I think I've had enough surprises for one day."

"Did you call the police?" she asked.

Bren looked across at the telephone he had returned to its cradle on the wall. "No. That was someone else who works for me."

"I should give you this," Latisha said, before handing over her copy of the deed Alan had given her.

Bren took it and scanned it carefully. "The weasel," he uttered, noting that it was a well-forged document. After a few seconds, he handed it back. "I don't need this," he told her. "But maybe you'd like to keep it." Seeing her amazement, he added, "In case we need to use it in court."

"Court?" Now Latisha was surprised.

"Breaking and entering, trespassing," Bren explained.

"Would I . . . be involved?" Latisha asked, in a voice that revealed her anxiety. "I mean . . ." She tried to think. "I wouldn't want my career affected by any of this."

Bren's gaze grew curious. "So what are you, a big shot or something?"

"Let's just say I really don't want to jeopardize everything I've worked for so far," Latisha told him.

Bren stared at her for a brief, intriguing moment. Latisha Fenshaw looked truly angelic to him dressed in a long white, tunic-styled cotton dress with a simple collar and short sleeves. No jewelry, a fresh-washed face, and plain pale blue sandals on her feet. Like a bright sunny day in April, she didn't look like a threat to anyone. He would not dream of hurting this woman in any way. On the contrary, she was just the sort of woman he could easily fall for. She looked gorgeous enough for him to make love to.

"Look." His smile widened. "I'm not going to try and talk you into anything, and I certainly don't want to make things worse for you than they already are. If I can deal with Alan Clayton without you, I will. Okay?"

Latisha nodded in relief. "I would prefer that. You see . . ." She paused for breath and to clarify matters in her own mind. "Last night, I did a lot of thinking and I realized I did not feel secure in my relationship with . . . Alan. I also did not feel we had a genuine friendship. I did not feel like he wanted to get to know me as a person, or wanted a future with me. And I certainly did not feel special. I felt unhappy most of the time, isolated and emotionally neglected. It was part-time love. I was nothing to this man and really, there was nothing there for me. I feel more humiliated now than I did last night and . . . I want him punished, but not at my expense. I need to move on from this. I just haven't figured out how."

Bren was sympathetic. "This must be very hard for you," he concluded, leaning forward in his stool, his body language grabbing Latisha's attention. "I thought Alan Clayton would've learned from the last woman he hurt in this way."

Latisha's brow rose and her lashes flickered slightly as her gaze dropped to eye level with the hairs on Bren's chest. She swallowed and looked up to find the deep pool of lust lurking behind Bren's lazily seductive stare. "He's done this before?" she asked.

Bren clenched his teeth, partly to repress the quivering from his angry breathing. "You're a strong woman, Miss Fenshaw. You survived him. No doubt if you saw him again, you could handle the situation quite easily. Perhaps you might even have a conversation with him as though nothing had happened. You hold no malice and that's a good thing. Just cry him out of your system and get on with your life."

Latisha sighed a sultry breath of her own. "I just want to know . . . why me?"

"You mean why he picked on you?" Bren asked. For a moment he looked at her as though uncertain whether to answer her question. Then his expression changed to one of deep understanding. "He was greedy, pure and simple." Bren paused for affect. "You're a pretty face, young, fertile. Alan's forty this year. You made him feel young again."

"Forty!" Latisha gasped. "He told me he was thirty-five." Her breath caught in her throat. "That's another thing . . . he had a birthday last year and didn't spend it with me."

Bren's eyes narrowed on her in curiosity. "Didn't you ever wonder why Alan never shared any important occasions with you, but the day before or after?" he asked.

"Not the day itself?" Latisha finished. "Of course I wondered. I talked to him about it, too. But, like

I told you, he spoke in riddles. Sometimes we even made arrangements and then he would cancel at the last minute. I found him spontaneous on most occasions. If he canceled, he always had an elaborate excuse, mostly to do with his work."

Bren's brow arched. "Which is?"

"He told me he would soon inherit his father's company."

"That's true," Bren agreed, softly. "A shipping yard and marina in Guadeloupe. At the moment, I'm not sure what he does for money."

Goose pimples traveled up and down Latisha's neck as she made an enormous effort to pull herself together. She glanced pointedly at the gold Rolex watch on Bren's wrist—the only other item he was wearing—and wondered whether she had entered the twilight zone. Such information in addition to what she had learned the night before was beginning to leave her feeling overwhelmed once again.

"I need answers," she stuttered, her voice barely audible.

"For closure?" Bren asked, reaching out with one hand to take a hold of hers. He saw the mortified look on Latisha's face and realized this was no laughing matter. "Your life is not a game."

Latisha nodded with embarrassment, though the tingling pleasure of Bren's touch suffused her face.

"I'm afraid Alan Clayton does not see things that way," Bren went on, curling his fingers through hers. "He always had a back door, someone who he could be with when things did not work out with any of his girlfriends. He would go back and forth between the whole lot of them, never making up his mind what or who he really wanted."

"So he's a jerk," Latisha said, sensing the soothing feel of Bren's touch. "He always takes the easy way out?"

Bren nodded.

"Who was his back door?" Latisha asked in disbelief.

"His wife," Bren concluded. "Eventually, even she couldn't handle it."

"You know her?"

Bren nodded again.

Her backbone stiffened. "And?"

"He'll never have a sense of what he wants," Bren said finally. "So you see, he can't give you any answers."

Latisha understood. "He's gone through the back door?"

Bren nodded a third time.

Latisha felt a fresh bout of tears welling up in her eyes. "He was misguided from day one?"

"Alan Clayton never saw one woman at a time," Bren clarified, squeezing Latisha's hand to offer reassurance, more because he enjoyed the sheer pleasure of touching her. "In his world, he's a single guy who happens to be married. He's exclusive to no one."

Latisha placed her coffee cup on the nearby bench and rose from her stool. Feeling the dent in her pride and the drooping of her shoulders, she could hardly breathe. Knowing that the answers had been provided by such a handsome man, Bren Hunter, made hearing the truth even more humiliating and unbearable.

"You must think I'm a complete fool to have a

relationship with a man who ultimately tricked me into accepting a house that wasn't even his to give."

"On the contrary, I don't," Bren informed her slowly, refusing to let go of her hand. "Alan makes it very hard for anyone to see past his smooth, charming exterior to the true rot beneath. And his friends and family are very weak. You just got caught up in his deceitful behavior and you're very lucky to be out of it."

The color of Latisha's copper-brown eyes was lost behind a film of tears. "I've only been here a few times. That's why I don't understand why he gave me the deed. To pacify me, I expect. I don't understand what he wanted from me."

Bren eyed her, confused. "Sex."

"Then why do I feel so . . ." The tears fell once again in a flurry.

Within seconds, Bren rose to his feet and Latisha felt strong, consoling arms encircle her body. The strength of a new man was against her. She felt Bren's physical impact the moment he embraced her. It was instant and instinctive. Tucked into his body, she felt able to sob without fear, to wash the whole, ugly ordeal out of her body and release the heartache. And Bren did not let her go. He didn't seem embarrassed by how distressed she seemed. It was all too much, too much for one person to absorb in such a short space of time.

"Shhh," Bren whispered in encouraging tones that allowed her to weep knowing that he was there for her. "It's going to be all right."

Latisha believed him. She knew in her heart that she would be fine. She had decided to leave his wonderful home. She could not impose upon his hospitality any longer. What she needed was time alone to get over Alan Clayton.

Finally, Latisha pulled away and felt the soft strokes of Bren Hunter's hand smooth away the strands of stray hair away from her face. Even his warm fingers felt comforting to her, their soft movements against her cheekbones and temple a telling sign that she would be just fine. She swallowed as his gentle motion brushed away the last remnants of spent tears. And then his gaze was on her. Dark, brooding, and mysterious. A forefinger slid down her cheek and rested on her top lip.

The soft flesh trembled at his touch, but the sensation did not stop there. Her whole body felt it, too. It was a sudden tremor that rippled its way all the way down to her groin and back up again. Latisha was startled. This couldn't be happening to her while she was getting over another man. But it was. Suddenly, her gaze was fixed on those dark, brooding, mysterious eyes. Latisha felt unsure of the caring tenderness she saw in them, of the long, lingering, lustful gaze that flickered ever so slightly. She could not trust her own judgment. Yet every inch of her body was aware of the strange connection. A part of her was fascinated. The other part was scared. She did not know what it meant or whether it meant anything.

"Mr. Hunter . . ." Her voice failed as she felt her heart slam into her rib cage.

"A man only has to look at you to know there's no place he would rather be," Bren whispered, moments before his forefinger dropped to her lower lip and began to rub the soft flesh persuasively.

"Bren . . ." Her mouth quivered beneath his touch. She wanted to protest, but her heart was pounding so madly Latisha feared she would faint.

"Don't say anything," he drawled softly. His forefinger now on her chin, he tilted her face upward. "Don't think anything. Just let me kiss those tears away."

Transfixed, Latisha met Bren's gaze and positively felt herself swoon as his eyes closed. Bren grasped her lips and in one swift movement, took sensual control. His kiss was sweetly bruising and deeply provocative, stirring something deep inside Latisha that had once felt wounded, but was now shaking with emotional healing. Bren's tempting, pulsing lips skimmed over every inch of soft, wet tissue, transferring something inexplicably tender, until they met at the tip of Latisha's tongue. His eyes closed. He savored the electric breath that passed between them, then stopped. Latisha gasped. The sudden loss of warmth, of intimacy, of closeness left her moved as it did Bren Hunter.

"Shhh," he whispered a second time. He opened his eyes and saw the wet glistening of tears. But they were no longer tears of sorrow. These were new tears. These were tears that sparkled with a newfound awareness. The kind that only a man can give a woman. "No man is ever going to hurt you again, Miss Fenshaw," he promised. "Now that you've been kissed how you're supposed to be kissed."

Latisha was suddenly dazed, uncertain, and unsure of everything she had gone through. "I should go pack," she muttered, saying the first thing that entered her head as the reality of her situation hit home.

Bren seemed surprised, more by his own response to her, the weakness of his burning flesh, than by his lack of self-control. "You don't need to leave right away."

"Yes, I do," Latisha insisted, aware that her heart had not yet recovered from the pounding it had been subjected to minutes earlier.

"Where will you go?" Bren asked, concerned and seemingly just as dazed.

"To my sister's home in Florida," Latisha explained. "Then back to England."

"You live there?"

She nodded.

"Born there?"

Latisha nodded again.

Bren seemed defeated by the situation, aware that he had lost his grip on a woman he had wanted to hold on to in certain ways: her shapely body, her curious mind, the key to her heart perhaps.

"In that case," he exclaimed, shaking his thoughts away, "allow me to make you breakfast before you go. No doubt you'll need time to pack your things and there are certain arrangements to make, so if you need something to eat later, I can do that, too."

"I'd like that," Latisha agreed, looking around the kitchen, feeling somewhat awkward at leaving the house she thought had become her home. "Would you mind if I use your phone?"

"Of course not," Bren told her, softly.

* * *

It was all a cruel awakening when six hours later she was seated in a taxicab staring at the old place. She could not imagine a circumstance that would bring her there again, where she could sit in one of the deck chairs and gaze out over the waters of Long Island Sound. The disappointment was such that Bren could see it in her face. In the short space of one night and one morning, he had come to learn just how much Latisha Fenshaw loved his house. It was a cruel awakening to him, too, that he could not imagine a circumstance that would allow her to revisit.

"I'm sure it would be best if you forgot you ever came here," he told Latisha, as he leaned across to talk to her through the open window at the passenger side of the car, repressing the sudden urge to give her a farewell kiss and retake a slice of pure heaven. The taxi driver was running his engine and seemed anxious to get on with the business of taking Latisha to JFK Airport. "Forget you ever met him and get on with your life."

Latisha gazed up at Bren and knew he was right. She should forget she had ever met Alan Clayton. "I just want to know one thing," she asked, stifling the compulsion to kiss Bren Hunter one more time. "How do you know so much about Alan?"

Latisha saw the stiffening of Bren's shoulders. "He's married to my sister," he confirmed in a deadly serious tone.

Her mind struggled to grasp what he had said, barely hearing his final words. Latisha blinked long and hard. "What?"

"Good-bye, Miss Fenshaw." Bren tapped the hood of the car, an indication that the driver should go on his way.

Wait! Latisha's mind screamed. But no words would come out. As the car sped away and she felt a fresh well of tears rise in her eyes, she turned and looked back through the car's rear window to find Bren Hunter standing at the gate of his house, now dressed in jeans and a jersey, his majestic frame dwindling as the distance widened. The brief bond that had existed between them stretched further away with every second until Bren's figure became just a speck, no longer distinguishable.

It was the last thing Latisha remembered, seeing the despair in Bren's eyes, feeling the shattering of her heart, and recalling the confusing effect of his kiss. If there was ever a time in her life when events took over to the point where everything turned out so badly, leaving New York had to be it. But she knew, in time, Bren Hunter would be someone very much forgotten.

Later, as she walked toward the tail section of the plane and sat down in a window seat, regret swept over her at the thought of Bren's kiss. It should never have happened. Not like that. Not while she was so vulnerable and in pain. Looking out the window, she could see the geometric configuration of the streets below, the complex image that made up New York City. Latisha made a vow to herself that she would never go back to Rye. She would never see Bren Hunter again either. And if Alan Clayton had the nerve to show his face in her life one more time, it would be too soon.

Chapter Three

Three months later

"Your father would've been proud of you," Lady Sarah Fenshaw whispered in Latisha's ear on having watched her complete another circle of the room. "I'd say you've raised at least 250,000 dollars."

"All for a good cause," Latisha added. "And right now I'm exhausted. I don't think I can force another smile. My feet are killing me. I can't wait to get out of these shoes."

"Or that dress." Sarah chuckled. "I swear, I can't imagine how you got into it."

"I might need a chisel and a hacksaw to get out." Latisha laughed about the violet-colored velvet gown that clung to every bit of spare flesh to accentuate her womanly curves. "If the designer will allow me. It's on loan." That was not quite the truth, but Latisha did not want to burst the bubble.

"You have to give it back," Sarah reminded her, aware that there were fledgling fashion designers who sought publicity for their gowns by carefully selecting a suitable candidate to wear one of their most exclusive creations. Latisha had told her

that a leading African-American magazine
wanted to supply some media coverage for the
event, so Lady Sarah was very much aware that
her stepdaughter wanted to make a good impression.

"Believe me, it'll be misery to wear it again."
Latisha giggled. "I haven't taken a full breath all
evening."

Both women laughed as Latisha looked around
the stateroom. The remains of a Caribbean-style
buffet lay in evidence among a scattering of
empty wineglasses that were discreetly being
cleared away by the two local women Lady Sarah
had hired as waitresses for the evening. She
watched them quietly before taking in the small
cluster of people standing around in groups, talking among themselves while sipping Dom
Perignon champagne.

The room featured a unique raised-platform
dining area with leather seating. There was rich
cherry-wood cabinetry, which added a certain
warmth and beauty to the space, and the floor
was solid teak parquet. It was a superb summer
party with an impressive group of dignitaries and
notables with their wives, all much older than
Latisha. Delicious tropical cocktails had cooled
down most of the guests who were still chatting.
As hostess with Lady Sarah, Latisha was happy to
accommodate them all within the confines of the
Caribbean Rose Salon.

The forty-two-foot Carver yacht had been
owned by her father, Sir Joshua Fenshaw, before
he had passed away. At first, Latisha had loathed
spending time on it, but when she had decided
to become a trustee and supporter of his various

charities and trusts, that included the yearly cocktail soiree on the yacht that was anchored in the west-end harbor at Tortola in the British Virgin Islands. Two years into the job and Latisha was still happy with her choice. The West Indian Servicemen and Women's Benevolent Trust had a lot to thank her for.

"Another drink?" Sarah inquired, throwing back her long locks of curly black hair while one of the waitresses passed by them.

"I couldn't," Latisha said, as she noticed the tall man from across the room. "Who's he?" she immediately inquired, discreetly pointing the man out.

As she did so, he caught her attention. Latisha immediately recognized something about him. The eyes. That was it. His soft, brooding, mysterious eyes seemed to transmit a bolt of energy her way. He seemed familiar. She felt they had met before. Yet, she could not be quite sure. This man had a full beard that covered most of his face. And his Afro was very short, cropped close to his scalp. The indomitable physique was familiar, but . . . she could not be sure.

"He's from America," Sarah replied. "I don't recall his name."

"I think we've met," Latisha said, quite absently.

"I don't think you would've met him," Sarah said. "He's a very powerful man in politics."

"Hmm," Latisha responded, surprised to find the man had begun to walk in her direction. She continued to stare. "He's coming over."

"Don't gawk at him," Sarah insisted, annoyed to find Latisha suddenly entranced. "Pretend to be talking to me."

But it was too late. In seconds he was within eye contact. Latisha became even more aware of his tall frame, of his dark brow, of the expanse of his broad chest beneath his lightweight cream jacket, and of the imposing manner in which he stood. All aroused her senses. This was no chance meeting. She had indeed met this man before. She looked into his pewter-colored eyes and her senses grew sharper. The scent of his musky aftershave caught her attention and suddenly she thought of Colombian coffee.

"Hi," he announced, extending his hand, taking delight in the way she had held her head high, keeping her slender spine as straight as an arrow.

Latisha languidly took it and felt the brush of his familiar warm fingers. Electricity immediately sizzled through her veins as she felt a wild rush of dizzying fascination. She tried to look past the beard, tried to imagine the face beneath it. The deep voice was distinct. Smooth as silk. "Do I know you?"

"We met in Rye," he told her, before fixing the collar on his open-necked navy shirt. His eyes remained fixed on Latisha, taking in the sensational view in front of him. "Just outside New York City? I believe you once enjoyed the view of Long Island Sound."

Latisha felt her face flush with blood.

"Congressman Bren Augustus Hunter," Sarah blurted out instantly, in recollection. "Now I remember. You're one of the five newly appointed members on the board of governors for the Joint Center for Political and Economic Studies in Washington, D.C."

"Congressman!" Latisha coughed, embarrassed. "Excuse me, please."

She immediately took off and hurried through a set of sliding doors that led her onto a large side deck stretching almost the full length of the boat. The warm breeze of the Caribbean immediately ruffled the soft curls of her hair, but she could not appreciate the seductive nature in which the long tendrils tickled around her earlobes. Latisha was gasping in shock. Could it be possible that Bren Hunter was on her late father's yacht?

She tried to absorb the night air of the west-end harbor, tried to appreciate the breathtaking views of Tortola and its surrounding islands, but she could not. The beautiful scenic views, the island's red sunset, the hills and forests, palms and tropical flora, and even the neighboring yachts she could see ahead of her made no impact on calming her jittery nerves. Latisha was overwhelmed with embarrassment.

And then she heard footsteps behind her. Latisha spun on her heels to find Bren Hunter standing directly in front of her. The slight sway of the yacht on the cool waters made her feel less steady on her feet than she had minutes earlier. At least that was the excuse she was giving herself. In truth, Bren Hunter's very presence was the real cause of her dizziness. Latisha had thought she would never see him again. Then she remembered the last time she saw him and the circumstances of her leaving flooded her memory.

"What are you doing here?" she gasped, the humiliation of their last meeting surfacing to torment her.

"I was about to ask you the same thing," he responded, in a light tone, his brows arched at the déjà vu. "I was invited."

"By who?" Latisha demanded.

"Linford Mills, governor of the U.S. Virgin Islands," Bren replied, his chest suddenly taking a tight hold of his breath. "He asked me to come along—"

"This is a private cocktail party," Latisha interrupted, nervous. "Trustees and their partners only, with a few select invitations."

"I didn't know," Bren revealed. "I was told the trust was looking to raise money with a charity auction. I tagged along with Linford, though I'm sorry I didn't bid on anything." He took a step forward and Latisha took one back, appearing more startled as his explanation unfolded. "How have you been?"

She nodded in the affirmative. "Fine. And you?"

"Busy," he breathed, aware that his body was fine-tuning his heart. "I'll be taking a short golf vacation before I fly back to the States. You?"

"I have business to attend to here," Latisha replied, swallowing the constriction in her throat. "Then it's back to Florida."

Bren nodded his understanding while laboring under his breath.

Latisha felt the unpleasant pause and filled it immediately. "You didn't tell me you were in politics," she began. "That's . . . that's great."

"And you didn't tell me you were a trustee on the board of directors for the West Indian Servicemen and Women's Benevolent Trust," Bren answered, his eyes lighting up. "What kind of charity work does the trust do?"

"Retirement homes, financial security, funeral expenses, that sort of thing," Latisha explained. "Currently, we've just raised enough money to build a place where old war veterans can go and relax. It will also be a place where their friends and family can visit." Latisha knew she was waffling, but it was all she could do to take her mind off Bren Hunter. "There'll be places for them to sit, plenty of flowers, a water fountain, and a lawn they can picnic on."

"Nice idea." Bren nodded, placing both his hands in the pockets of his navy-colored trousers while he contemplated Latisha Fenshaw more closely.

"And what does this . . . Joint Center do?" Latisha queried, in a desperate attempt to calm her nerves.

"It's a nonprofit organization," Bren began, closely scrutinizing Latisha.

She had not changed. Not to him. Her hazelnut complexion remained just as brown, her copper-colored eyes just as dark, and her lips seemed just as kissable. The only difference was her hair, which was stylishly swept up away from her face with tiny tendrils falling about her earlobes, and her choice of dress. This time, he felt more enamored seeing her in front of him, dressed like a model who had just stepped off a Paris runway.

Bren's breath was still lodged in his chest. "We conduct research and do analyses on public policy issues that are of concern to African-Americans and other minorities." His voice was beginning to sound hoarse and he tried to correct it. "We promote involvement in the governance process and create coalitions with business and other diverse communities. I offer support on an ad-hoc basis."

Earlier, he had not been sure it was Latisha he had seen from across the stateroom, even as he watched her walk around the room. He had told himself it was impossible. Lightning did not strike twice. But he had not been able to convince himself. His gaze had shifted from her admittedly exquisite profile to the revealing one of the man she had been talking to and back again. She just looked too familiar to him.

Had it not been for the way she had styled her hair, the way in which her makeup had been applied with such perfection, or the clothes that she was wearing, he would have recognized her instantly. The Latisha Fenshaw he last saw was a very simple, but very attractive woman. To his surprise, the woman who faced him now was someone far more alluring. His loins experienced a stinging kick that forced him to draw in the muscles around his manhood for fear of the obvious.

"The institution was founded in 1970," he concluded, realizing he was stalling for time by providing information he could not imagine would be of any interest to Latisha Fenshaw. "And we publish a wide variety of materials on politics, elections, social issues, economic policy, and international affairs."

"I must get back to my guests," Latisha said, swallowing another bout of nerves.

But as she made a step forward, Bren held her

back. The simple gesture of his hand on her left wrist was enough to cause Latisha's nerves to spiral in all directions. In fact, his touch was such that she felt a gasp leave her throat. Her mind was instantly thrown back to the kiss—the one that never should have happened. She had been too vulnerable. Too upset. And when reality had hit home, she came to discover that as phenomenal as the kiss may have been, Bren Hunter should not have taken advantage of her.

"Wait?" His voice filtered into her thoughts. "I would like to know how you've really been."

Latisha gulped, noting that Bren's glance veered ever so slightly over her head and out toward the dark waters of the marina. She knew that if she could she would have disappeared into them and never surfaced again, if only to save herself the humiliation of facing the one man who knew how deeply Alan Clayton had deceived her. If only to avoid the subject of how much she was now attracted to Alan's brother-in-law. Well, she had faced all her demons in one way or another, Latisha told herself. What could possibly happen to her, having to explain herself to Bren Hunter one more time?

"I'm reconciled to you kissing me under false pretenses," she accused, her voice raised slightly.

Bren stepped back on his heels. "What?"

"You were Alan Clayton's brother-in-law," she continued, annoyed. "And yet you kissed me."

"Now hold on," Bren drawled, amazed. "I was trying to make you feel better about yourself. About who you were."

"Yes, I was pretty messed up back then, wasn't I?" Latisha admitted solemnly. "Enough to be provided with one final humiliating piece of information as I was leaving."

"You're trying to imply that I had a sinister motive," Bren told her, his voice wounded. "If I've offended you, I'm sorry. That was never my intention."

As he turned to leave, Latisha felt the sting of his reaction. It made her aware that she still harbored some anger about what had happened. That within the depths of her emotions, there was still a place that needed healing. And while the wound was still there, she did not want Bren Hunter to just disappear. As complex as her feelings were and as astonished as she felt seeing him again, a perverse part of her wanted to endure their conversation a little longer.

"Did you find the lying, double-cheating rat?" she spat out instantly.

"He's here," Bren told her calmly.

"Alan's here?" Latisha was stunned. Her immediate response was to hate him. To hurl all the bitter reproaches she had fostered for so long at him. But all she could do was inquire, "Where?"

"At the hotel."

Her gaze was fixed. "What is he doing in the British Virgin Islands?"

"The situation's a little delicate," Bren told her calmly. "He's here with his wife."

"Your sister?" she gasped.

Bren nodded.

Latisha felt sick. "She must be an idiot to put up with him," she said coldly. "What kind of woman is she?"

"A pregnant one," Bren said in a shaky breath.

"She's having a baby!" Choked, Latisha was thoroughly thrown.

"The baby's fine," Bren explained, "but my sister is very weak with morning sickness and not feeling too well. She's under her doctor's supervision and needs to get plenty of rest without any distractions."

Latisha noted the flicker of movement in Bren's eyes and understood his implication implicitly. "I'm not going to make a scene," she insisted in annoyance. "I'm here another few days, then it's back to my sister's home in Florida."

"Only a few days?" Bren inquired.

"Three to be precise," Latisha told him. "So I would very much appreciate that during the rest of my time here on Tortola, you, your sister, and your brother-in-law stay a good distance away from me."

"I shouldn't be punished for what Alan did," Bren protested mildly. "Surely we can at least remain friends?"

"It's best that we don't," Latisha confirmed. "I've forgiven myself for Alan. He truly doesn't know how to be a man on an emotional level and it wasn't my job to teach him. I've stopped blaming him for not being the person I needed him to be and gave myself a pat on the back for not being the woman he wanted me to be either—a stupid one."

"You've handled yourself rather well, Miss Fenshaw," Bren acknowledged with a faint smile, "as I knew you would."

"I've come to learn that what changes with age and experience is how you deal with pain,"

Latisha revealed. "Like you said, Alan's intimacy cycle will always include more than one woman and I've accepted that. Whatever I had with him is something I now regard as an event that has helped shape my life story. I achieved closure and what happens now is up to me."

"You're amazingly optimistic," Bren remarked in honesty.

"I'm looking for a good man," Latisha proclaimed. "And they *do* exist. That is not optimism. That is what I deserve."

"And a man who dreams of a feast may wake up and cry Confucius," Bren declared.

"At least Confucius believed in perfecting one's own moral character," Latisha said, recognizing that Bren was implying that she was perhaps looking for too much. "That's an obligation every person should have."

"I think he understood human behavior, which has been predictable for the last three thousand years," Bren clarified. "Which is why——"

"You forgave your brother-in-law," Latisha interrupted, in disappointment. "I now see you in a new light, Mr. Hunter."

Bren felt the weight of her remark. In some way, it left him feeling defeated. This was one woman he desperately wanted . . . no, needed to see his good side. His compassionate nature, his generous qualities, his sincerity and loyalty. But how could he explain to Latisha Fenshaw that his sister's health and very life depended upon him keeping Alan close to her? That he had no choice but to ignore the transgressions of Alan's ways so that his sister could give birth to her child with the knowledge that her husband was nearby.

Not that any of it mattered to Latisha Fenshaw. She had been hurt. There was no room for her to understand the delicacy of the situation he was in. And she had made it clear he and his family should stay as far away from her as humanly possible for the remainder of her stay in the Virgin Islands. Whether he could keep to that resolve was another matter. But for now, Bren felt some duty in honoring her wishes.

"I hope it's not a dim light." He sighed. "And I will ensure that Alan does not know of your presence here."

"Good," Latisha agreed, "because I may not have been savvy about the deceptions that account for modern romance, but I am now."

Bren's eyes narrowed slightly. Without warning, a new, quite frightening emotion washed over him. It was a sweltering, primitive, almost nauseous flush of pure, heated adrenaline that sank its roots into his masculine psyche. "Some people would say that the love game is an unpredictable casino of chances and improvisation, but—"

"Most of the time, it's about as casual and offhand as the well-practiced triple flips of an Olympic high-diver," Latisha interrupted, disliking his point of view. "And the more shallow and impromptu the love is, the higher its appeal, wouldn't you say?"

"I see you would prefer to have a pretty good feel for how certain intimacies and maneuvers will play out before you start," Bren observed carefully.

"Absolutely," Latisha agreed, relieved that he could now see her point. "There's a certain skill in knowing when to press the attack and when to lie back and let the normal rhythms of deceit pass on by."

"Then again, you could become skillful and learn to ride the waves of romance like a surfer instead of being toppled," Bren responded, deciding to provocatively feel his way around Latisha's way of thinking.

"I think that explains the patterns and precepts that skilled liars live by," Latisha retorted. "I am not like some people who treat life like a game to be won or lost, Mr. Hunter. You said so yourself, once. I see it in terms of standards, ethics, and a system of values. Take your pick. Either way, it's what I want that counts, which is why I made a promise to myself to get precisely that."

"Of course," he agreed, inclining his head as a gesture of his impending departure. "And true power is the ability to make something happen or to keep it from happening to get what it is that you do want." He glanced at his watch. "I hope you keep to your promise, Miss Fenshaw, and on that note I'll have to bid you good night."

Latisha watched him take the length of the side deck to the stern and disembark onto shore. As a new breeze caused her hair to tickle the back of her neck, she became aware of the tangible loss of Bren Hunter. But the circumstances of knowing him were not ideal. He was part of the horrible mess she had left behind in New York, of the lies and deceit she had been unable to live with. It was simply cruel that a large part of her still liked him so much and a deeper part longed to be kissed by him again. But it was not a possibility.

In that moment, Latisha made a bargain with herself. Each time she thought of Bren Hunter she would replace his image with an imaginary picture of a green-eyed monster. And whatever happened, she would never let that image go.

The sun was intense and the beach was baking. Latisha was reclined on a towel under a shady umbrella, her eyes closed, without a care in the world. She was convinced that Tortola, "land of turtle doves," or Chocolate City, as it was sometimes known by the locals, had the best beaches in the world. Sitting in the sun on Smuggler's Cove, with her brain a complete blank, Latisha was now taking a little time for herself.

It was just what she needed after the late-night cocktail party that did not end until well into the early hours of the morning. Now alone with Lady Sarah, who was suffering a hangover on the towel next to her, she thought perhaps she could catch some sleep before attending the dinner party she had been invited to that evening, something she was not looking forward to in the slightest.

It was a while before she felt the presence of a new arrival. The slight noise, the shift of sand beneath her towel, and the sense that her own shade had become much darker made Latisha open her eyes slowly. Beside her was a newcomer who was staking out her measure of the beach. The British Virgin Islands, Tortola being the largest among them, proved popular with foreign tourists in July. Although there were many beaches, only the discerning made a point of finding a good location to sun themselves.

The woman standing above her was quite slim, with long, brown, shapely legs, equally long dark-brown hair, and all the alluring features of a woman who wandered the beach hoping to catch the eye of a monied man. Her own father, Sir Joshua Fenshaw, had subjected her at an early age to such women who competed for his attention. As a young child, she had watched in fascination at the many inventive ways they had sought to garner his attention.

Lady Sarah had once been such a woman before her father had taken her hand in marriage. He had found happiness with her in the last few years of his life before he died of natural causes in his sleep. His widowed wife was now Latisha's closest friend, and it was always a pleasure to see Lady Sarah whenever she vacationed on the yacht her father had bequeathed to her, Josette, and his widow. Latisha loathed being on the beach, else she be perceived as someone seeking romance.

Earlier, she had acknowledged the male attention that had come her way. But she was not in the market for any flirtations with the kind of men she had often met in her twenty-seven years. But Lady Sarah loved the beach and Latisha had promised they would spend some time together. With that in mind, she squinted her eyes to deflect the sun's rays and welcomed the newcomer.

"Hi." Latisha smiled.

"Hi there," the woman replied in a rich American accent. "You don't mind me taking this spot, honey? I just gotta lie down."

"No," Latisha lied. "Go right ahead."

She dropped a cotton rattan bag and a handful

of other items onto her towel. Then like a sleek black panther, she lowered herself onto her back and stretched out her entire body. Clad in a yellow halter-neck bikini, the woman had a great figure, Latisha had to admit. Not unlike her own either, only there was more on the hips and thighs. And a tad more around the bustline, too.

Aware that she herself had covered most of her assets in a simple costume, Latisha now wished she had been more daring, even though that would have invited more unwelcome attention. Even Lady Sarah was in something that revealed more flesh. But Latisha could not see the point in baring all when there was no one special adoring her. And the last thing she wanted was to attract any playboys, who preyed on the beaches of the Caribbean before moving on to other islands for more game.

"I'm taking it easy," the woman said casually, while staring up at the flawless blue sky. "We girls have to pamper ourselves every once in a while."

"I'll second that," Sarah muttered from beneath her own umbrella. She was lying on her back on a large beach towel with her eyes closed and a damp face cloth across her forehead. Close by was a good book and a cocktail glass half-full of rum punch, both items untouched.

"You're awake?" Latisha was surprised.

"Still hungover," Sarah replied on a sour note.

"Was it a great party last night?" the woman with the shapely legs inquired curiously. She tried to look over and get a glimpse of Lady Sarah, but all she could see was her long, olive-colored legs.

"I laughed too hard, drank too much, and was

lucky not to have passed out," Sarah began in explanation. "And boy, am I feeling it now!"

"You had yourself a ball," the woman assumed, chuckling. "My name's Veronica. I'm on vacation for a week. And you are?"

Latisha raised herself on one elbow to begin the introductions. "Latisha Fenshaw, and this is my stepmom, Lady Sarah Fenshaw."

"Less of the stepmom," Sarah chastised. "I was married to her father before he died," she added. "His second wife. Latisha is my closest *friend.*"

"Right," Veronica acknowledged with a smile, noting that there were not many years between the two women. "You're on vacation, too?"

"Sort of," Latisha said, prevaricating. "Then I'm meeting my sister in Florida. She lives there."

"I live in the States, too," Veronica enthused. "Boston. Ever been there?"

"No." Latisha shook her head. "I've been to New York though."

"Boston's nice," Veronica continued. "Very clean. Quiet. A lot of greenery, if you like that sort of thing. Great place for kids. I've decided I'm gonna have a large family."

"That's nice." Latisha nodded, finding their entire conversation taxing.

Once upon a time, she had found herself having similar dreams. A man, a home, and children. And at the tender age of twenty-seven, she had thought she would have attained much of what she wanted about now. But every time she had set her sights on someone, something happened. He was too lazy, a workaholic, could not commit, drank too much, or in Alan's case, married.

"Do you have a man?" Sarah intruded. Still on her back with her eyes closed, she had refused to scrutinize the woman.

"Oh yes, and he loves me," Veronica answered, assuredly. "We've been married three years and two months. I'm a very lucky girl."

Don't rub it in, Latisha thought. "That really is nice," she said with ease, raising her body until she was seated on her bottom. Hugging her legs, she added, "It's hard to find a faithful man these days, even within marriage."

"My man would never cheat on me," Veronica interjected quickly. "I mean, just take a look. Where else is he gonna find fine goods like this?"

Latisha chuckled. "Sometimes it's not about how a woman looks."

"You don't say," Veronica proclaimed, offended.

"Don't get me wrong," Latisha persisted, feeling the urge to explain. "What I mean is . . . a man becomes accustomed to how a woman looks after a while. And if he's not in love, he takes her beauty for granted and moves on."

"And you would know, would you?" Veronica demanded, while raising herself onto her elbow to stare at Latisha with full scrutiny.

Latisha was aware that Veronica was absorbing into her mind's eye every facet of her features. Her oval-shaped face, rounded cheeks, black hair swept up into a bun on her crown, and the layers of sun block she had creamed on to protect her against skin damage. With no makeup, she probably appeared plain to the highly maintained

Veronica, who was decked out in waterproof mascara, eyeliner, luscious clear-glossed lips, and a well-maintained weave.

"I have a male cousin who, for some years now, has been throwing out a comment or two to me about men," Latisha began in a halfhearted voice. "I wasn't paying attention until a few months ago, when I discovered I was dating a married man. He led me to believe he was single. Since then, I now realize that marriage doesn't make promises. It's the people who are committing to each other who do."

"He was married and you didn't know?" Veronica probed.

"I didn't," Latisha told her.

"You never suspected?"

"I suspected," Latisha replied, "but I'd met his family. There was no reason to believe he could've been lying to me."

"He sounds like he was a smooth operator," Veronica went on, without further comment. "My man wouldn't do that to me. You see, his mama, she didn't want us to marry. She thought I wasn't good enough for her boy. But my brother, he helped me. I have a florist shop now and a nice home. My man dotes on me and—"

"I'm sorry," Latisha interrupted. "I wasn't trying to project any of my insecurities about men on you."

"Latisha has a hard time because she's an intelligent and beautiful human being," Sarah suddenly declared from beneath her shade. "She intimidates a lot of them, only she won't admit it to herself."

Veronica's eyes narrowed. "What do you do?" she asked with a faint smile.

"I'm a trustee and custodian to several charitable causes," Latisha confirmed, before turning toward Lady Sarah. "I *do* know what the problem is."

"And she earns too much money," Sarah added.

"No, I don't." Latisha chuckled. "My work allows me to travel, that's all."

Veronica's brows rose. "And you think what . . . that men are faithful to wives who are beautiful, but dumb?" She almost coughed as she made the assumption.

"A man wants control," Latisha explained impassively. "If she can live her life independently without him, he'll not feel needed and he'll cheat."

Veronica's mouth fell open. "I worked hard for over a year to get a florist shop. I want to help my man provide me the kind of home I would like in Boston. If things are what you say, that means he's gonna cheat. That my beauty and the fact that I love my man won't count for much to him at all. Well . . . Latisha, my man is nothing like that. The acid test was his mama, and now that I've proved to her that I'm keeping my man, I have nothing to worry about." Before Latisha could open her mouth, Veronica was picking up her things.

"I'm sorry," Latisha intoned, watching in alarm as the woman rose to her feet.

Within seconds, Veronica had folded her towel and her umbrella. "I'm done here." Then she was gone.

"You've made an enemy there," Sarah mouthed casually.

"What's *her* problem?" Latisha asked, training her eyes on Veronica, who had marked a spot farther along the beach where she began to deposit her things.

"Maybe you hit a nerve," Sarah suggested before rolling onto her side, her manner indicating that she had not the slightest care in the world.

"A very sore one," Latisha mused, noting that Veronica had removed her bikini top. Topless, the offended woman disappeared beneath the umbrella she had positioned on the sand. With a sigh, Latisha returned to her own towel, closed her eyes, and allowed her brain to reach another blank.

Chapter Four

On Latisha's returning to the yacht, her mind was no longer a blank. Her seriousness was back with a vengeance. Congressman Bren Hunter now filled her mind. She wondered about him. Which hotel he was staying in. Whom he was with. What was his birth sign? His mother's maiden name? Why he had grown a beard? What political party did he belong to? His favorite color. His shoe size. What book was he currently reading? Did he have a girlfriend? Or was he himself a married man?

Her curiosity remained at its peak as she opened the door in her cabin suite that led to the bathroom. It was marble, in soft shades of blue veined with yellow and green. The floor was pale blue marble tiles, which felt wonderfully cool beneath her feet. Gold fittings attached to the walls were filled with bars of soap, small jars of aromatic oils, and perfumes to bathe her skin. Latisha stood under the warm shower for a long time, thinking . . . contemplating, as every trace of sweat and sand was rinsed from her body. Then, blotting herself dry, she wondered if Bren had enjoyed kissing her in New York.

He's probably forgotten all about it, she thought

cynically. Latisha then thought about how rude she had been seeing Bren again. Suddenly she giggled. No point in repressing it. She did not feel guilty at all about her behavior. She felt relieved. Why pretend otherwise? Now she could debate in her mind whether they could be friends, if she saw him again, or would Bren want more, as she did? Only she refused the thought of admitting it to herself. She quietly thought instead about the likelihood of crossing paths with him again, given that Tortola was such a small island. It was a probability. Bren Hunter was very much someone unforgotten.

But with the memory of him came a maelstrom of deceptions. Alan Clayton. Her heart trembled with the knowledge that the louse was somewhere close by. In a hotel room, with his wife, enjoying his tranquil homey life as though he had not destroyed the romantic dreams of a girl who had grown up wanting to be loved. Still she could not get over how deceitful he had been. Alan Clayton had no scruples whatsoever when it came to his own behavior.

What was more appalling to her was that Bren Hunter had chosen to turn a blind eye. Because his sister was now pregnant with Alan's baby, he had decided to forgive his brother-in-law. This from the man who had promised he would deal with the two-timing, yellow-bellied liar. She should have known not to believe anything he had told her either. After all, Bren Hunter worked in politics. In the ultimate game of power, a man had no business playing ball or politics in Washington until he had learned to keep a straight face and lie.

Hugging herself in the dry towel, she went into her elaborately decorated bedroom. The portholes were closed against the late afternoon heat, but Latisha opened one slightly and peeped out. Another rich sunset gazed back at her. Nearby were neighboring yachts, some filled with the sound of laughter, others the soft bellowing din of music. The local residents were enjoying their vacations. If only she felt as lucky. Her evening was destined to be spent mostly in the company of people older than herself, with whom she had very little in common. They would likely bore her to sleep, as her own guests did the night before.

Latisha walked over and sat at the small ivory-colored vanity unit that was a feature of the large cabin suite. Overhead were more than a handful of tiny lightbulbs embedded in the frame, designed to illuminate her face while she looked in the mirror. Her sober image revealed a woman who had taken control of herself and her life. Someone who saw plenty of virtues in being the person she was. *You're never going to settle for second best,* Latisha told her reflection as she heard a knock at her door.

"Who is it?" she inquired.

"Your stepmother," Sarah joked.

"Come in."

The door slowly opened and a more excited woman entered, barefoot. Lady Sarah was dressed in a fresh white bikini with a multicolored sarong hanging loosely around her waist, both complementing the olive tones of her skin. The long locks of her curly black hair were freely dancing around her shapely shoulders and her dark, doe-shaped eyes were glowing with mischief.

"I'm not coming to the dinner party with you tonight," she announced on a light note, while she entered the cabin. "After you left me on the beach, all alone, I might add, I met the most adoring man. His name is Monsieur Piers Lapare and he's invited me to a beach party later."

Latisha turned from her vanity unit in amazement. "But . . . but—"

"You'll be just fine," Sarah enthused, perching herself on the edge of Latisha's queen-sized bed.

"I won't know anyone there," Latisha protested at once. "It was your idea that I go and see the Wrights. They were more yours and my father's friends, and—"

"You need to meet new people," Sarah assured her. "Besides, they remember you. Nancy always liked you and your father. He told me he used to take you to play there when you were a little girl with your sister."

"I'm a grown woman now," Latisha gasped. "The last time I saw her was two years ago. She might not even recognize me."

"Why don't you take along your friend, Congressman Hunter?" Sarah encouraged. "He's—"

"Not a friend," Latisha returned.

Sarah dipped her brows. "You never did tell me what last night was all about," she probed, curiously. "You rushing out onto the side deck like that. And the congressman leaving so suddenly afterward."

"It's nothing," Latisha said.

"In that case . . ." Sarah rose to her feet and made for the door. ". . .I can rely on you enjoying yourself tonight, shall I? A girl of your age should be having more fun."

Easier said than done, Latisha thought as she waved her farewell. Lady Sarah was thirty-nine years old—twelve years separated them—though she looked much younger, and seemed on the verge of starting her life all over again. Latisha could hardly blame her. They had both been devastated at the sudden death of Sir Joshua Fenshaw. He had been an exceptional man. A generous person who had been the instigator of many worthy charitable causes. If this . . . Piers Lapare was someone who could make her happy, Latisha saw no reason why Lady Sarah should not want to choose to spend her time with him.

Pulling on her clothes, she combed her hair. Defeated by its newly washed silkiness, she allowed it to hang to her shoulders, sighing slightly as she noted her ends required clipping. From her makeup bag, she dug out a bright brown lipstick, slicked it over her lips, and slowly brushed on a burnished gold blusher across her cheekbones. With a brown liner, she outlined her copper-colored eyes and dark brows before peering into the mirror to assess her handiwork. Latisha saw the natural look she wanted. Nothing pretentious or glamorous.

She took the hired Jeep. The dinner party was to be at Highfields, the Wrights' summer villa. Nancy had not only been a longtime friend of her father's, but she had also kept in touch with Lady Sarah during her painful grieving. Nancy had lived on Tortola for fifteen years and had grown to love the place, making it her home with her scatterbrained husband. Though George

Wright was an adorable old man, Latisha was reminded that he was often difficult to understand. Her last conversation with him at her father's funeral had been a tedious affair, something she cared not to repeat.

Still, her arriving for dinner would be a good distraction from the boring life that she was living. Highfields was a fifteen-minute drive from the west-end harbor, and it gave her time to reassess her thinking. Her life had moved on. She now felt able to socialize again after hosting her own event the night before. There was something deeply intimate to be learned from a failed relationship, Latisha even decided, while briskly driving along.

Deep in thought, she was drawn away from the winding and hilly roads that had made her rent the four-wheeler. Narrow and steep, they had been carved out of what were once trodden dirt trails, traveled not only by foot, but also by donkey. But Latisha was oblivious to the rough, bumpy bounce of her journey. She had learned more about who she was, what she wanted, and what she did not want.

This had to be a good thing, she silently decided. By knowing what she needed in her life, she would know what to look for next time. *Next time!* Latisha allowed those two words to roam around inside her head. Next time, she would not be a fool. Next time, she would not jump into a romance like a love-struck teenager. Next time, she would find out exactly whom she was dealing with. Next time, she would ask a thousand and one questions over and over to check that she got the same answers. Next time . . .

All at once, Latisha stopped dead. She had arrived outside the villa. She paused in the driver's seat to take a breath, before allowing her eyes to slide upward across the property overhead. Highfields had been built by local architects and was tucked into the hillside, an intimate hideaway on the private Belmont Estate on Tortola's northwest coast. Set above a palm grove, it afforded some of the most beautiful panoramic views over Smuggler's Cove, a five-minute walk away down a private path. Cutting the engine and dropping her car key into a white polished leather Gucci handbag, Latisha opened the car door, stepped out, and began to negotiate the stone steps that led upward to the villa that was set among one acre of landscaped grounds.

Highfields was one of just a handful of private villas on the dead-end road where she had parked the rented car. No one seemed to remember the road's name. There was little traffic—human or otherwise—though the last time she had been there to escape the hustle and bustle of civilization, Latisha was to find some goats and chickens wandering along, aware of nothing except the rhythms of the sea down below.

There was something tranquil and peaceful about the place that touched her in a beautiful way when she reached the top step. Tortola was a place where the words "no worries, mon" rang true. As Latisha took in another breath of air, she was reminded that she was now on "island time." Although into the third day since her arrival, only now did she feel her body slipping into a slower pace. Her mind was beginning to ease out of the frenzied thoughts of knowing that Alan

Clayton and Bren Hunter were somewhere close by. It was the breathtaking view in front of her that caused the mood shift.

The island was not only hilly, but mountainous, too. On an upper elevation, she could see traces of the rain forest. There was also the view of the surrounding sixty islands or so, though Tortola was quieter and less developed than the others. As a visitor, she had always enjoyed its desire for less tourism; Tortola was an escape from the commercial souvenir shops and glittery night life. It was this special secret charm of gentle lapping waves and cool sea breezes that had kept her returning time and time again. Once the hideaway of buccaneers and brigands, it now attracted yachting connoisseurs like herself, who were drawn by the steady winds, the privacy, and the lure of total relaxation.

Another minute, and Latisha walked toward a set of wide French doors on a covered veranda overlooking Smuggler's Cove and Jost Van Dyke. The doors were already opened and led directly into a dining porch. Latisha peeked in, her gaze immediately connecting with a twelve-foot-long custom-made mahogany bar and peninsula that was joined to the room. A ceiling fan was working overtime and she could hear voices in the distance, moments before an inner door opened and a familiar face instantly beckoned her inside.

"Latisha, is that you?" Nancy Wright greeted, placing two salad bowls into the middle of the well-laid-out dinner table before rushing over.

The two women hugged before pulling back to assess each other.

"A little thinner," Nancy noted.

"Spectacles now?" Latisha noted as well. The old lady had aged, but not dramatically. The face was still round and chubby, and the body even more so, but the hair had now grayed and the violet-colored eyes seemed much smaller. The smile nonetheless was as wide as ever.

"Where's Sarah?" Nancy asked.

"At a beach party," Latisha explained, aware that a rum punch and a good book on the beach earlier had not been enough for Lady Sarah. "She'll be dancing under the stars to live music by one of the local steel bands in the arms of a man by nightfall."

Nancy's eyes lit up. "A man?"

"She's met someone. I think he's French," Latisha expanded. "A Monsieur Piers Lapare?"

Nancy shook her head. "I don't know him." She shrugged. As a local among some sixteen thousand residents who lived on the island, Nancy had come to know most people in her years of living there. "He must be new."

"Hmm," Latisha mused. "How many for dinner tonight?"

"Twelve," Nancy said, making her way toward the kitchen while Latisha followed close behind. "You're the fifth to arrive."

"Where's George?"

"Out by the pool," Nancy told her, walking directly toward the large side-by-side automatic ice-making refrigerator. She opened the door and operated the ice dispenser while Latisha placed her white handbag on the floor and took the nearest chair.

The professionally designed kitchen was laid out to accommodate several chefs working simultaneously and seemed too large for Nancy's short, chubby frame. It contained a large stove, prep sink, mahogany cabinets, coffee machine, toaster oven, blender, granite counters, and enough pots, pans, dishes, glasses, and silverware to cater to a small army. Latisha recalled that the door by the stove led to a work pantry containing a large double sink, dishwasher, microwave oven, more counters, cabinets, and enough storage space for a little girl to hide in.

A smile tugged at Latisha's lips when her mind took her back to the games she had played as a child among those very cabinets. It was so unlike the kitchen she had grown to love and left back in Rye. The memory of it caused Latisha to blink, heavy hearted at the loss of the comforting time she had spent in the house overlooking Long Island Sound. Recoiling from it, she plunged herself back to the present.

"Is George sleeping?" she asked Nancy, with a touch of concern. He would be at least sixty-seven by now, Latisha reckoned. A war veteran who had retired after years of working in England as a miner, digging coal.

"No. He's with the other guests." Nancy nodded, pouring ice into a bucket and taking it over to place on the bar. "So how are things with you?" she probed.

"Me?" The question took Latisha by surprise. "I'm fine."

"I haven't seen you since the funeral," Nancy went on. "Two years now. You've lost weight."

Man trouble, Latisha told herself silently. "I've been busy," she offered. "It hasn't been easy taking over my father's charity work. Between being a new trustee of the Association of Jamaicans Trust and the West Indian Servicemen and Women's Benevolent Trust, there's also the Black Cancer Care he set up in New York before he died and my patronage of the Sickle Cell and Thalassemia Society, not to mention the other minor charities, all of whom require my support. I seem to be on an airplane more often than I am at home."

"What about Josette?" Nancy asked, annoyed. "Can't she help?"

"My sister is enjoying her life with her boyfriend in Florida," Latisha explained. "Teaching is what she wants to do and Steadman's job as a nurse keeps her busy doting on him after hours. There's no use in the two of us disrupting our lives to continue my father's charitable causes. Besides," she ventured, "I was at a dead end pursuing a singing career that wasn't going anywhere. I haven't got what it takes to be a soul singer."

Nancy chuckled. "And what about your love life?"

Latisha coughed, suspicious of the question. "Why are you asking?"

Nancy walked over to the stove and pulled out a large tray of hot, spicy jerk chicken. "Some of my guests tonight might interest you."

"All in their forties and fifties," Latisha said deridingly. "I've had it with older men. I'm beginning to question whether I am trying to replace my father, and no one can ever measure up to him."

"Latisha," Nancy began, just as there was a knock at the French doors from the dining room. "In here," Nancy hollered, before redirecting her attention. "No one can ever replace Sir Joshua Fenshaw. Your father was everything to you, but life has to go on."

"I know that." Latisha nodded, disliking that the conversation had turned on her. She marveled at how older women were able to do that. Lady Sarah had the knack, too. "It's just hard to find someone who's secure and nurturing. Tall, dark, and handsome men do not fall at my feet."

"Ah, Linford," Nancy greeted, looking above Latisha's head. "I'm glad you could come."

Latisha's eyes widened at the familiar-sounding name. Aware that there were further footsteps behind her, she turned her head to discover the man standing to her left, with the sound of another person approaching close by.

"Linford," she said, disappointed that she was to share yet another evening with the talkative fifty-two-year-old man, who had done nothing but leer at her the night before.

The governor of the U.S. Virgin Islands was about five-nine, with a pomaded silver, wiry Afro that he liked to brush backward over a balding crown in the center of his head. With blue-brown eyes and a café-au-lait complexion that belied his multiethnic Caribbean roots, he was dressed like Hollywood's idea of a black political puppet—a plain suit, neatly pressed; polished black shoes for appearances' sake, and possessed of very little rhetoric, save for a good few lines that could lend credence to his role. Linford Mills was no Colin Powell.

Though he was often described by her father as a lady killer, Latisha failed to see how he became accustomed to acquiring the legendary number of women he was renowned for, especially as there was a Mrs. Gloria Mills, who would not take kindly to the news. But she smiled gaily and accepted his greeting with a dose of refined manners.

"How nice it is to see you again," she said, with pretended sweetness.

"Hello again, Miss Fenshaw," he acknowledged, shaking her hand. "We should stop meeting like this. People will talk."

"Will they?" Latisha chided.

"Wonderful cocktail party you hosted on the *Caribbean Rose* last night," he began in conversation, ignoring her remark. "I can't wait to use those golf clubs I bought at your charity auction. Did Tiger Woods really donate them?"

"Yes," Latisha confirmed, moments before she swung around on Bren Hunter, who seemed to materialize from nowhere and was looking down at her, expressionless. A bolt of energy frizzled between them. Latisha stared. "Hello!" she blurted out unexpectedly.

Bren Hunter was dressed in a pair of white linen trousers with a black and white cotton Lacoste jersey and white moccasins on his feet. The beard was gone, freshly shaven, she suspected, that very afternoon. Latisha was now able to recognize more fully the man she had left behind in New York: his square face, cool pewter-colored eyes, and the straight patrician nose that seemed more noble now that the facial hair was gone.

He advanced a step forward, his eyes still trained on her, then suddenly, and it was an amazing surprise to all concerned, he tripped over. Latisha gulped in horror when, to her chagrin, the congressman flew into the air and landed quite awkwardly on his bottom. She was out of her chair in an instant, rushing immediately to his aid. Looking none the worse, save for the startled expression on his face, he had not hurt himself, she was relieved to see.

"What happened?" Bren demanded, his deep, silky voice filled with annoyance as he propped himself up on to the beautiful Mexican-tiled floor by his elbows.

"My handbag," Latisha said, apologetic and suppressing the urge to burst with laughter bubbling in the pit of her stomach while she picked up the offending Gucci. With her free hand, she took a hold of Bren's left arm, detecting a whiff of his musky aftershave. "It was stupid of me to leave it on the floor like that. Are you all right?"

"Silly girl," Bren remarked, taking his time to stand to his feet.

"I'm sorry," Latisha said, gulping, her laughter suddenly replaced with trepidation. "It was an accident."

"You're capable of all manner of blunders, aren't you?" Bren snapped, now standing. Linford and Nancy were at his side, brushing him off and ascertaining that he was indeed capable of seeing the evening through.

Latisha felt the instant prickle of tears behind her eyelids. Bren's cruel comment—a reminder of her nightmare in New York—was uncalled for. He need not have taken her back to that awful, embarrassing moment of discovering that she was trespassing in his house. It had not been a blunder. She had been duped, pure and simple.

Of course, this now led Bren to the impression that she was naive and prone to all kinds of misfortunes.

"My . . . blunders, Mr. Hunter, involve someone who's been given a pat on his crooked shoulder and a total reprieve for his actions."

"Miss Fenshaw—" Bren began, schooling his eyes on her. She was dressed in the same tunic-style white dress he had last seen her in, appearing totally innocent and angelic. He became suddenly annoyed at himself for having been harsh with her, but it was apparent Latisha was not so forgiving.

"And absolved of all his guilty shenanigans," she continued, in direct reference to Alan Clayton. "I guess that's how things are done in Washington. Covertly."

"You've met before?" Nancy noted, her brows raised.

Bren Hunter appeared nervous. "It was—"

"A mishap," Latisha ended.

She did not miss the narrowing of Bren's eyes moments before a flurry of late arrivals entered through the dining room's French doors. While Nancy went over to offer her greetings, Latisha watched as Bren threw a derisive glance at her before his attentions were taken by the cluster of people who immediately sucked up to his indomitable and powerful presence. Her thoughts were still trained on how easy it was for him to command such attention when Nancy came over.

"What was that you were saying about men never falling at your feet?" Nancy whispered, deliberately pursing her lips to suppress the giggle that threatened to erupt. "Seems one just did."

"Yeah," Latisha croaked, unmoved. "And the devil pushed him."

There was a constant, prickly awareness of Congressman Bren A. Hunter during dinner. As he smiled and argued a point with George Wright, seated next to him, a foot—sometimes both—would carelessly brush Latisha's as he leaned back into his chair, which was facing her across the table. Then there was the scent of his musky aftershave, which teased her nostrils like drifting smoke, causing her to discreetly raise her eyes from her plate to gaze at him, disturbingly aware that beneath was the far more basic aroma of the male animal.

Once, they had both reached for the last of Nancy's hot West-Indian-style dumplings in the silver epergne at exactly the same instant, their fingers touching unexpectedly. Latisha had drawn back sharply and he apologized softly and allowed her to take it. She accepted, acknowledging that his nature had now softened toward her with the incident of her handbag behind them. But his brief smile in no way penetrated the guard Latisha had placed around herself.

Now, with the dinner over and Nancy serving coffee and mints, Latisha watched and listened while he advanced his point of view. She noted how his nostrils flared with every impassioned word spoken. How his brows dipped and peaked when he contested a remark that displeased him. And while she had silently eaten most of her dinner, refusing to throw in any comments of her own, save for the odd passing declaration about her father's continuing work, she was aware that Bren Hunter's conversation had heightened to involve other members seated at the table.

"But it's the constitutional right for any country to defend its borders," he insisted in the hard-charging manner of a politician stating his view.

"But it doesn't have to mean war," the ambassador to St. Vincent maintained. "There is always a compromise. That is why we have the United Nations."

"So what if a country threatens to invade?" Bren asked, pressing further his case.

"What country?" George asked innocently, having once been a soldier and understanding nothing. In his day, a man took orders without question. He still did not comprehend, even in his advanced age, to what depths his allegiance was measured and whom his actions affected. He had simply been told by his father to serve the motherland, Great Britain. That was what young men from the Caribbean did for king and country. To him it was all about His Majesty's sovereignty. There was never the issue of what was really being fought for. And so he added, "There isn't such a thing."

"Any taking of land is war," Bren challenged, his brows narrowing as though to assert the point.

"You are talking as though the world is working its way toward another big war," Linford said nervously, "where land will be taken and negotiated at will."

"A new world order," the high commissioner for Jamaica tossed in.

"It could happen," Bren claimed, calmly allowing his eyes to scan the eleven faces glaring at him from across the table. "What do you think?"

Suddenly, Latisha realized his question was aimed directly at her. "Me?" She was startled and her heart rate doubled immediately. "I don't know anything about politics."

"But you are trustee to a trust that serves the men and women who fought the last big war," Bren reasoned. "I'm sure you must have an opinion about their experiences."

"I think it was all very sad," Latisha debated in a quiet tone. "You see, many of the servicemen and women in the Caribbean fought on behalf of a crumbling British Empire. And when the war was over, many felt a strong loyalty to a country who did not value them in the same way. This is something I've discovered being a trustee of the Association of Jamaicans Trust. It's all very sad."

"But we are part of a commonwealth now, headed by the monarchy of Great Britain," the high commissioner announced in a wounded tone. "Even in independence, we haven't been completely abandoned."

"But had it not been for men like my father," Latisha asserted with pride, "who had to fight the government to gain status and give recognition to the worthy causes he was pioneering to see that Caribbean war veterans were looked after, they would have been ignored. That's why I think war is very sad for everyone involved."

"We know it's sad," George muttered, "but do you think it is necessary?"

Latisha, never being able to understand

George when he spoke, offered him a blank
stare.

She saw the man she had known from when
her father had first taken her to Highfields as a
child. His dark chocolate-brown skin that was always sweaty around his forehead. The mass of
curly white Afro which had not thinned with age.
The broad nose, well-built shoulders, huge ears,
and thick neck that always made him appear
physically strong.

But there was the deep, penetrating hazel-col-
ored eyes that always made her feel small and
fragile. And the round pink lips that moved in
such a fashion that she always missed the mum-
ble of words that fell from them whenever he
spoke directly to her. It was hard to believe that
he was now an elected executive of the West Indian Standing Conference, representing the
British Virgin Islands and the contributions of its
Caribbean people to the motherland. A man
now able to command such worldly people to be
seated at his dinner table.

"I . . . I don't know what you mean," she said,
certain that George Wright had a problem communicating whenever she had tried to have a
conversation with him.

"Do you agree with the congressman's views
that the protection of one's borders means war?"
Linford asked.

Latisha immediately imagined a green-eyed
monster. It had lizard-shaped eyes and sharp yellow teeth and a lurid, cheeky smile that was
comical enough to make her want to laugh. Instead, she narrowed her eyes and paused long
enough for the entire table of people to take

their attention from Bren Hunter and train it on her. Keeping her facial expression fixed and her voice sweet, she confidently aired her position.

"I think Mr. Hunter's opinions are about as redundant as are his promises," she responded, after some thought. "Therefore, I cannot wholly be supportive of his views."

"Whoa!" Linford chuckled at Latisha's raw audacity to be so bold and blunt. He eyed her closely and licked his lips. Members at the table also did not miss the frizzle of sheer energy that passed between Latisha and Bren Hunter.

"The girl was asked," George reminded them, not realizing that Latisha's answer was related to a subject that only she and Bren understood. "But we do not wish to alienate the congressman tonight." He laughed, lightheartedly. "After all, this is only dinner." He turned and faced Bren. "You must be used to more serious debate in the U.S. House of Representatives?"

"Of course," Bren acknowledged, forcing a smile.

"A man like you, representing the tenth congressional district in Brooklyn, needs drive," George continued. "That's what we soldiers had in the war. Drive."

"George," Nancy crooned. "Mr. Hunter is not a soldier." She smiled sweetly at Bren. "Is it right what I hear that you've been twice designated legislator of the year by the American Association of Community Health Centers for your work with mental health?"

Bren nodded, shyly.

"And that the National Association of Rural

Health Clinics credited you for successfully opposing budget reductions in their program?"

"I don't agree with federal budget cuts in that area," Bren declared softly.

"So you're no puppet on a string?" George asked pointedly.

Bren chuckled. "No."

George nodded his approval. "That's what I like to hear. You're a fighter. You've got a fighter's spirit."

"He recently obtained 153 million dollars for a new federal courthouse in downtown Brooklyn," Linford volunteered to the conversation. "That's good."

"It's also my job," Bren said, trying to downgrade the intense probing into his life.

He glanced over at Latisha, noting her sudden silence as she absorbed every minute detail. He wondered whether she was impressed, surprised, indifferent. It was difficult to decide with the way she hid her emotions, as though her thoughts were elsewhere. He did not imagine for one second that her view of him had changed. If there was one thing Bren had learned about Latisha Fenshaw, it was that she was a person who stuck to her guns.

"You shouldn't be so modest." Nancy's voice filtered into Bren's thoughts. "After all, you're also a member of the Congressional Black Caucus, I'm told."

"And the New York State Council for Elected Black Officials," Linford added. "And what's that other one?"

"The Coalition of One Hundred Black Men,"

Bren said, placing his napkin on the table. "I think that's it for me for the night."

"Oh." Nancy panicked, standing immediately to her feet as though aware her small party had overwhelmed the congressman. "Is it that time already?" She consulted her watch, which read fifty minutes after midnight. "We don't usually turn in so early."

"I'd like more dessert," Linford said, his tone indicative that he did not wish to leave just yet, though it was Bren he had come with.

"I have a meeting with a friend early in the morning," Bren said politely, as he too rose to his feet to face Nancy from across the table. "It was very nice of you to allow Linford to invite me along to dinner." Turning to George next to him, he added, "And thank you."

He began to work his way around the table toward the French doors, expecting Linford to follow. Latisha's heart did a rapid patter as she watched him do so. She knew it was her own earlier response to the conversation that had really troubled Bren Hunter. He had been holding his own ground very well before she spoke. Now, it seemed, he wanted nothing more than to get back to his hotel room and put the evening behind him. Guilt shadowed her mind. It was like a strange, waking dream when she found herself suddenly inquiring about his return journey.

"Do you need a ride?"

"It'll mean I can chill out here a little longer," Linford encouraged immediately, with pleading eyes leveled on Bren.

Latisha realized Bren seemed about as startled

as she was at her offer. "If it's no trouble," he replied smoothly.

"It's no trouble," Latisha returned. "I'm ready to get some sleep myself."

Bren shrugged. "Okay."

Latisha heard from somewhere inside the little strangled gasp that left her lips, the warning that she had behaved impulsively. But she tried not to worry. After bidding her farewells to Nancy and George and the other guests, the clearly functioning part of her brain was muttering a solemn vow, as Bren followed her out onto the veranda and down the stone steps toward the road below where she had parked the Jeep, to listen and learn.

Listen and learn, she mused, as Bren gazed at her before entering the car. While he silently buckled his seat belt into place, she started the Jeep's engine. Latisha was certain there was a conversation to be had, judging by Bren's expression thrown her way. And whenever or whatever Bren Hunter chose to speak, she knew one thing. She was ready to take him on . . . all the way.

Chapter Five

"So . . ." Bren began, unable to endure the silence a moment longer. He looked across at Latisha, who was steering the four-wheeler down the unmarked road with the darkened sky casting shadows from the trees into the distance ahead of them, and got right to the point. "That's quite an opinion you have of me."

"I can't imagine that would bother you any," Latisha answered, steering out onto a main road. She was aware that she was in awe of Bren Hunter, that she was nervous at sharing her car with him, and hated herself for it.

He kept his gaze fixed. "I can safely say you think I'm a person with the morals of a stone," Bren returned, his voice steely cool.

"Isn't that the standard all politicians aspire to?" Latisha chided, noting the coldness in Bren's tone. "Or is it what most men are?" She could not decide.

A silence hung over them before Bren spoke. His voice sounded flawed, as though a sudden dawning had worked its way to his brain. "Alan really hurt you, didn't he?"

Latisha felt the truth trembling in her veins. It was not so much that she had been in a relationship with someone so deceitful, or that he very much belonged to another woman, but the idea that Bren Hunter had ignored everything the moment she left New York. Of course, there was the family tie since his sister was married to Alan, but in Latisha's eyes that was not reason enough to turn a blind eye.

"He brought out the worst in me," she said simply, not wanting to debate or continue talking about the subject. "It was a very bumpy ride. I hadn't fastened my seat belt, so I got thrown."

"You seem to have learned to deal with it and quickly move on to the next phase of your life," Bren offered admirably. "Breakups are not failures, just stepping stones toward that aim. You said so yourself."

Latisha noted his mellowed expression and decided the sooner she got rid of him, the better. "Where to?" she asked, irritated by his kind words. This was very much like the conversation they had undertaken the night before on the *Caribbean Rose*. She had remained levelheaded and in control, even though it had been an enormous surprise to see him again. Now it appeared Bren was trying to gain the upper hand and she was not going to allow it.

"Sebastian's Hotel," he said, carefully measuring her.

Bren realized Latisha was not going to give anything away. She had kept her voice calm, her gaze fixed ahead with her shoulders straight and her head held with a certain degree of pride. He liked her stance, her dignity, and the determined way in which she was not going to let her past affect her. Of course, he had only been a minuscule part of that past, playing no large part, save for the fact that he had promised Latisha he would do something about Alan.

Bren knew that, in her eyes, his doing nothing was seen as a betrayal. He could not understand why he needed to explain the reason to Latisha, only that he wanted to try. Maybe he could strike up a conversation first, he thought, deciding to go with it.

"Nice yacht," Bren began.

"Yes," Latisha acknowledged.

"Yours?"

"Not quite."

"Then whose?"

"Mine, my sister Josette's, and my father's widow, Lady Sarah," Latisha replied, reluctantly engaging in small talk.

"I'm sorry about your father."

"Thank you," Latisha said. "He didn't suffer."

"And your mother?"

"She's still alive."

"In England?" Bren asked, confused.

"Yes."

"So . . ." He began to do the math. "Your mother was his first wife?"

"Yes," Latisha confirmed.

Bren nodded his head nonchalantly. A silent pause hung in the air before he spoke again. "Nice group of people tonight."

"If I were in my forties, perhaps," Latisha remarked, annoyed. "Maybe then we would have something in common."

Bren actually chuckled. "Like what?"

"Midlife crisis," Latisha declared, enjoying the sound of Bren's chuckle.

"And there I was thinking life begins at forty," he joked.

"How old are you?" Latisha probed, keeping her eyes on the road for fear that she would appear to be interested.

"Thirty-eight," Bren told her. "Not quite ready for a walking stick yet."

Latisha smiled at his humor while mentally filing the information. "So," she began, taking a hold of the conversation. "How do you fit in all the work that you do? There's not enough hours in a day to accomplish everything."

"I have a staff of twenty at my Washington office," Bren explained lightly. "All of whom have no qualms about relentlessly latching on to a congressman like myself to expand their opportunities."

"They're relentlessly ambitious?" Latisha asked.

"It is rampant on Capitol Hill," Bren remarked. "Sometimes, it feels like a bit much, but I rely on my staff a great deal to carry out my public platform. It's a little different at my office in New York. Only seven aides work there."

"Was that your childhood dream, to become a Congressman?" Latisha asked him.

"No," Bren answered.

"Oh . . ." Latisha hesitated. "You'd like to become something more like an attorney general?"

"No."

"Senator?"

"No," Bren confided smoothly.

"Governor?"

"Actually," he confessed, "I hope one day to become president of the United States."

Latisha choked. "That's pretty ambitious."

"And attainable," Bren responded quickly. "My father, Edgar Warren Hunter, was elected, as a Republican, to the U.S. Senate in 1967. He also served on the president's Commission on Civil Disorders, investigating the causes of race riots. No one ever expected a black man to attain such high positions in those days. Anything's possible if you really want it bad enough."

Latisha nearly slammed on the brakes in shock. Something inside her brain instantly began to see Bren Hunter in a different way altogether. As they cruised along, he suddenly did not seem like the green-eyed monster she had invented in her head, nor the silent collaborator of Alan's misdeeds. The light no longer seemed so dim. He had become a human being. A thinking man with an inquiring mind, and a desire to learn new things. To learn about her.

"Is he still alive . . . your father?" she asked candidly.

"He'll be eighty-five years old four months from now," Bren answered. "My mother just turned eighty. I was their only child."

Latisha immediately became confused. "I thought you had a sister," she probed, curiously.

Bren shook himself. "Yes," he admitted, after a short pause. "She was born to someone else."

The revelation dropped with a loud bang. "Your father had a mistress?" Latisha scoffed, scornful at the revelation. "I now see what yardstick you measure yourself by."

"My father was a good man," Bren replied, a touch annoyed. "I rather suspect equal to your own father before your parents' divorce."

Latisha felt the aim of his retaliation. "It happens." She shrugged, noncommittally. "They were happier apart and Josette and I benefitted from that. It was important to them both that we were happy."

"And are you?"

"What?" Latisha asked.

"Happy?"

Latisha refused to take the question seriously, knowing full well that Bren Hunter was more than aware of her circumstances. "I'm content," she admitted, carefully. "It feels good to be getting on with my life without any complications."

"Male complications?" Bren corrected.

"No lies or deceit," Latisha amended, homing in on the area that mattered to her most.

"Something tells me I'm included in that assessment," Bren drawled, slowly allowing his gaze to drift across Latisha's face.

"You said things you didn't mean," she reminded him, seeing the hotel ahead of them. "And I don't like people who do that, who find it far easier to tell the truth only when a lie will no longer do. Not that any of it matters now."

"It matters to me," Bren confessed, annoyed that the conversation seemed destined to be cut short as Latisha turned the Jeep into Sebastian's parking lot. As she pulled up the hand brake and kept the engine running, he felt desperate for more time with her. "Why don't you join me in the lobby for coffee?"

"I really need to get back to the *Caribbean Rose*," Latisha said. "It's late."

"Tomorrow then," Bren persisted. "Allow me to explain."

"It really doesn't matter," Latisha breathed,

about to add her reasons. But before she could do so, a familiar person made her way over toward the Jeep and tapped hard on the passenger-door window. Latisha recognized her immediately and wondered how the woman came to know Bren. "Is this your . . . wife?" she asked, mortified, as Bren instantly rolled down the window.

"Latisha, I'd like you to meet my sister Veronica," Bren announced, returning the introduction. "Veronica, meet Latisha Fenshaw. She was at the dinner party tonight."

Veronica's deep, penetrating gaze locked like a snake directly on Latisha. "I suppose I should say hi or something," she offered, making no mention to her brother that they had met earlier on the beach. "But I really need to talk to Bren."

Latisha realized that Veronica seemed agitated and somewhat disturbed, and nodded her head in acknowledgment. "Of course," she conceded, turning to Bren. "I'll take a rain check on that coffee."

Bren did not disguise his disappointment. He reached forward and took a hold of Latisha's left hand, squeezing it gently with his own. The gesture was secretive, tangible, and deeply meaningful. "Another time, I hope?"

"Perhaps," Latisha said, carefully releasing her hand.

As he walked away from the Jeep, Veronica gripped Bren's arm. "I can't find Alan," she whispered.

Latisha heard the words clearly as Bren closed the door and bade his farewell. Up until that moment, it did not register that Veronica was in fact Alan Clayton's wife. That this beautiful woman to

whom she had told her failed love story had the
unfortunate luck of being married to the liar,
cheat, and adulterer she had been discussing.
Latisha felt the instant panic rise up in the pit of
her stomach moments before she reversed the
Jeep and took it onto the main road.

Veronica was pregnant with Alan's baby. That
was the next piece of information to filter.
Latisha could hardly believe it. It had to be the
mother of all coincidences that she had even met
the woman. She had expected Alan's wife to be
much older, more plain and fat. She had gone so
far as to imagine her ugly. But reality proved otherwise. Latisha pumped the gas like a maniac to
quell the thought that her rival had always been
someone as physically attractive as herself.

The pain was back when she finally dropped
her heavy body into bed. Lady Sarah was not on
board, so there was no one except the captain
with whom she could gossip about her terrifying
discovery without being judged. The nightmare
suddenly seemed more real and Latisha lay
awake for a long time spinning events around in
her head. Finally, just as she had resolved to
avoid any confrontations on the small island, she
heard the faraway giggles of Lady Sarah's arrival.

Someone was obviously with her. Piers Lapare,
Latisha remembered, sensing that Lady Sarah had
obviously enjoyed her night. Latisha would no
doubt be told about it all in the morning when she
could also fill in the gaps with her own news.
When sleep finally came, only one lasting memory
lingered, causing an uncertain sensation to invade
her body: Bren Hunter's affectionate squeeze of

her hand. In her hazy dream, something deep down told Latisha that she liked it.

The moment dawn broke, a knock at Latisha's door roused her instantly. She turned in her bed, then looked through her porthole, where a clear, flawlessly blue sky gazed back at her. Then with her head still stuck in her pillow, she murmured an impassioned plea that she required another half hour in bed. But Lady Sarah burst into the cabin suite like a woman in full bloom and made a declaration that had Latisha sitting up against her pillow immediately.

"I'm in love!"

The three words echoed like bells. "What?" Latisha was shocked.

"He's everything I'm looking for," Sarah began, perching herself on the edge of Latisha's bed to begin the wonderful tale of having been wooed into submission. "He's adorably sweet, good-looking, charming, has these amazing roaming hands . . ." She giggled like a teenager. "I'm being swept off my feet and I've never felt this way since your father."

"Sarah," Latisha warned, thinking back to when she had been wooed into a wild romance fourteen months ago. "This may not be a full sweep. It may be a bit of a dustup."

"Somehow, I don't think so," Sarah protested, between bouts of giggles. "I think he's going to reach every nook and cranny with his broom."

"You only met the guy yesterday," Latisha said, alarmed to see Lady Sarah appearing so carefree, impulsive, and joyously young.

"Love at first bite." Sarah chuckled, while tilt-ing her neck to proudly display the red mark caused from smooching with her French ad-mirer. "Piers Lapare is sooo . . . magical," she went on. "He's picking me up in half an hour and we're going shopping together. I can't wait."

Latisha realized that Lady Sarah was fully dressed in a pair of embroidered stone-washed jeans and a red T-shirt. Her long, curly black hair was swept up into a ponytail and her face seemed colorful and bright. The woman that faced Latisha this morning was definitely much younger than her thirty-nine years. Latisha en-vied Lady Sarah's spirit, but was happy that her father's widow had moved on since his passing.

"He's coming here?" Latisha asked.

"Yes." Sarah jumped up from the bed. "So I'm going to have some breakfast and then meet him on the harbor. Don't wait up for me."

And with that answer, she was gone.

Latisha blinked, reclined in her bed, and rolled over. An hour later, there was another knock at her door. Latisha was now out of her bed and had just taken a shower. With a towel around her body, she padded over and held on to the doorknob, pulling the door ajar. She imagined Lady Sarah had gone on her date, so was expecting Nigel, the captain. He was equipped with his satellite phone, which he promptly handed over, apologetic for having disturbed her.

"It's Mr. Linford Mills," he told her.

The captain waited at a discreet distance by the door while Latisha took the phone. "Hello."

"Hello there," Linford leered on the other side. "How are you today?"

"Okay."

"I enjoyed your delightful company last night and wondered if you'd like to repeat the experience over lunch today."

"Actually . . ." Latisha paused long enough to concoct a lie. "I'm already booked for lunch."

"Are you free later?"

Latisha felt ill at having to invent another plausible lie. Quickly deciding no explanation was required, she said, "I have plans."

"Plans?" Linford objected.

"Yes," Latisha affirmed.

"Okay," he conceded quietly. "Maybe I can catch you another time."

"Thank you for calling," Latisha told him, handing the phone back to Nigel. "If he calls again, I'm not in," she ordered. "He's far too old."

He nodded. "Yes, ma'am."

As she closed the door, Latisha heaved a sickly breath before walking over to the porthole to take a second glance at the sky. It was now a much deeper blue, with a glaring sun beating down. The day was indeed hot enough for her to relax in a lounger on the sundeck with a good book and breakfast. Actually, she decided, consulting her watch, which read 9:33 A.M., a snack would probably be more appropriate.

Forty minutes later, she reclined on her back in a Cacharel toile push-up rose-colored bikini, which she had borrowed from Lady Sarah's room, with dark shades over her eyes and a sheer gloss on her lips. High overhead, the sky was a flawless blue and the sun was hot on her bare arms and outstretched legs. The marina with its array of yachts bustled about her and Latisha was happy to do nothing except bathe in the sweltering hot sun.

She had oiled her arms, neck, face, and legs with enough UVA protection to allow the glowing undertones of her skin to glisten like velvet. Latisha also kept her hair down because she was too lazy to do anything else with it. Besides, she had reasoned before going up on the sundeck, she was not expecting company today. So it was of some surprise when a few minutes later, Nigel was back in front of her, his tall frame blocking the gaze of the sun as he stared down and roused her attention.

"What is it?" Latisha asked, annoyed at his disturbance. She had half expected him to announce that Linford Mills was on the phone a second time, now aware that the man had his eyes set on her.

"There's a Mr. Bren Hunter to see you," he exclaimed softly. "Would you like me to send him up?"

Latisha sat up immediately. "Who did you say?"

"Congressman Hunter."

"Oh my God," Latisha breathed, amazed. "Where is he now?"

The captain smiled. "I left him—"

"I'm right here," a silky deep voice interrupted.

Latisha's heart stopped beating the moment she saw Bren Hunter emerge from the lower deck and walk across the teak floor toward her. He seemed even more handsome than how she remembered him from the night before, now dressed in beige-colored shorts and a white T-shirt, with brown leather sandals on his feet.

Freshly shaven and his hair groomed into place, there was no mistaking him. He was the man who had filled the dreams that had kept her tossing until dawn.

"Good . . . morning," she said waveringly, unsure that her eyes were not playing tricks with her.

"Hello again," Bren responded with a smile.

His mood seemed bright and open, and Latisha felt unsure how to take him. Natural courtesy took over. "Would you like a drink?"

"No," Bren deliberately told the captain.

Nigel nodded and disappeared instantly. As he did so, Bren came closer, standing directly above Latisha's cushioned recliner, deliberately blocking the sun as his tall shadow loomed over her. Latisha removed her shades and stared up at him, her instincts sensing the movement of Bren's eyes as he charted the sensual fleshy curves of her body. The bikini she was wearing left little to the imagination and she consciously reached for the flimsy pink caftan she had tossed at her feet and plunged her arms into it.

Bren's eyes flickered at every movement, leaving Latisha unnerved as she spoke. "What are you doing here?" she asked, in a tone slightly objecting to his uninvited attention. "I thought you were meeting a friend this morning."

"I came to apologize about my sister," Bren began, his own tone sorrowful that Latisha had witnessed Veronica's erratic outburst the night before. "And—"

"We don't want her finding out that I was the unfortunate woman to have been duped by her husband," Latisha interrupted, feeling sick that such awful events should catch up with her while she was vacationing on the British Virgin Islands. "Don't worry. I'm not going to say anything."

Bren was silent. "What will it take to put Alan behind you?" he asked suddenly.

He took a step forward and Latisha was more than aware of his towering presence hovering over her. She also knew that her summarization of her current malaise was not sitting well with Bren Hunter. It had been three months since she had made her discovery about Alan, and Bren had been the shoulder she had cried on. Three months after, she realized it must now appear to him that she had still not let go.

"He is behind me," she insisted.

"Then why do you talk of him as though you still care?" Bren probed, folding his arms against his chest.

"I don't," Latisha affirmed, staring up at him until she made contact with his eyes.

Bren's gaze intensified. "No?" he responded. "Prove it."

Latisha laughed with a certain degree of irony. "I don't have to prove anything to you," she said, offended at his very boldness for suggesting it.

"You're right. You don't," Bren agreed. "But you do need to prove it to yourself."

"Is that why you're here?" Latisha asked him, curiously. "To tell me how I should feel today?" She slowly rose from her recliner, a touch more than offended as she walked around him to put distance between them. "I'll tell you how I feel, shall I?" Latisha faced Bren from where she was standing by the bridge, where the captain steered the yacht, and looked him right in the eyes. "Sorry for your sister, that's what. Sorry that's she's pregnant for a man who doesn't know her worth. Sorry for all womankind that men like Alan exist. And sorry that you're here, spoiling my day with your fretting and worrying that I may let something slip to Veronica."

Latisha was amazed when Bren immediately seemed affronted. "And I feel sorry that you're not prepared to open your heart again to someone new," he fired back in lame defense of his sister.

"My heart is open and ready for love with the next available person," Latisha declared defensively.

Bren took a step forward, his interest primed to know more. "Is that the promise you told me you made to yourself?"

"Yes." Latisha nodded. "So you see, I'm not as screwed up as you think."

"I don't think anything." He shrugged, coolly contemplating her.

"Oh yes, you do," Latisha said hotly. "You came here to see if I was crying my eyes out, didn't you? Or did you think I wanted to scratch your sister's eyes out instead?" When Bren remained quiet, Latisha realized she had hit a nerve. "You surprise me, Mr. Hunter."

"I wanted to be sure that you were all right," Bren finally admitted, on a more professional level. "That's all."

"And why shouldn't I be?" Latisha demanded, folding her arms against her chest.

"Because . . ." Bren almost seemed lost for words as he stared at Latisha's fiery face. "I want you to keep that promise you made to yourself."

"Like the one you made to me?" Latisha reminded him, twisting her lips into a hard line. "The games on the playing fields of political combat may be different, Mr. Hunter, but I'm not a fighter in your arena. I play in the real world."

"I'm sure you do," Bren acknowledged, his gaze softening slightly as he advanced another step toward the bridge. "But there are games that are vital to the effective functioning of our lives, and others that tie us up in knots and stall the whole process of getting to know someone."

"And there's the blame game where dumping on the other side means someone hasn't really absorbed the lessons of his own experience," Latisha responded, her lips still curled despite the jitters Bren's dark eyes evoked inside her.

"Alan and Veronica's marriage is more complicated than you think," Bren attempted to explain, his heart pumping heavy as he became enthralled by the delicate twist of those lips. "Her health is at stake. We have to watch her blood pressure and—"

"This is what you wanted to tell me last night?" Latisha interrupted, zoning in on the soft, lazy, sympathetic tones resonating in Bren's voice. She forced a slight smile to indicate an end to the conversation. "As you can see, Mr. Hunter, I'm all right. I'm not going to tell Veronica anything, so you can go now."

Latisha expected Bren to retreat and leave. After all, she had made it plain she had survived the ordeal of meeting his sister. But to her chagrin, he took several steps forward until he had filled the space between them, his gaze penetrating with a smoldering flame flickering brightly and defiantly at her.

"No," he said, looking down into her face and boldly using the back of his hand to gently stroke her cheek.

Latisha stared, shaken that Bren's very closeness should pluck at her heartstrings so easily. She imagined this was what politicians were—dashing, daring, and dangerous. That only a powerful man could walk onto her yacht and make such a bold gesture within minutes of his arrival.

"I'll take that move to be a form of your style?" she remarked, gently brushing his hand away. "I also think you have suffered a little sunstroke to think I'm going to be sucked into some sort of ploy. I've already told you, I'm going to keep quiet."

"The only stroke I seem to be suffering is from the loss of kissing you again," Bren returned, refusing to be deterred.

His admission rocked Latisha to the core. "That was then and this is now," she stuttered, taking a few steps backward, shocked at his brazen declaration. Shocked that something deep within had delighted at his sweet confession.

"Time changes everything," Bren sensibly acknowledged. "Here we are again, unexpectedly meeting on the British Virgin Islands. I would say that has to mean something."

"It means the devil likes to play tricks," Latisha told him sternly, "which I'm not going to fall for a second time."

"You don't feel the tremor, as I do?" Bren asked

suddenly, his face masked in confusion as he obliterated the last bit of distance between them with three short steps.

"I'll have you know, Mr. Hunter, my emotions run on a personal Richter scale and you haven't measured so much as a blip," Latisha lied profusely.

Bren seemed surprised. "Not even a murmur?"

"Not even a twitch," Latisha exaggerated, taking yet a farther step back until she felt the hard glass of the bridge window against her backbone. "You came about your sister. Your apology has been noted. I'm not voting today, so I think it's time that you—"

But before she could end her sentence, Bren had lunged forward. The kiss came just as quickly, in long, tempting mouthfuls. Her eyes wide open, Latisha was shocked to find herself in his arms. There was no escaping the shaking of her legs, the quiver of her heart, or the butterflies that were causing havoc in her stomach. Bren Hunter was most definitely causing a stir, one she could not deny.

Her eyelids tried to remain open. She tried to keep her expression fixed, but to little avail. The moment Bren's kiss deepened, Latisha was melting. Every brush of his lips, every fluid movement, every joyous second of potent indulgence had flung her into another existence, where an awakened feeling was vying for control. She had not meant to kiss him back, but something that could only be attributed to the power of nature had taken over.

Without quite realizing it herself, Latisha was returning the small shifts and movements that

Bren's mouth was encouraging within her. She matched his momentum measure for measure, adjusted to the pace of his rhythm, and allowed herself to mirror the way in which he was adapting to her lips. The kiss was as phenomenal as it was unexpected, and when she was finally able to tear her mouth away, Latisha realized she had fallen for the sheer volume and velocity of Bren Hunter's power.

"That'll rock you," he told her, his voice bringing her back to the present with a slight thud.

Latisha almost felt her feet weaken beneath her when Bren released her from his arms. Her voice was constrained and confused when she spoke, yet the aftershock prompted her to raise a defiant guard. "You haven't succeeded in getting my vote."

"I don't need to," Bren told her, in the manner of a politician who had scored enough points to win. "I've caused a tremor on that little Richter scale you got going on, and that's enough for me."

"Not for me," Latisha lied through tight lips, annoyed that she had fallen for Bren Hunter's seduction so easily. "I'm flying back to Florida the day after tomorrow. I doubt we shall have occasion to meet again."

Bren appeared surprised, but composed himself quickly. "The world is a very small place, Miss Fenshaw," he said quietly. "I'm sure there's every likelihood that we shall meet again."

Latisha was not deterred.

"Why are you doing this?" she asked, bemused.

"I'd like to be your friend," Bren revealed.

"You can't change the past," Latisha told him.

"No," Bren admitted, his brows raised with confidence. "But I can do something about your future. And believe me, I intend to."

"Not if I can help it," Latisha returned firmly. "Let's get one thing clear. I don't particularly care for your ethics or the fact that you seem preoccupied with winning or losing my friendship. My life is not open to manipulation of any kind. So, in your own words, forget you ever met me and get on with your life." With that answer, Latisha pointed toward the stairway that Bren had emerged from, which led down toward the lower deck.

Bren was startled. His brows dropped immediately. He conceded, accepting defeat. "As you wish."

Within seconds, he was gone, leaving Latisha to confront herself with the one resounding truth. Bren had caused a shock wave on a magnitude she had never known before and what she had effectively achieved was to refuse Bren the power to do it again.

The time read 8:01 P.M. when Lady Sarah rushed into the dining cabin like a woman on cloud nine. She seemed chattier and more forthcoming than ever with her face lit up like a woman raring to go.

"Look what he's bought me," Sarah enthused, holding her right hand up into the air to reveal a very expensive ring on her index finger. "It's a Tahitian black pearl," she boasted, pointing at the stone embedded in eighteen-karat gold. "From the lagoons of French Polynesia, the queen of all pearls." Kissing the ring, she added, "Handmade by the famous Hans Eberle."

Latisha was seated at the dinner table, polishing her plate with what was left of a wonderful chicken Caesar salad. She was still unnerved after the experience of Bren Hunter's devastating kiss, but her gaze followed her stepmother as she walked around the table and deposited herself in the nearest chair. On closer inspection, Latisha realized the ring was made on the premises of the exclusive Caribbean jeweler and most likely cost a small fortune.

"This is beautiful," she gasped, on seeing that the ring was also sprinkled with tiny bright diamonds. "It must have cost him a pretty penny."

"Yes, it did," Sarah confirmed, "and he said I'm worth it."

Latisha nodded. "I would agree. But isn't this relationship moving a little too fast?"

"Fast?" Sarah sighed. "I can hardly wait to see him again."

"I just want you to be careful, that's all," Latisha cautioned. "I can see this man obviously likes you, but it is still early."

"I know what I'm doing," Sarah said, a little peeved. "Piers and I are going scuba diving in the morning and then out for a spot of lunch."

"No chance of you spending the day with me then?" Latisha inquired, feeling a touch neglected.

Lady Sarah adopted a sorrowful expression. "I'm sorry," she mumbled apologetically. "I didn't plan to ignore you like this. It's just that—"

"You're in love," Latisha finished, in a sardonic tone.

"Latisha?" Sarah reached out and touched her stepdaughter's hand. "I hope you don't think I've forgotten your father. You do know nobody could ever replace him in my heart. He still has a special place there."

"I know." Latisha swallowed, forcing back the lump in her throat as the memory of him flashed in her mind's eye.

She had always known that one day Lady Sarah would move on and find love again with someone else, only she had not expected it to happen so soon. Two years felt like such a short time, but of course different people healed in different ways. Naturally, it seemed right that Lady Sarah should live her life again in a manner of her own choosing. She was still a young woman, after all. Not so unlike herself, a woman also hoping to find love.

"So you don't mind?" Latisha heard the question, but it was seconds later before she comprehended it.

"My father would want you to be happy," she answered, holding back the stinging tears in her eyes. "And I want what he would have wanted for you."

Lady Sarah reached out and gave her an affectionate hug. "I'm the luckiest person in the world to have someone so wonderful in my life as you." She chuckled, kissing Latisha on her left cheek. "I must arrange for you to meet Piers Lapare before you return to Florida."

"Invite him over for dinner tomorrow night at 8:00," Latisha suggested, by way of affecting a formal introduction. She hoped the activity would also keep her occupied and her mind off a certain congressman who seemed to shadow her every thought from the moment they had kissed. "I would love to meet him."

"Then it's settled." Sarah smiled, her eyes sparkling with emotion. "Believe me, you'll love him."

"Hmm." Latisha sighed.

"What's the matter?" Sarah asked, on seeing the combination of mystery and misery in Latisha's eyes.

A casual shrug. "Bren Hunter came by today," Latisha told her.

"The congressman?" Sarah gasped. Observing Latisha's forlorn expression, she added, "That's not a good thing, is it?"

Latisha shook her head in the negative. "No, it's not. He kissed me."

Sarah arched her well-marked brows. "On the lips?"

"It shouldn't have happened," Latisha said, aware her body was still hungover from the impact of it. "In fact, it was bizarre."

"Dreamlike," Sarah corrected, with a smile on her lips.

Latisha's eyes narrowed at her. "He came onto the yacht, we talked, we kissed. He left."

"Just like that?"

Latisha nodded. "Exactly like that. Except I gave him the brush-off. Dating him would just add to the existing complications."

"What complications?" Sarah inquired, intrigued.

"You wouldn't believe," Latisha remarked, deciding to come clean. "Remember I'd told you how I discovered I'd been dating a married man?"

Sarah nodded. "Yes, you told just about anyone who had ears to listen, including that woman you offended on the beach."

Latisha felt the ripple of that memory vibrate down her spine with the awful knowledge of whom she had been speaking to. "This married man told me his name was Graham Jefferson," she went on, "but his real name is Alan Clayton and he's Bren Hunter's brother-in-law."

"But kiss me neck back to rhatid," Sarah cussed, in what was, to her, uncustomary usage of the Caribbean lingo. "They're related?"

"Yes," Latisha confirmed. "It could only happen to me."

"They're related!" Sarah repeated, as though she needed to hear herself say it a second time for accuracy. "That's—"

"Why I can't get involved," Latisha finished. "I think he expected to try and get to know me in some way, like a friend. He was aggressive, like this . . . Piers Lapare you've met, and I would much rather he wasn't."

"Because you could find yourself bumping into Alan Clayton at some point?" Sarah surmised.

"Exactly," Latisha agreed. "And I really wouldn't want to find myself facing charges of murder, which is why I showed Bren Hunter his cards."

"Forget Alan," Sarah enthused with an air of excitement, as though she was seeing a new picture altogether. "If Congressman Hunter has his eyes set on you, you'd better know now I've heard he's a man who usually gets what he wants."

"That's what I'm afraid of," Latisha responded. "I don't want my heart played around with again. I can't take another letdown."

"You'll take a chance if you thought you'd met the right person," Sarah proclaimed. "When your father passed away, I never expected in my wildest dreams to feel this way again. But look at me now."

"How can I love again when I've been so hurt?" Latisha insisted on knowing the answer to that question.

"You will," Sarah promised. "If it's not Congressman Hunter, it will be someone else just as determined as he is. Love finds us all eventually, whether we like it or not."

Chapter Six

Love finds us all eventually, whether we like it or not.
Those were the words on Latisha's mind as she
awoke the following morning. Her cynical sub-
conscious found it hard to believe them. *Why
should anyone love me?* she wondered. Though the
frustration could clearly be seen on her face, her
hazelnut-brown complexion glowed with health,
the copper brown of her eyes sparkled with life,
and her pink rosy lips were smooth like silk, having witnessed how skillfully Bren Hunter had
kissed her. But there would be no thought of that
happening again, she told herself while getting
dressed. She had shut him out of her life and he
had gotten the message loud and clear.

Half an hour later, Latisha was at the breakfast
table with an absent Lady Sarah. She was bored.
Breakfast of ackee and saltfish, fried mushrooms
and onions, prepared by the local cook who
boarded the *Caribbean Rose* every morning armed
with a basketful of fresh supplies, did not look appealing in the slightest, so went uneaten. She had
no idea how she should spend her day, though
Latisha recalled that Lady Sarah and Piers Lapare
were expected for dinner later that evening.

With that in mind, she decided to go shopping.

Town Road in Tortola was the place for picking up the best cultural artifacts to take home. She had promised to buy Josette a Boscoe painting to fill a wall space in her living room, and herself a Land handbag from their fine leather collection to replace the old one she had. Then there was the El Dorado rum she had intended to pick up for her mother. With an image of pink or red flowers for the dinner table dancing around in her mind, Latisha went to the shore intending to also buy a bunch of bougainvillea from the nearest florist shop.

She took the Jeep. Latisha needed the drive to clear her head. Her thoughts were mostly on how she had behaved when she saw Bren Hunter. She was surprised that she had been so forthright and firm. Latisha realized this was a new side of herself she had not seen before. There was a sense of determination, and yet there was also a levelheadiness she was unable to ignore. Was Latisha Fenshaw finally growing up?

If so, why could she not get Bren Hunter out of her mind? After leaving New York, she had tried to forget him. There was no possibility of her ever seeing him again, she had thought. But fate had taken over and he was back in her life. Yet she had pushed him away. In fact, she had been rude. With the lingering sense of his kiss still on her lips, she had told him to forget her and get on with his life, just as he himself had once told her.

Latisha pumped the engine, frustrated at her bewilderment. She felt confused and upset by her confusion. The sensation was as though she were reaching for something, and whatever it was

it constantly evaded her. She could see it and just
about feel it, but it was not quite there. And
adding to her confusion was not knowing what
on earth it all meant. She tried not to worry. It
was not in her nature to dwell on matters she
could not solve, but when she finally parked the
car on the main road and got out, she soon
found that her brain was having difficulty grap-
pling with things.

She quickly propelled her mind to the task at
hand—spending money. That would soon do the
trick and bring her back to her former self—a quietly confident, funny, and generous person. At
least that was what Latisha wanted to believe.
Dressed in a pair of luminous blue cotton trousers,
a white cotton tunic, and patterned canvas es-
padrilles on her feet, her white canvas and leather
handbag hung loosely over her shoulder, she
began to window-gaze while gingerly strolling
along.

The hours flew by in much the same way as
Latisha's shopping spree, in a daze. She had allowed herself several indulgences, purchasing a
hat and several tropically designed clips for her
hair, then the audaciously expensive perfume
that had caused a discreet gasp at the checkout
counter when she charged it to her American Ex-
press card. She had not forgotten Josette, or her
mother, and was sufficiently laden with enough
bags and a large painting beneath her arm when
she began the slow walk back to her car.

Her mood was positively giddy. Latisha felt she
was back to the woman she had recognized in the
mirror on awakening that morning, the one who
had momentarily disappeared, but was now back

in full form. Her spirits had lifted and she could feel the smile dancing on her lips as she opened the Jeep's door and began to load her wares. Besides her self-indulgence, there were several more items that she had decided would decorate her home in England, and a small present for Lady Sarah.

With everything inside, Latisha slammed the door shut and turned to find herself recognizing the woman from across the street. The woman appeared distressed. It was not difficult to see that she had been crying. Latisha was paralyzed for all of three seconds contemplating what to do. She was unsure whether Veronica Clayton needed help. It was only her recollection of what Bren had told her that made Latisha cross the road.

"Veronica?" She approached the woman whose teary gaze welcomed her timely presence. "Are you all right?"

"No," Veronica whispered. Her hands were trembling and she was gently rubbing her stomach. "I don't feel well."

Latisha became concerned, especially on seeing how hot and flustered Veronica seemed. "I have my Jeep across the way," she said, pointing to it from where they were standing. "Would you like me to take you back to your hotel?"

Veronica nodded as more tears spilled from her eyes.

Latisha held out her hand to offer support and began to safely guide her across the road. Only when Veronica was comfortably seated in the passenger seat did she start the four-wheeler. As she entered the flow of traffic, Latisha briefly spied Veronica's expression. Alan Clayton's wife was nothing like the friendly, lively, and feisty woman she had met on the beach. The woman who was now silently whimpering, but who did not seem to be in any real physical pain, betrayed a melodramatic flair Latisha could never have expected.

"Your brother told me you're expecting a baby," she disclosed, feeling she should check on whether a diversion to the nearest hospital was required.

"Bren told you that?" Veronica gasped in amazement.

"He's . . . looking forward to becoming an uncle," Latisha quickly lied. "I was just wondering if you would like to see a doctor."

Veronica shook her head vigorously in the negative. "Just take me back to the hotel," she ordered soberly. With an impassioned plea, she added, "Please."

Latisha was more than aware of the overwhelming anguish in Veronica's voice. It occurred to her that Alan Clayton was not far behind it. To her chagrin, Latisha felt a tremor of her own anguish begin to surface. It seemed she was suddenly on a slippery slope headed for a terrible disaster having Alan Clayton's wife sharing her Jeep. Veronica was the woman she had not known existed, the one Alan had abandoned her for. The one he had gone back to and impregnated with his first child. Alan's back door.

Latisha chewed on this as she drove on, realizing that the source of her difficulty was becoming more apparent. It was a struggle to silence the alarm bells that had begun sounding inside her head. What Latisha realized was that Veronica needed to know the truth about her husband.

Someone needed to sit this woman down and tell her about the man she was married to. Tell her what a piece of scum he was. Tell her that her love would be appreciated more elsewhere. But it could not be done. She, Latisha Fenshaw, was not the person to level such accusations.

"How many weeks pregnant are you?" she asked, attempting to make conversation.

"Twenty weeks and two days," came the muffled reply.

Latisha nodded, closing her eyes briefly to blink back the sudden pain of reckoning: Alan had still been attempting to formulate a relationship with her during the time his wife's conception must have taken place. It was a further revelation. More confirmation that she had indeed been his mistress with no knowledge of her status. She felt the deep anger swell at the pit of her stomach at his brazen audacity. Several large breaths later to steady her breathing, Latisha was rankled.

"What's your husband like?" she queried, with a perverse need to suffer more pain.

"My man's name is Alan," Veronica muttered, overwrought. "And he's about as elusive as the tooth fairy." She was clearly disturbed before she spouted off. "And if I ever catch up with whoever it is he's been seeing behind my back, Miss Thang is gonna need more than Botox injections to put her face back together again."

Latisha was stunned. "You think he's having an affair?"

"He's had the personality of a refrigerator ever since we got here," Veronica said, stifling her distress, "but I'm gonna cook him up good. Like the old song goes, 'who's making love to your old lady while you were out making love?' Yeah, I'm a-gonna cook them both up real good."

Latisha heard the declaration of war and felt her body tremble. "Surely, he wouldn't know anyone here. You're both on vacation."

"That's what I thought," Veronica revealed, tears now rolling down her cheeks. "So where's my man?"

Latisha sighed her relief. At least Alan was not with her. "You should talk to your brother," she said on a sensible note. "Maybe—"

"Bren?" Veronica laughed. "All he cares about right now is his big position in Washington, D.C. He's hoping to run for that Senate seat in New York in the next election. Did you know that?"

"No," Latisha said in shock. "What's he doing wasting time here?" she queried further.

"He had to visit an offshore bank," Veronica divulged, drying her eyes with the back of her hand. "And . . . keeping me company, I guess, between golf games. He's a good man though. And he needed a break. It was his idea that we come down here so I could get me some rest. I'm under doctor's orders, but I just want to go home, back to Boston."

The Jeep was pulling into Sebastian's Hotel when Latisha recognized everything about the tall man pacing the forecourt. He was dressed casually in a pair of stone-washed jeans and a pale blue Versace short-sleeved shirt with tan-colored moccasins on his feet. He looked anxious and worried as the car came round. She saw him momentarily flash a glance at her, moments before their eyes locked dead center. Bren's expression changed to one of mere amazement as he glimpsed his sister seated in the Jeep. Latisha saw the brief smile play along his lips as she cut the engine and watched him run around to the driver's side. She rolled her window down, keeping the door closed to effect a barrier between them.

"I found Veronica in town," she explained, catching the sparkling color of his eyes. It signified how happy he was to see her again. "She's not feeling well."

Bren glanced across at his sister. "It was very kind of you to bring her here," he replied politely. "How is she?"

"Distressed and anxious about finding her husband," Latisha revealed, her lips held pert at having to say it. "But, to be honest, I think she's also running a temperature."

A fickle glance shot between them. "Will you help me get her inside?" Bren asked suddenly.

"Well . . . I . . ." Latisha began, not wishing to become involved. It was more than her sanity's worth to see Alan's wife in such a state and she wanted nothing more than to get back to the *Caribbean Rose*. "I'm expecting company at 8:00 and it's already 5:30."

"I just want you to sit with her until I call a doctor," Bren persisted.

Latisha lowered her voice discreetly. "Please don't ask me to do this," she whispered. "I can't—"

"Oh my God," Veronica lamented suddenly. "I think I'm going to vomit."

Latisha's head spun round. "Not in the Jeep," she screamed, clicking her safety belt and slipping the gear lever into park before quickly jumping from the driver's seat. She was at the

passenger door in an instant, almost rudely helping Veronica disembark. Bren was two steps
behind, his face growing with immense concern
at seeing Veronica looking so anemic and helpless.

Latisha expected that this fragile image was not
what Veronica wanted people to see. It looked
pitiful. Her face had paled, her eyes were weepy,
and the lines of anguish were marked in her face
in even more tangible distress. Here was pain.
Alan's wife was suffering and Latisha felt drawn
to her in sympathy.

She took a hold of Veronica's right hand.
"Breathe deeply," she advised, sensing that Bren's
warm body had inched closer. Latisha did her
best to ignore the strong magnetism of his prox-
imity and kept her eyes on Veronica. Bren's sister
was not paying any attention, but Latisha pursued the rescue by gently forcing her to bend
over and face the ground to aid her recovery.
"I'm going to help you get to your room and
Bren is going to have someone take a look at
you."

"I don't need a doctor," Veronica insisted
weakly. "I need the father of my baby." The tears
began to fall hopelessly.

"I'm sure he'll be along soon," Bren explained,
taking a hold of his sister's left hand. "Let's just
get you inside, out of the sun."

Latisha was mindful that her hand did not
relax, nor did it curve into Veronica's. As they
worked their way through the hotel lobby, she
kept her clasp light on the short journey until the
moment they made it to the room, where she
pulled it free. It was symbolic that a good part of

her was uncomfortable with seeing another woman look so feeble and that behind the facade the real damage had been caused by a man. As Veronica began to lie slowly on the bed, Latisha's one thought was to leave and dismiss the awful scenario from her mind. But Bren was not going to allow her to depart so easily.

"You help her into bed," he sounded out in a flat and weary tone. "I'll be right back."

"But . . ." Latisha objected, slicing a glance at her watch. "I'm expected—"

"Ten minutes," Bren begged, his gaze sending a plea in her direction. "Please?"

Latisha conceded the moment his pewter-colored eyes swayed her into submission. "Ten minutes."

It was two hours before the doctor arrived. Another twenty before he left. He had diagnosed dehydration and hypertension, and prescribed a sedative that would cause no harm to the unborn child, but would help Veronica get through the evening. Latisha was outside on the veranda waiting for the verdict when Bren finally joined her to break the news. She felt both relieved and exhausted, and was looking forward to returning to the yacht.

"So, Veronica's going to be all right?" she asked, careful to show the right amount of concern.

"A good night's rest and she should be okay," Bren responded, wiping his forehead in relief. "Thank you."

"For what?" Latisha was bemused.

"Being here. Sitting with her," Bren told her. "It must have been very hard for you and an imposition for me to ask. If I could've changed the circumstances to save you from going through this, I would have."

"She seemed frightened," Latisha said, nervous at the reminder of some of the things Veronica had said. "I couldn't leave her, despite knowing . . ."

"That she's Alan's wife," Bren finished. He appreciated her difficult position. Latisha hardly knew Veronica and he suspected she must've felt some embarrassment at facing the nameless woman who had always been a constant in Alan's life. But Bren appreciated Latisha's courage, too. That she did not abandon his sister—a person in a moment of distress—out of spite or hatred. Within seconds, he felt his admiration for her swell his heart. "You're remarkable, do you know that?"

Latisha smiled weakly and shrugged. "It's a known fact." It was her bravado talking. Deep down, Latisha knew she felt frightened being this close to Bren.

"I'm sure it is," Bren agreed, returning an equally friendly smile. But a layer of sadness lay behind it. He had not forgotten their farewell conversation. Latisha had told him to get on with his life and this was an indication that she did not care to see him again. But after all she had done, he felt obligated to at least offer her coffee, and if it was at all possible that they could part on more friendly terms, it would mean more to him than her simple dismissal the last time they had spoken.

Latisha's voice suddenly broke into his thoughts. "I should leave."

Bren immediately stalled her with a gentle tug at her wrist. "As a good Samaritan, I should at least reward you with Sebastian's finest cinnamon coffee to send you on your way."

Latisha felt the churning of emotions in the pit of her stomach the moment Bren's warm fingers curled around her wrist. The sensation worked its way quickly to her chest and spread like a rash across her shoulders, down her arms, and lingered at her fingertips. She shook immediately, knowing that Bren would have felt the tremor. The twinkle in his eyes indicating he felt the surge was the answer she needed to withdraw her wrist.

"I can't."

"Latisha," he whispered, the wounded loss of her reflecting briefly in the dip of his brows. "Don't pull away from me."

The soft, moaning tone in his voice worked its magic to weaken Latisha, but she resolved not to be pulled into Bren's spell. "You're asking too much from me to even be here," she proclaimed, annoyed that Bren saw things too easily. "Alan could walk in here at any moment. We're outside his hotel room, the one he shares with his wife, remember? I don't want to be here a moment longer than I have to."

"Of course." Bren nodded, blinking as though he were coming out of a trance. "I'm not thinking straight. You must find me insensitive about this whole matter."

"I do," Latisha informed him breathlessly. "Where *is* Alan anyway?"

"I don't know and I don't much care," Bren said abruptly.

Latisha stepped back from him, seeing a good measure of frustration marked in Bren's face. "I should leave."

"I don't want you to leave," he admitted, his tone hoarse and firm. "I want to . . ." Bren hardly knew where to start to convince Latisha Fenshaw how much he needed to be with her. How much his heart yearned to get to know her. *If only you knew how much I want you,* his heart yelled out silently. "I want to say good-bye properly," he amended, desperately calming his voice. "Yesterday was . . . not how I'd wish it to be."

"It was what you told me in New York," Latisha reminded him, the pain of leaving there suddenly rising up to torment her.

"I'm sorry," Bren said.

"I'm sorry, too," Latisha replied, unsure as to why.

They both paused and took a breath. The silence enveloped them and a new, much deeper emotion swept over Bren and Latisha as they looked at each other. It was absurd. It was bizarre. It was uncanny. But at that precise moment, a new understanding developed between them. There was no mistaking it. No explaining it. As their eyes locked and the chemistry rocketed in the space between them, something happened. And whatever it was, Latisha and Bren both knew.

"Don't try to intellectualize this," Bren told her, his hand unconsciously reaching out to touch her waist.

Latisha felt the strong sensual pull toward him,

felt Bren's soft fingers against the strip of flesh at her waistline, and knew of his all-consuming power. She also knew of her vulnerability, even as his lips came closer and she accepted the brief brush of them against her own. "Not here," she whispered, the split second Bren tried to savor the taste of her.

He raised his head and followed her gaze to the double French doors behind him that led directly into Veronica's bedroom. Bren nodded his understanding. "This is tactless."

"It is," Latisha agreed. "Now you see why I have to leave."

"One coffee," Bren urged.

Latisha hesitated. "I . . ."

"You fly away tomorrow," he said, bristling, disliking the finality. "One coffee to say good-bye."

Latisha swallowed the lump in her throat and gave in.

"Nice hotel," she said moments later as they were seated at Sebastian's coffee and cocktail bar. "I've never had occasion to visit here before."

Against the polished wooden floor were bamboo tables and chairs for diners to partake of the scenic view. Adorning the perimeter of the small area were palm plants of varying sizes and height, adding a lavish Caribbean ambiance to what essentially looked like the sort of place newlyweds would hide out during their honeymoon. Latisha envied the couples she spied from where she was seated on a bar stool next to Bren. If she could write her life over, this was what she would have. A moment of true passion and romance in such a place as this while in love with someone she could cherish.

"Do you always stay on the *Caribbean Rose?*" Bren probed, clicking his fingers to summon the bartender.

"Yes, for as long as I can remember," Latisha disclosed, unable to take her eyes off two smooching couples.

Hearing her distant tone, Bren looked across and found Latisha distracted. He took the opportunity to scan the outline of her face, reminding himself how much he liked what he saw. To him, Latisha Fenshaw was a beautiful woman. He liked everything about her refined features, her hazelnut-brown, almost flawless complexion, the copper color of her eyes, and more importantly, the way she wore her hair pulled back into a ponytail and the neat curve of her kissable lips. She was just the sort of woman who could . . . possibly fit into his life. If only she would allow it.

"What's the attraction?" he queried, seconds before her gaze resettled on him.

"Nothing." Latisha dismissed her wishful dream in an instant. Seeing that Bren did not quite believe her, she added, "I was just thinking. I've been coming to the British Virgin Islands since I was twelve with my father and Josette, my sister. That was when my father started dating again, after the divorce. We used to stay at Nancy and George's villa in the Belmont estate, before he bought the yacht."

"Which is how old?"

"Fifteen years."

"So you're . . . twenty-seven," Bren surmised.

Latisha nodded.

Bren discerned the faintest twinkle in her eyes. *Did Alan know you like this?* he thought, treacherously. *Did he know those eyes of yours when in the throes of an orgasm?* He wondered further what was going on in the back of Latisha's mind as he ordered them both coffee. Was she uncomfortable, worried, or confused at being with him? Had she told Veronica anything she ought not to? Quickly, he decided against this. If there was one thing he had learned about Latisha Fenshaw, it was that she was a woman of her word. He could not imagine her looking forward to seeing Alan again, even to check out whether he still measured on her secret Ritcher scale. There was only one man he wanted to register an ultimate quake and that was him.

"So," Bren drawled, turning in his stool to face the curvy frame of the woman seated next to him. He detected the faraway expression on her face and wondered if she was thinking about her father. "Tell me one thing he clearly loved about you."

Latisha's mind went blank. "Who?"

Bren felt his heart drop. Maybe she was thinking about Alan after all. "Your father," he breathed, resting his left elbow against the bar while he scrutinized her more closely. He could see that the attraction between them was still strong, though neither of them at that moment was capable of addressing the issue.

Latisha smiled a little. "He liked the way I pinched the crust off my bread," she confessed with a deep, relaxed sigh in remembrance of the one man she had truly loved. "He liked it because he would do the same thing, too."

"Tell me more," Bren encouraged, eager to learn.

"He was born in Antigua, unlike my mother, who came from St. Kitts," Latisha revealed. "Before he passed, he was hailed as one of the greatest West Indian players in cricket history."

"A legend," Bren cooed.

Latisha's face was filled with admiration for her father. "He'd also been inducted into the Cricket Hall of Fame and was knighted by the queen for his services to cricket."

"That's amazing," Bren enthused. "Of course his name is familiar. I'm more of a golf person myself, but I recall . . . Wasn't Sir Joshua Fenshaw honored by the Antigua Cricket Association at a special function at the governor's mansion four years ago?"

"Yes," Latisha confirmed. "How did you know?"

"I was there," Bren announced. "It was one of the first of many invitations I'd received when I was elected to Congress. I didn't meet him, but I heard his speech. He paid tribute to another player whom he described as the 'coolest dude' as far as the game was concerned."

"That would be his best buddy and fast bowler, Flip Rowland," Latisha divulged, shaking her head incredulously. "I can't believe you were there."

"I tagged along with a friend," Bren went on. "You do look like your father. It was before—"

"He was in Trinidad when it happened," Latisha interrupted solemnly. "He was due to attend a West Indies Cricket Board–sponsored conference aimed at updating and standardizing a coaching manual. As a former West Indies captain and world record holder for the fastest test century, his views mattered. But he never made that conference. Sarah, his wife, found him. He'd died in his sleep."

"I'm sorry," Bren responded, reaching out to take a hold of Latisha's left hand. "It couldn't have been easy for either one of you, and your sister. How is Sarah now? She seemed happy when Linford Mills introduced us both at your charity party."

"She's doing just fine." Latisha chuckled. "In fact, right now, she's falling in love all over again with someone named Piers Lapare."

"At least she's moving on," Bren declared softly. "You should follow her example."

Latisha flinched and removed her hand from the safe haven of Bren's large one. "That would be difficult, considering I'm leaving for Florida in the morning," she mocked, annoyed at his suggestion. "And I'm sure you must have a lot of work to attend to. I'm told you might run for the Senate in the next election."

"Not this year's election," Bren corrected, while the bartender placed their hot coffees on coasters at the bar. "Maybe in four years' time." He paused. "Veronica told you?"

Latisha nodded, reaching immediately for her cup.

"I thought as much," Bren acknowledged. "I've only confided in her so far."

"What's it like . . . being a congressman?" Latisha pried, wondering whether she was about to hear something spectacular.

"When I first came to Washington four years ago, I thought I understood how the place worked," Bren began. "Textbook-wise, I knew that the president and his cabinet ran government, that Congress declared war and passed budgets, that the Secretary of State controlled foreign policy, voters elected one party to govern and that the parties determined how members of Congress voted, except for southern Democrats, who often teamed up with the Republicans. Then somewhere along the line, I discovered a serious game was being played with high stakes that often involved people's lives."

"People's lives?" Latisha repeated the two words.

"For instance," Bren expanded, "I learned that the power of the southern committee chairmen goes beyond the challenge of junior members. That a black man still has a fair way to go and that Washington can be a very lonely place."

Latisha chuckled. "I can't imagine you being lonely for a minute," she said, unaware of the flicker that passed across Bren's eyes.

"If you don't love the clubbiness of the members' dining room or Capitol Hill watering holes, like the Democratic Club, then you're at risk of not being part of a select group," Bren stated, tersely. "I'm not the type to rub shoulders or swap stories where the movers and shakers have regular tables. It's easy for a man in my position to make a mistake and become involved in something he wished he hadn't."

"But your job does have its perks?" Latisha delved, not detecting Bren's forlorn mood or the hint that he was unhappy with a certain situation, the pockets of discontent attached to being a congressman.

"It can be influential," Bren pronounced, with a hint of power in his voice. "Take my trip to sub-Saharan Africa last year, a top foreign policy priority in my mind. I have been urging the president to try and end the conflict in Africa by suggesting that we create a task force to study the continent. It should be made up of experts both in and out of government so that we have a clearer idea of what we are dealing with outside our borders."

"Why?" Latisha asked, noting a certain steeliness evident in Bren's tone.

"America has a rich history of bringing about peace and stability around the world," Bren began, working his way into the topic with ease and confidence. "Our work has included stopping the violence among ethnic and religious factions in Eastern Europe, we've tried to solve issues in the Middle East, and now I believe we have an obligation to the people of Africa."

"So you're a . . ." Latisha sipped her coffee. ". . . Proponent of closer U.S. and African ties?"

"Of course," Bren responded, reaching for his own coffee. After taking several sips, he replaced his cup and continued. "I've conferred with high-ranking government and elected officials, representatives from nongovernmental organizations, relief workers, American missionaries—many of whom are members of my constituency in New York—and ordinary citizens in Central Africa. We all agree that there should be a U.S. policy regarding Africa."

"And what would be the purview of this task

force?" Latisha ventured further, intrigued that Bren held such strong views.

"To offer practical and strategic insights into the promotion of democracy, prevention of the spread of disease, economic development, education, human rights, and other aspects of improving the quality of life," he insisted sternly.

"This all sounds very interesting," Latisha marveled, drinking more coffee. "Did the president listen?"

"He might go with my recommendation to approve a full-time, high-profile envoy to try to bring about peace to the war zones," Bren said, sounding a touch unconvinced.

"High-profile?"

"Maybe the inclusion of a former Secretary of State or a U.N. ambassador."

"Right." Latisha nodded, gulping more coffee.

"And of course I'd like to see appropriations made under the Arms Export Control Act and the Foreign Assistance Act of 1961 for the Department of State. I keep insisting in Congress that we need more weapons control at home and overseas."

"To counter terrorism?"

"Exactly." Bren approved of Latisha's question. "Which is why we should take more interest in African affairs. Congress cannot legislate laws for the Supreme Court to interpret and then have enforced by the executive branch of the Constitution if we ignore our foreign policy."

"Is this why you're a Democrat?" Latisha asked. Bren stared at her. "What?"

"Your father was a Republican senator," she recalled from what he had told her, "but you're a Democrat."

"We're father and son," he admitted candidly, "but I don't subscribe to his views on many things. I've always been my own person."

"I've come to realize that," Latisha noted, equally candid. "I can see now your main objectives in life are far removed from issues closer to home. Perhaps that is why there isn't a Mrs. Bren Hunter."

Bren felt his breath escape him as his composure slipped. "That's debatable," came his reply with a wicked slant to his lips. "There have been times when I've thought 'she'd do,' but it just keeps escaping me."

"So if I were to read your autobiography, I'd find a few minor scandals appended to your name?" Latisha chuckled, curious as to how many women had come close.

Bren chuckled in return. "You'd have to look very hard."

"So you pay attention to Gallup's public ratings on the honesty and ethics of politicians?" she asked.

"Absolutely," Bren proclaimed. "I'm one of the new breed in government. A dedicated person, like yourself in a way. You're also trustee of the Jamaicans U.K.—"

"The Association of Jamaicans Trust," Latisha corrected.

"And what's the charity about?" Bren asked.

"We sponsor lectures, conferences, and other meetings to educate the public and to improve the mutual understanding between Caribbean and British people," Latisha explained. "It's a very small charity and most of our funds are raised with donations and an annual membership fee."

"Sounds interesting," Bren intoned, lightly.

"It's satisfying and rewarding," Latisha continued. "We hold a membership meeting twice a year to decide where and how the funds should be spent. Last year we supported the Caribbean Affairs Forum, which allowed them to debate the issue of a Commonwealth member state ID that could be used by Caribbean nationals to protect their identity while in a foreign country."

"Wouldn't that person have a passport?" Bren inquired, suspicious as to the need for a secondary document.

"The forum was debating the rise of Caribbean criminals using false names and other people's identities to widen their activities," Latisha explained. "Their plan was to suggest a separate document to Home Office officials that would remove suspicion from law-abiding citizens, making it easier for them to travel or take up temporary residency in another country."

"To help the law enforcement agencies keep track of them," Bren stated. "I'm not sure I like the idea of infringing on people's civil liberties when a passport should be enough."

"Our trust would simply provide the opportunity to allow such conferences and debates to take place," Latisha clarified. "We do not necessarily represent the views of the topics under discussion."

"You don't have objections of your own?" Bren asked.

"I'm not a politician," Latisha reminded him,

with a smile. She downed the last of her coffee and glanced at her watch. "That's your job and I wish you luck in all that you do, but I really have to go. I'm going to have to find a suitable excuse to give Sarah why I missed the dinner party I'd planned for her and Piers Lapare tonight."

"I'm sorry," Bren said, on that note. He did not want to see her go, but the time was late and he knew at some point in the morning Latisha would be boarding a plane to Florida. "Why do you need to leave so soon?" he asked her lamely.

Latisha assumed Bren was referring to her departure from the island. "My sister and I are accepting an honorary award in recognition of our father's contribution to world cricket," she breathed, her own voice losing momentum. "So, I need to go. You'll be here for . . ."

"Two more days," Bren clarified.

"Two?"

"I have a score to settle on the golf course with Linford Mills, then it's back to the rat race at my Washington office."

Latisha nodded and jumped off the stool in preparation for another farewell. Bren jumped to his feet, too. Without expecting it, she was suddenly embraced in a strong hug. The embrace was such that Latisha could not force down the stinging of tears behind her eyes. She did not know why they were there. It was not as if she knew Bren Hunter. He had no place in her life that she needed to make room for. He was simply a man who had not yet earned his value to her.

"Look after yourself," Bren said, pulling away. He made no attempts to kiss her and Latisha felt the disappointment. "I wish you all the luck, too

and . . . offer my apologies to Lady Sarah for
keeping you to myself."

It was the last thing he said before she hopped
into the Jeep and made her return journey to the
Caribbean Rose.

Chapter Seven

Latisha boarded the yacht with a heavy heart and her hands laden with shopping bags. A light beneath Lady Sarah's cabin door and the soft murmur of voices within alerted her to the fact that her stepmother had company. No doubt Piers Lapare was scheduled to stay the night, and not wishing to disturb them, Latisha went immediately to her own room, vowing to offer an apology in the morning before going to the airport.

Unable to reach for the light switch, she entered into the darkness of her own cabin and began to unload one bag after another from her weary arms. The painting slipped, and she was just able to catch it before it fell to the floor. Leaning it up against what she sensed to be the bottom of her bed, Latisha gently dropped the rest of the bags and heaved a steady breath. She wished she had not said good-bye to Bren Hunter. She wished there would be another opportunity for them to meet so that he would kiss her again. She wished that she could have kept him in her life in some way. Reflecting on what her short visit to the British Virgin Islands had been like, Latisha went over to her light switch and flicked it on.

A short gasp left her throat the moment she saw that there was a strange man in her bed. Not strange exactly. Cheeky might be more accurate. Outrageous would be right on the ball. Her father had once joked that the list of his lovers had spanned three continents, wide-ranging by profession, race, color, creed, and religion, and happily discarded once their use was no longer required. But Latisha had no interest, nor the slightest inkling of relishing the sight in front of her. Another married man was far from what she needed in her life right now.

"Who let you on board?" she demanded, annoyed at finding herself in such an undesirable predicament. "Nigel?"

"Lady Sarah," Linford Mills answered triumphantly.

"And she asked you to wait in here?"

"No. I sneaked in."

"Are you wearing anything?" Latisha asked with an annoyed tone.

"Just the suit I was born in," Linford replied with a lustful grin, moments before pulling the sheets back to reveal his flabby naked body, wreathed in fat. Just one part of his anatomy stood out, hard, toned, and beckoning to attract her attention.

"Put your clothes on," Latisha ordered, disgusted that he had the nerve to do this.

"I thought you'd like a little something before leaving us tomorrow," Linford persuaded, undeterred. "A good send-off?"

"I said put your clothes on," Latisha insisted, reaching for his shirt, which she spotted at the edge of her bed, and throwing it at him.

"Latisha?" His voice was wounded.

"I can't believe you're doing this to me," she responded angrily. "You were a friend of my father's. I could never imagine you wanting to make a play for me, his daughter."

"I thought—"

"Strike that," Latisha interrupted, watching as Linford clumsily seated himself up against her pillows and quickly inserted his arms into his shirt. "You didn't think."

"I may have made a slight error of judgment," he said sheepishly.

"I'd say, 'lady killer,'" Latisha bleated, referring to the nickname her father often used to describe him. She was also to recall that she had never heard a reference to Linford Mills without the word *asshole* attached as either a suffix or a prefix. "What on earth could possibly be going on inside your head?"

"Nothing," Linford muttered weakly. He reached for his underpants and trousers and began to plunge his limbs into them. "I just thought you needed company."

"Really?" Latisha said angrily. "With a man old enough to be my father?"

"It happens," Linford defended, in the way only a jaded politician could.

Latisha did not want to be convinced. "Just go." She blinked hard, wanting nothing more than to dismiss the awful event of him being in her cabin. "Let's just pretend this never happened."

"I don't want to pretend," Linford suddenly fired back. Then he smothered a grin and had the audacity to pose sitting upright. "I may be old enough to be your father, but I look good for my age, right?"

Latisha was fuming, but stuck to getting him to leave. "You'll do," she said, guessing as to what sort of exposé a news reporter could reveal about Linford Mills's life. She suspected it would be colorful enough to make an inside story for *Playboy* magazine.

His lips curled while he patted a vacant space on her bed. "Come and sit next to me."

Latisha looked at him sternly, feeling her heart begin to race in alarm. Yet caution prevented her from calling out to alert Nigel, Lady Sarah, or her lover. Pulse pumping and her mind whirling, she decided instead that she could deal with her sleazy intruder amicably on her own.

"Linford," she cautioned, shrugging off his behavior, purposefully keeping her voice calm. "You need to go home."

His blue-brown gaze laughed at her. "Are you sleeping with Congressman Hunter?"

The directness of the question caught Latisha by surprise. "No!" she hollered firmly. "I'm surprised you imagine I would be."

"He's a handsome man," Linford opined. "Why shouldn't I think it? I just want to be certain I'm not treading on his territory."

Latisha heard the hint and retreated two steps immediately. "What do you mean?"

Linford Mills rose from the bed and began to make his way around it toward Latisha. "Congressman Hunter is a very important man," he began, "and a man like Hunter likes to have a certain woman at his disposal to ease him into his day and relax him at the end of a rough one."

"Like a concubine?" Latisha scoffed, outraged at his suggestion.

Linford shrugged his shoulders. "It goes with the job."

"Bren Hunter and I are simply . . . friends," Latisha continued, offended. "Who do you take me for?"

"Someone who would not want to get in the way of his ambitions," Linford continued astutely. "He already has his sights set on a suitable person to help boost his candidacy with the political hierarchy. Miss Vanessa Harper, chief operating officer of the Democratic National Committee, has all the credentials Congressman Hunter needs."

"What are you saying?" Latisha felt her voice weaken.

Linford was within inches of her when he spoke. "I'm saying that if, on the slightest whim, you have any wishful dreams or fantasies of a romance or relationship with Bren Hunter, forget it. He needs a pedigree to reach the heights he's going. It's all in the breeding, and let's face it, the daughter of a twice-married, deceased ex-captain of a cricket team isn't what the U.S. voters want to see as part of a winning team."

Latisha felt the sting of tears in her eyes as all her earlier musings about Bren Hunter, or his kissing her again, dissolved. "Get out," she railed, returning to the concrete present.

Linford touched her shoulder with ill-timed concern. "I saw the way you looked at Bren across Nancy's dinner table," he drawled slowly. "And, out of respect for your father, I feel it my duty to make sure you don't raise any hopes of . . . being with him. Bren's my friend and I know he's aiming high."

Latisha removed his hand and bent it backward until Linford winced in agony. "Give me one excuse not to cause you more pain," she seethed through clenched teeth.

"I can replace Bren Hunter whenever you need me." Linford offered his lurid enticement with enough relish to send Latisha over the edge.

Letting him go, she picked up his jacket from the bed and tossed it at him. With her gaze fixed, though she was thoroughly shaken and liked nothing of what she had heard, she marched over to her cabin door. Opening it wide, Latisha pushed an astonished Linford through it. "Let me personally escort you off the *Caribbean Rose*," she gibed, nursing the idea of throwing him overboard instead. "I don't intend to see you on it again, ever."

"But—"

"Give my regards to your wife, Gloria," Latisha uttered, in a low threatening tone. "Tell her that should I find you making advances toward me again, she has my kind permission to castrate and pickle you in a bottle for posterity." Watching Linford Mills disembark the gangplank onto shore, she added, "With a label reading 'beware of the dog.'"

Linford grimaced and turned his back on her. As he began to disappear into the distance toward his car parked up ahead, Latisha felt the burning scar of his words. Linford was right. It should have been plainly obvious to her that Congressman Bren Hunter's entire existence could in no way identify with her own. She was a girl from England, whose only achievements in life were those of her father's work. Had he not made those gateways possible, she would probably have amounted to nothing of significance.

Latisha bowed her head wearily and felt the tears in her eyes as she began the short walk down the side deck toward her cabin door. Had she chosen to, she might have become a passable singer. That was really what she had wanted to do. It had once been her main objective in life, too. But practicing every day was another matter. Doing chorus lines, session work, and background vocals was a drag. And the determination to compile demo tapes to send to A & R executives at record companies, or even tour to build up name recognition, simply wasn't appealing enough to garner her full attention. So that had all gone by the wayside.

Now a woman in her late twenties, she saw a new purpose in charity work, the perfect remedy to validate her existence. There was no hardship in what she was doing. She liked meeting the various people who had been affiliated with her father's causes. She liked the opportunity charity work gave her to travel. Latisha felt her very involvement was merely another part of the grand adventure of her life. Another story, another layer of the many experiences that had helped her evolve. And to know that Linford Mills could so easily try to crush everything she had cultivated in her life, to dare compare her to some well-bred, politically ambitious potential wife, summoned more angry tears to her eyes.

Her appeal to Linford was only as a pretty girl could appeal to an aging man. Suddenly, Latisha had the frightening thought that Bren Hunter probably saw her in that same way, too. With his formidable figure, his strong views on policy, and his position as a legislator with a Washington office full of underlings, she felt clearly now that her notion to get on with her life and allow Bren to get on with his was the right one. So why did she feel so . . . wrong?

Latisha paused outside Lady Sarah's cabin suite for further reflection when the door was suddenly flung wide open. She blinked once to refocus her mind, a second time to refocus her gaze, and a third to double-check that her eyes weren't actually deceiving her. The man who was planting his final seductive kiss against the lips of her stepmother was pulling off his next double act to Latisha's amazement. Her mouth fell open. And when he raised his head and discovered her standing within inches of him, Alan Clayton was struck dumb.

"Latisha," Sarah squealed, oblivious to anything except the fantasy of having fallen in love. "You missed dinner."

Latisha was too shocked to respond.

"I'd like you to meet Piers Lapare," she introduced, heady and happy as a playful puppy.

Latisha could not move.

"What do you think?" Sarah enthused, showing him off. She mindlessly rubbed gentle strokes against Alan's chest, looking sensual and elegant in her flimsy white floral robe, her gaze locked approvingly on the one she considered to be her man.

No matter how good Alan was to look at, Latisha had not forgotten what a cold, calculating, and merciless man lurked beneath all that raw testosterone. *I think he's from the deep cesspool of sin where God has sent all His guilty rejects to fester in the filth of their lies and deceit, their misdeeds and misdemeanors, and where they shall be forever condemned for their transgressions against womankind,* she mused in satisfaction.

"He's marvelous, isn't he?" Sarah chuckled.

Latisha paused, considering that. She remembered everything about Alan Clayton. An almost imposing six feet, medium-build frame, short brown hair, beige complexion, and the emerald green of his enchanting eyes. Dressed impeccably in one of his designer suits—mint-green linen trousers and jacket by Armani—with a deep blue shirt beneath and white sandals on his bare feet. It would be hard for any woman not to consider him marvelous. But Latisha was no longer any woman. Since knowing Alan, a part of her had grown up, and she was now someone with a lot to say.

Narrowing her eyes scornfully, she said, "I think—"

"Where were you?" Sarah cooed, kissing Alan briefly on the cheek before linking her arm through his. "Piers and I were worried something had happened to you."

Latisha stared at the demon she had hoped never to see again and replied with a bland answer, making direct reference to Alan's wife. "I was rescuing that woman we met on the beach. You remember? Her name was *Veronica.* "

The code word worked its magic. Alan's posture was erect and his eyes flickered nervously. "What happened?"

"She was distressed about trying to find her husband, apparently," Latisha said, keeping her gaze fixed, and her jaw clenched. "I drove her back to her hotel."

Alan immediately removed Lady Sarah's arm and sounded out his excuse. "Sugar, it's late. I have some paperwork to deal with back at my hotel. Catch you soon."

Lady Sarah's face melted in disappointment. "How soon?"

Agitated, Alan pronounced, "I'll call you."

Lady Sarah's eyes narrowed as she watched him leave. "What was all that about?" she muttered, confused.

"Like he said, he's probably busy." Latisha shrugged. "I'm going to turn in. Good night."

"Wait," Sarah pleaded. "You're leaving tomorrow. Don't we get to chat before you go?"

"In the morning," Latisha replied hurriedly. "I'm really tired."

"Sure?"

"I'm sure."

"Okay. Good night."

It was only when Lady Sarah had closed her cabin door that Latisha made a quick detour. She could not say what alerted her to follow Alan. Her sixth sense, her woman's intuition, or a second insight. But the moment she went ashore, there he was, waiting for her patiently at the marina parking lot. Latisha broke into a cold sweat the moment she saw him. She was not ready for a scene, but knew a showdown was inevitable.

"Alan Clayton!" Latisha immediately lashed out, panting as she came within inches of him. She pushed her hand hard against his left shoulder, causing him to stumble several steps backward. "What the hell do you think you're playing at?"

Alan reacted instantly. "Lauren? Lurline?" He had clearly forgotten her name.

"Latisha!" she corrected angrily.

"Right." He nodded, displaying a churlish grin. "Small world."

"Very." Latisha's voice was urgent and serious. "New York wasn't big enough for you. I see you've gone international with your bag of little tricks. That's my stepmother you're sporting with. I want you to leave her alone."

Alan noted Latisha's tensed energy and considered her another neurotic female seeing everything at its darkest and most dramatic. "I'm just company for her, which is what she asked for," he relayed, discounting everything Latisha had said.

"Did she also ask that you refer to yourself as Piers Lapare?" Latisha asked hotly. "Or maybe it would be kinder if I fill her in on your activities. Amelika, your fake wife. Graham Jefferson, another pseudonym. That you're forty and not thirty-five. And let's not forget how good you are at forgery. That false deed was almost passable until the real owner showed up."

Alan's face paled.

The flicker of his eyes told Latisha something she did not know, but which she discerned quickly. "So Congressman Bren Hunter hasn't confronted you yet," she said, leering at him. "Perhaps he's biding his time until an opportunity arises where he can string you up by the balls."

Alan retreated two purposeful steps backward. "I didn't—"

"Want Lady Sarah to know how devious you are," Latisha interrupted by way of a diversion, locking Alan with a steadfast glare. "That you were using her?" She went on in a flurry of questions. "I wonder exactly how much of your loving attention she actually received. I mean, I went totally neglected, didn't I? The ring you gave her. Is it real?"

Latisha detected a movement in Alan's jaw seconds before he shook his head.

"I thought not," she assumed, on a disgusted note. "You're still shamelessly acting on behalf of your johnson. Faithful to no one, not even your real wife, Veronica."

He listened to her stiffly. "How is she?"

"Distressed," Latisha continued, unable to believe she had once pledged herself to this man. Now it seemed hard to even conjure up the memory of a time when she had thought he had been worth it. "I think she's sensing that she's getting leftovers." Latisha waited for Alan to respond, but he didn't. It was clear he was not going to talk about his wife or their relationship. "What is it with you?" she pursued, wanting to know, if only to make some sense of it all in her mind. "Is it all a joke, you feeling important when your life is full of women?"

"As long as they go for what they can get and not for what they want, I'll give it to 'em," Alan bragged. "It's all gravy."

His blatant remark shook Latisha to the core, but she realized she had become incredibly calm. Her manner was just as Bren Hunter had said it would be. "No doubt if you saw him again, you could handle the situation quite amicably. Perhaps supply him with a conversation as though nothing had happened." Bren had told her she would hold no malice, and she did not. Quite the opposite, in fact. Not only did Latisha feel she had undergone a very lucky escape, a good chunk of her psyche had absorbed the clear view that women were simply pawns in a game of chess to men like Alan Clayton.

She acknowledged the truth. "I didn't mean anything, did I? I was nothing?"

Alan shrugged. "Veronica's always gonna be there."

"So you can take the easy way out?" It was all clear to her now, his wife being the back door. She sighed heavily. With her tone equally astringent, she asked, "Why marry? Why put Veronica through everything she's going through when you can see that she's in love with you?"

"I got married to be certain of the paternity of my children," Alan returned without a moment's hesitation. "Now that Veronica's pregnant—"

"You can return to your casual way of life," Latisha interrupted sadly. "Veronica will open her eyes eventually, as all women do," she revealed sternly. "And when she does, she will see everything I see. Someone who doesn't know how to make love. She will realize she feels more unhappy with you than before she ever met you. The dawning moment will arrive when she takes a good look at her marriage and realizes that she and her baby are the only two people in it. And she will leave when, one day, another man makes her see that he can repair the damage you've done."

"What damage?" Alan chided in a defensive tone, disliking everything he heard.

"Making her feel worthless," Latisha rebutted. "You see," she confessed, "that's how I felt. There I was, telling you what I did not want in a man, and there you were, being everything that I didn't want. You're as false as that expression on your face and you brought out the worst in me because of it."

"You knew what you were getting into," Alan defended suddenly. "I told you I was married."

"If you want a conversation that does not involve me putting my fist down your throat, you'd better stick to the truth," Latisha threatened, stepping forward until she was right in Alan's face. "Having a relationship or a marriage based on secrets and lies is doomed to fail. So take this as a friendly warning." She took a hold of his scrotum and squeezed it until Alan squealed like a hog being branded with a red-hot poker. "Come near my stepmother one more time, and there are three guys I know who'll make sure it'll take more than three plastic surgeons to sort your body out." She let him go, her mouth forming a flat little line of stiff disapproval meant to convey a warning that if he said another word, she would probably harm him herself.

Alan bent his body forward, wincing in pain. His voice carried through the night to the car parked less than half a block away. Linford Mills was inserting his car key when he heard the sound and looked over toward the marina to where the *Caribbean Rose* was docked. He did not mistake that it was Latisha he saw conversing with a man. A smile crept along his lips as he glanced at his watch and concluded that he was witnessing a midnight rendezvous.

His eyes caught Latisha patting a soft touch against the man's cheek, unaware that she was acting out in mock sincerity for the torturous pain she had just caused. "You'd better run along to your wife," she said, smiling devilishly sweet as a tiny mean-spirited part of her rejoiced in the fact that Alan was in agony. "I would love to tell Lady Sarah that a shark ate you for breakfast, but I'm sure I'll think of something else to let her down lightly."

Alan looked dejected.

But Latisha waved her hand and watched him walk away, knowing that neither he nor anyone could ever make a mockery of her womanhood again. She looked behind at the *Caribbean Rose* and thought of Lady Sarah. Her heart sank, realizing that after tomorrow, she would not be there to protect her. Latisha's heart skidded to a halt as she also realized she would have to call Bren Hunter. Only he could help to keep Alan Clayton away from her stepmother during her absence.

Ten minutes later, she was on the satellite phone on the bridge patching a call through to Sebastian's Hotel. "You're not going to believe this," she finally told the sleepy congressman, her heart flipping on hearing Bren Hunter's voice again. "Piers Lapare is Alan Clayton. I think we should talk."

They made an appointment. They would meet at dawn.

Chapter Eight

The time was 5.22 A.M. Latisha awoke with her heart thudding and one thought trailing across her mind. She had arranged to meet Bren Hunter before leaving Tortola that morning and she had no idea how she would react on seeing him again. Her bones felt like jelly as she rose out of bed and gazed through the porthole. Dusk was gently parting the sky and a glimmer of the dawn was breaking. The two extremes were symbolic of her own circumstances when, one hour later, she found herself at Smuggler's Cove.

The place had once been a legendary meeting spot for pirates. Latisha was not far from feeling like a sea wolf herself about to cause havoc, only it was with her heart, as she waited in the Jeep on the pier overlooking the beach. She had less than four hours before her flight and there she was, at 6:33 A.M., waiting for the man whose very image had kept her awake for most of the night.

The feelings were familiar, too. There was the usual rush of adrenaline, a level of mistrust, and the anticipation of seeing him again. And combined with the swirl of emotions in the pit of her stomach, a sign of her annoyance at having seen

Alan Clayton, Latisha hardly knew what she would say. There were no rehearsed lines, no pre-emptive sentences formulated in her head. No words suitable to arrive at a plan on what to do about a cheating married man.

But Bren had agreed to the meeting. She had told Lady Sarah nothing of what was going on. Latisha had thought it best to first hear what the congressman would suggest. After all, he was used to making important decisions. Someone who turned the wheels of Congress, and the world. This time, he would have to do something about his brother-in-law, she told herself. This time, he would have to take action.

Action came sooner than Latisha could think. As she began to look around and absorb the lush scenery, the small tremors of the still seawater, the solitude and serenity that only an early morn-ing breeze could bring in Tortola, she saw Bren. He was heading toward her on foot, across the soft plains of the empty beach dressed in a blue jogging suit. Her heart thudded to a halt.

Latisha instantly jumped from the Jeep and slammed the door shut, shaken at how quickly everything about Bren materialized before her very eyes. The nutmeg brown of his complexion, the square-shaped face, and the straight, patri-cian nose so familiar to her now. His firmly shaped cheekbones and the dark, brooding mys-teriousness of his pewter-colored eyes soon came into focus. Up close, she could just about sense the musky scent of his aftershave. Latisha could not deny the breathlessly excited feeling perme-ating her body as he looked at her.

"Bright and early," he said casually, by way of a

greeting, as he slowed his pace and came to a halt within inches of where she was standing, frozen by his presence.

Latisha felt the sudden rush across her body as her womanly instincts responded to his presence. But she repressed any desire to throw herself into Bren's arms, decidedly leaning her back against the Jeep door instead for blessed support.

"I'll get straight to the point," she said hurriedly, chagrined that her voice sounded hoarse and sexy, instead of firm, "You need to keep Alan away from Lady Sarah."

"Slow down," Bren cautioned, noting the strong words that came out on a panting breath. "I got your call and I'm here. What's happened?"

"I told you what happened," Latisha said, knowing that the level of her panic had little to do with protecting her stepmother from a broken heart. At that precise moment, she felt more concerned with the dictates of her own. "Piers Lapare. That's who he's calling himself now."

"Okay, calm down," Bren said, taking a stride toward Latisha and then folding his arms beneath his chest to scrutinize her more closely. "What would you like me to do?"

Latisha leaned on her heels and faced him. "I want you to do what you should've done three months ago," she said in annoyance. "That was when you should've dealt with Alan. Now he's loose, causing all kinds of mayhem, and I don't want my stepmother involved."

Bren nodded, though Latisha realized his attention did not appear to be on the subject at hand. She felt Bren's penetrating stare and became aware that he had schooled his gaze on her, allowing it to travel the whole length of her body. The quick flicker of his eye movements absorbed the simple pink floral dress she was wearing, the fuschia-colored mules on her feet, and the flimsy multicolored shawl wrapped around her shoulders to provide a thin layer of shelter from the slight breeze. She had swept her hair up into a topknot and she wore no makeup. Latisha could sense Bren liked it; seeing her face bare made it easy for him to read her thoughts.

"You're right," he acknowledged, sensing that she was struggling to hold on to some form of composure. It told Bren that the chemistry between them had not weakened, but had grown stronger in every way. "Had it not been for Alan, the temptation to kiss you right now would not be such a difficult thing," he said clearly.

Latisha felt her spine lean hard against the Jeep at Bren's sudden admission. "What is this?" she asked, foolishly thinking she could camouflage her emotion. "A new strategic initiative to—"

"What's going on between you and me can no longer be ignored," Bren cut in, leaning slightly forward until he could see the dancing color in Latisha's eyes.

She retreated backward against the hardened steel of the car. Even so, only two inches separated her from Bren's lean, muscle-hardened chest. She looked up at his carefully chosen expression and felt the crackling rush around her system as she tried and failed to resist the hypnotic pull of him. Bren exuded it, pulsated it, affirmed it. And splaying herself on the Jeep was all Latisha could do to handle the situation.

"Bren, don't," she whispered in a weak protest

to save herself. "I'm here to talk about this . . . Piers Lapare pseudonym and Lady Sarah."

He drew back slightly. His gaze flickered and danced with hers. "Why are you punishing yourself?" he asked, bemused as to why she should be denying her feelings. "Punishing us both?"

Latisha shook her head and momentarily stared out to where the faint colors of the sunrise had stained the sea to a pale papaya yellow. The scene was so romantic, it seemed almost daunting to deny anything at all. "We're to discuss what to do about Alan," Latisha reminded him firmly.

"And I promise I will deal with him," Bren declared calmly, "after I've dealt with you."

His reply shot straight to Latisha's heart like a splinter, piercing and embedding itself. "Me?" she gasped. "There's nothing to deal with."

"I think there is," Bren said levelly, locking his eyes to hers.

The silence that followed sizzled with hesitation. It burned in Latisha's chest and hacked at her senses until she felt the veil of tears in her eyes. She clung tight to her shawl and felt her body huddle into it, all for fear that Bren could read the slightest ounce of the plainly obvious feelings of vulnerability she displayed. "What do you mean?" She swallowed, not understanding him.

"You're in denial," Bren told her in a quiet, calm manner. "You *know* you want me to kiss you again, but you refuse to allow yourself to let go and enjoy it."

Latisha had no idea what his eyes were telling her as he held her gaze. "Bren—"

"Of course I realize seducing you right after

Alan would be difficult," he interrupted her coolly, "for what good would a single night of passion be if you are not willing and believing that being in my bed is the only place you want to be?"

Latisha frowned at his simple analysis, deciding she really did not *want* to understand, but knowing she could not help the fact that she did. It was the long-term seduction that was the real aim to Bren Hunter, she deduced. It seemed he had set himself the target of making her want him enough and trust him enough to need him more than she had ever needed anyone in her life. And it was her understanding of this that suddenly tied Latisha into an emotional knot.

"I don't know if I can go through all this again," she said in a sensual breath.

Latisha was shaken when Bren uncrossed his hands and reached out to her, his fingertips brushing against her shawl ever so lightly. "Through what?"

Latisha was shaken as the movement of the soft fabric responded to his touch. "Letting somebody else in," she admitted, attaching a light smile to her answer, though it took everything she had in her to force it through. "Can I trust a man again?"

Bren was sympathetic to her question, but he felt almost happy, too. For deep down, he knew he could be the man Latisha needed. He knew he had everything in his heart that could make this woman happy. That he could fulfill her needs and yearnings in a way that would make her beg for more. Most of all, he knew that eventually she would come to see this. See that not all men were like Alan Clayton.

"If you want it badly enough, you'll try," he told her, working his left hand down the length of her flimsy multicolored shawl until it connected with her fingers. Curling them into his own, Bren gently rubbed against the velvety texture of her skin until he felt Latisha relax.

"Being with someone . . . sex . . . is a very precious thing to share," Latisha explained, aware that she had the congressman's full attention. "I want it to *mean* something to the person I'm with. I don't want to feel like I'm nothing."

"And you're not, to me," Bren reassured her. "I believe in taking things one step at a time."

Latisha was hurt by the memory of what Linford Mills had told her. "I think your prospects would require you to select someone with political ties, with whom you can share a life and further your career," she said slowly. "Someone like Vanessa Harper."

"Vanessa Harper!" Bren laughed. "You've been listening to too much media gossip."

"So you do know her?"

"Of course I know her," Bren admitted, chuckling. "We grew up in the same neighborhood once upon a time, before her family moved."

"Is she your girlfriend?"

Bren laughed again. "No. Though I believe there are people who would like to believe that she is."

Latisha backed down. "I heard through the grapevine that you two could be—"

"Just friends," Bren insisted firmly. "We have

A SPECIAL "THANK YOU" FROM ARABESQUE JUST FOR YOU!

Send this card back and you'll receive 4 FREE Arabesque Novels—a $25.96 value—absolutely FREE!

The introductory 4 Arabesque Romance books are yours FREE (plus $1.99 shipping & handling). If you wish to continue to receive 4 books every month, do nothing. Each month, we will send you 4 New Arabesque Romance Novels for your free examination. If you wish to keep them, pay just $18* (plus, $1.99 shipping & handling). If you decide not to continue, you owe nothing!

- Send no money now.
- Never an obligation.
- Books delivered to your door!

We hope that after receiving your FREE books you'll want to remain an Arabesque subscriber, but the choice is yours! So why not take advantage of this Arabesque offer, with no risk of any kind. You'll be glad you did!

In fact, we're so sure you will love your Arabesque novels, that we will send you an Arabesque Tote Bag FREE with your first paid shipment.

* Prices subject to change

THE "THANK YOU" GIFT INCLUDES:

- 4 books absolutely FREE (plus $1.99 for shipping and handling).
- A FREE newsletter, *Arabesque Romance News*, filled with author interviews, book previews, special offers, and more!
- No risks or obligations. You're free to cancel whenever you wish with no questions asked.

INTRODUCTORY OFFER CERTIFICATE

Yes! Please send me 4 FREE Arabesque novels (plus $1.99 for shipping & handling). I understand I am under no obligation to purchase any books, as explained on the back of this card. Send my free tote bag after my first regular paid shipment.

NAME _____

ADDRESS _____ APT. _____

CITY _____ STATE _____ ZIP _____

TELEPHONE ( ) _____

E-MAIL _____

SIGNATURE _____

Offer limited to one per household and not valid to current subscribers. All orders subject to approval. Terms, offer, & price subject to change. Tote bags available while supplies last.

Thank You!

AN084A

ARABESQUE

Accepting the four introductory books for FREE (plus $1.99 to offset the cost of shipping & handling) places you under no obligation to buy anything. You may keep the books and return the shipping statement marked "cancelled". If you do not cancel, about a month later we will send 4 additional Arabesque novels, and you will be billed the preferred subscriber's price of just $4.50 per title. That's $18.00* for all 4 books for a savings of almost 40% off the cover price (Plus $1.99 for shipping and handling). You may cancel at any time, but if you choose to continue, every month we'll send you 4 more books, which you may either purchase at the preferred discount price. . . or return to us and cancel your subscription.

THE ARABESQUE ROMANCE BOOK CLUB
P.O. BOX 5214
CLIFTON NJ 07015-5214

PLACE
STAMP
HERE

THE ARABESQUE ROMANCE CLUB: HERE'S HOW IT WORKS

nothing in common, except maybe a few political aspirations."

Latisha tried to smile. "You must think of me as being somewhat too careful," she said at last. "But—"

"You got bumped and you're taking your next ride a little slower this time," Bren said, accepting her smile. "I just want to help you along with a farewell kiss and a promise that I can see you again soon. And I'm going to wait right here until you honor me with both."

Latisha stared up at him. Strange, she thought, how one person could become so important in such a short length of time. Three months ago, she hadn't even known of Bren Hunter's existence. Until a few days ago, hadn't known of his position. Three months ago, she had been alone and rejected, seeing nothing in her future she could build on. But now Bren Hunter was promising to be there.

"Are you vowing to change my life?" she asked, certain she was imagining what he was saying.

"I'm certain I want to try and make you happy," Bren amended, using his free hand to brush against the side of Latisha's left cheek. "Take care of you, protect you, make your life complete if you'll have me."

"You know nothing of who I am or what I want," Latisha told him, thankful that the Jeep behind her was supplying all the support she needed. For at that moment, her brain began to make an imprint of his loving face, of his adoring eyes and the tender expression that was marked in every feature.

"I know what you need," Bren assured her.

Latisha believed him, too. Even in his jogging suit, power seemed to exude from Bren Hunter in every way. It was difficult for Latisha because she also found him fascinating even without his smooth, silky voice washing over her like a tidal wave. And when his face came closer, she could not resist. Latisha almost groaned in agony feeling Bren's lips against her own.

A squeezing sensation deep down in her body was already making its presence felt. Latisha knew the telltale signs of attraction, of her yearning to be kissed by Bren again and again. Yet her fear kept her from yielding to the growing intensity of his lips. As his breath touched her lips, she pulled back into what little fraction of space was left behind her and faced him.

"I don't want you to kiss me," she lied profusely, her head light, her brain almost dizzy with self-deception.

"Too late," Bren dismissed her plea, gently gripping her neck with one hand, the other holding her arm in place against the Jeep. "You're mine."

His lips came crushing down. It was that quick. That sudden. A hot dive into total oblivion.

Latisha was instantly swept into the motion of Bren's torrid and fevered attack. Mouth straining against mouth, his tongue delving and entwining, she was lost to the scalding heat that touched her soul. Every part of her body responded to it. Her heart, her pulse, even her ears, for she was certain she could hear the rush of her fiery blood flood by like searing volcanic lava. Latisha groaned when Bren's hands tightened and brought her limbs beneath his fingertips. The thrust of her body left Bren doubtless of what she was feeling.

Bren could not believe that he was feeling this way. It was so unlike him—a reserved, sensible congressman—to behave so recklessly. But he wanted Latisha Fenshaw badly, and had it not been for the place they were standing, where no privacy was guaranteed, he would probably take the fevered kiss where he desperately wanted and needed it to go, for Latisha's sake as well as his own.

Her mouth tasted as he expected it would, warm, soft, fierce, and delightfully his for the claiming. And he wanted it all. The pleasure of savoring her, of gently biting her lip, licking against her teeth, and using his tongue to wrap around her own until she fell helplessly into supplication where she would deny him nothing. Nothing. That was to be his ultimate goal. That was where he wanted to take Latisha Fenshaw.

And so the kiss lingered. An endless stream of exquisite rapture.

It was the sound of a dog barking that eventually caused them to pull apart. As Latisha climbed down from the daze into which she had disappeared, she was astonished to find that the sun had crept into the sky and that they were no longer the only two people on the pier. Not so far away, a man was jogging along with his dog and farther in the distance on the beach were a couple of people, taking a leisurely early morning stroll.

She felt her face flush with embarrassment that some innocent observer may have spotted them in their fevered moment of frenzied passion. Seeing her pinned against the side of the Jeep by a devastatingly attractive man, whose very slaughter of her every sense with the power of his kisses had caused her to lose touch. Latisha frowned at her own weakness in allowing it to happen.

"This is highly irregular for a congressman," she panted, thinking it was time she began to compose herself.

Bren shook his head and moved his hand from her neck to the topknot on Latisha's head. "No, it's not," he whispered, pulling her head back until her mouth was directly beneath his. "For a man." One glance was all it took for him to take her lips again in the name of seduction.

Latisha's eyes flew shut. . . .

His hand snaked down her cheek to find a resting place at her nape, where it lingered. The other hand gently squeezed at her waistline, feeling the slender bone structure beneath the pink dress. Bren raised his head. Licked his lips. Savored the taste in his mouth. Inhaled a deep, long breath. Finally, he opened his eyes and looked down at the woman inches below his head.

Glossy black hair, hazelnut-brown complexion bronzed by the sun, dreamy, copper-brown eyes, and lips swollen from kissing were within his view. He cataloged each of Latisha's features in his head like a man planning a hearty feast. And as his mind imagined the sultry body and amazing curves that were still hidden beneath the pink floral dress, destined to be explored another day, Bren marveled at his self-restraint.

"When and where can I see you again?" he inquired, mindlessly planting a soft kiss at the tip of her nose.

Latisha could not decide whether another en-
counter with Congressman Hunter was feasible,
even after everything he had told her. "Washington," she blurted out, unsure as to why she had
chosen that precise destination. Why not? she decided, weighing the improbability of a rendezvous
there. Perhaps a part of her did not believe it
could happen, and that was just how Latisha saw
things—cynically.

But Bren nodded his approval. "That's great.
I'll be back at my office in a few days. You can fly
over from Florida. I'll arrange a ticket and your
travel expenses."

Latisha blinked. Was he being real? "I don't
know . . ." she began in hesitation.

"I'll book you into a hotel," Bren continued,
certain that he knew exactly what he wanted to
happen and making every effort possible to
achieve his objective. "Don't worry about the tab.
I'll take time out to show you around town, show
you the hot spots, wine and dine you, and make
you feel on top of the world. You'll get my full attention, your needs will be tended to totally, and
all that I require is for you to say yes, so I can start
planning your itinerary."

Latisha laughed. "You make me sound like a
business proposition."

"Oh, but you're more than that," Bren confessed, throwing her a cheeky grin until the smile
on her lips widened. "You'll be in Washington at
my invitation and it's my job to make sure you
fully enjoy your visit there."

Latisha sighed, unsure and yet so certain that
she wanted to run with this. What Bren Hunter
was offering was beyond her expectations, be-

yond anything she had ever experienced. He was placing romance on the table in all its technicolor glory. And she badly needed to be romanced. Needed his attention. Needed to know that this was one man she could truly trust. She closed her eyes and debated, though the smile never left her face while she did so.

Bren saw it and enticed her. "Say yes," he whispered, briefly brushing a kiss across her lips. "Let's take Washington."

Latisha opened her eyes and saw the deep pool of desire embedded in the silvery pewter color of Bren's own. Everything about the circumstances that had led them to this point was swiftly forgotten. Alan's deceit. Lady Sarah's impending heartbreak. Veronica's crushed spirits. They all vanished. The only thing Latisha saw was what she wanted. Before another moment could pass, she was sending Bren Hunter an affirming nod.

Chapter Nine

The limousine glided down the freeway. Ten lanes of traffic, five going in either direction. At times, when his driver crested a rise, Bren Hunter could see ahead a mile or more. Thousands of cars were in his view, speeding along the highway with the limo and towards it. Bren was used to the dangerous way that Americans traveled, so he was unfazed by the traffic.

Arriving at his office, dressed in a black suit and black shoes, his tie flat against a starched white shirt, and carrying his briefcase, Bren greeted his secretary with a welcoming smile.

"Good morning, Lucy," he said.

"Good morning, sir," she returned. "How was your golf getaway?"

"Fine." Bren nodded. "A little breezy."

"Mr. Chico Maccola is waiting in your office as you requested," she informed him, immediately scanning her desk for all the other messages awaiting his attention. She picked up a handful of yellow slips two inches thick and passed them to him. Bren thumbed his way through swiftly—Donald Steele of the Congressional Black Caucus; Edgar Warren Hunter, his father; Brian Lyons of the *Washington Post*; a Mr. Neil Wilson, another newly appointed member on the board of governors for the Joint Center for Political and Economic Studies—his eyes falling on all the many messages requesting return calls.

"What does the reporter want?" Bren asked, curiously.

"Mr. Lyons calls everybody in Congress," Lucy said, apologetically. "He's fishing for news. I don't usually add him to your messages, sir. I must've—"

"I'll ignore him then," Bren said dismissively.

"And Vanessa Harper would like you to let her know when you're back in town," Lucy continued, listing an assortment of other crises that required his personal attention and that Bren had no intention of dealing with right away. He returned the slips.

"Hold my calls," he instructed, acknowledging the details. "Unless it's the president, of course." He winked and Lucy's eyes lit up.

She chuckled. "Yes sir."

Bren closed the office door behind him and glanced across at the private detective standing by the couch directly opposite his desk. It was too early in the day for anyone to be sipping brandy, but Chico Maccola had already made his way to the oak cabinet in Bren's office and had helped himself to half a glass. Chico also knew the value of silence as he observed Bren's entrance and remained standing, sleek and as cool-eyed as a polar bear watching its cubs.

Chico was an investigator who did very little talking unless the occasion called for him to say something. Even his appearance seemed a touch out of the ordinary—dark Dolce and Gabbana shades, a black beret that hid most of his hair, except for the ponytail that hung down his back. He wore a dark suit that looked expensive. He was polished, just like his political and sometimes unscrupulous clients.

Bren placed his titanium briefcase on his desk and opened the combination lock. Removing a brown envelope, he handed it over. "He has a new alias," he said calmly, eyeing the detective. "And I'm not happy that you missed Latisha Fenshaw."

"The girl you told me about in Rye?" Maccola said apologetically. "I'm sorry. I guess since she lives in England, she slipped my net. It won't happen again, sir."

"I don't want to hear excuses," Bren asserted. "His new alias name is Piers Lapare and he ran amok while we were in the Caribbean."

"Piers Lapare," Chico Maccola repeated, rolling the sound of the name around on his tongue.

"I want you to find a way of getting rid of him," Bren protested, harshly.

"Adultery no longer outrages," Maccola said candidly, leafing through the fresh dollar bills in the envelope, another cash down payment on his fee. "As long as he's not a TV pastor or some aspiring politician, whatever your brother-in-law does will have little effect on you. The public will still give you their votes."

Bren paused for consideration. "Can we find something that could be taken before a judge?"

"Financial wrongdoing, blackmail, murder . . . that sort of thing?" Chico took a seat on the couch and crossed one knee over the other. "He's not a big fish."

"But we could take a look at his finances?" Bren queried thoughtfully.

"Ah, you mean find something that might interest the IRS?" Chico nodded, following Bren's train of thought.

"He's about to inherit a marina and shipyard in Guadeloupe," Bren said. "It used to belong to his grandfather."

"What does he do for money now?"

"Trust fund, I think," Bren answered, "which makes it very easy for him to move around. He's not tied to a job. What I want is something tangible. Concrete. Something that can bury him for good."

"You want him out of your sister's life?" Maccola asked, surprised.

"I'm not talking about threatening to break his legs or a payoff," Bren explained, moving around his desk to take a seat behind it. He wished things could have been that simple. "That would be too easy. What I need to find is a weakness. I've let this go on for too long, watching this guy destroy people."

"He's an asshole," Maccola spat out with a shrug. "Lots of 'em out there. But your sister Veronica, now, she's one special lady. She doesn't deserve a jerk like that."

Bren thought of one other woman who didn't deserve to be hurt either. "He's got that knack for spotting vulnerability and zooming in on it." He paused. "Can I get him on breaking and entering? Trespassing?"

Maccola shrugged again. "Depends. Did you give him a key to your house?"

Bren sighed. "He used the copy I gave to

Veronica. Helped himself to my country house in Rye while I was away here in Washington, and during my trip to Africa last year. He used my Bentley." Bren thought of Latisha and felt Alan's treachery in his heart rip wide open. "I want the man's jugular."

"I'm all in favor of going for the throat," Maccola agreed, sipping more brandy. "After how he treated Veronica, I'd like to rip it out myself. How is she?"

"Pregnant," Bren blurted.

Chico's body shook with shock. "She's having a baby?"

"She's three months already, maybe more."

"To Alan Clayton?"

Bren nodded.

Chico Maccola took a large gulp of brandy. "That's crazy," he said, shaking his head incredulously. "After that suicide attempt in March last year . . ."

"I know." Bren sighed, folding his arms against his chest. "So . . . whatever it takes to bounce that man out of her life, I want it done."

"There is something . . ." Chico hesitated, before moving on. "I could arrange for a pest control company to sweep your sister's home. He lives there, right?"

Bren strained forward in his chair, attempting to grasp what Maccola was saying. He knew the private detective was trying to convey a message, but was unsure as to what. "Pest control?"

"Yes," Chico affirmed. "I'm sure the house could be riddled with bugs and they're very technologically advanced these days. They get into the smallest places. Into buttons, even cuff links. Only last week I saw a bug on a woman's earring."

Bren smiled, fully understanding Chico's meaning. "I think you should go right ahead and call an exterminator," he suggested firmly. "Tell them we want the strongest insecticide they've got, because we have a large bug we want to get rid of immediately."

"You'd never have guessed it, would you?" Josette said, slamming her hands down on the kitchen sink for emphasis. "Lady Sarah getting burned by this . . . cunning, calculating—"

"I had to tell her the truth," Latisha said, cutting her sister off to avoid hearing the inevitable profanity at such an early hour in the morning. "I'm not sure the airport was the right place, but she took it better than I expected."

"She didn't cry?"

"No," Latisha related, familiarizing herself with her sister's curious expression. Josette was a woman without vanity, who accepted that her shoulder-length hair—hidden under a floppy hat for protection against the sun while gardening— huge brown eyes with their rim of long lashes, and her generous smile drew people to her like moths to a flame. "She was as calm as a lake. Maybe going through pain softens our nature as we get older."

"But you were both vulnerable," Josette seethed, trying to imagine the scenario while walking over to the breakfast table where Latisha was seated. "It's like . . . he could see it . . . your weaknesses and despair. You'd lost your father, and Sarah her husband."

"I know," Latisha agreed. "But what could either of us expect from a man with manicured nails?"

Josette laughed.

"Did you know he also made Sarah pay for the ring?"

"What ring?" Josette inquired, her unplucked brows raised.

"A Tahitian black pearl sprinkled with diamonds," Latisha explained, recalling that Alan had given her every indication that it was a fake. "Apparently, he told her he would return the money to her."

"Oh my Lord." Josette gasped with amazement. "You'd both put him on a pedestal."

"That's what Sarah said," Latisha acknowledged with regret. "And he abused the privilege. That's what she told me with a certain look in her eye."

"A look?" Josette said.

Latisha shook her head. "No, her eyes . . . darkened. Maybe she was just hurting and didn't want to see me go."

"Where is this man now?" Josette queried.

"Back in Boston, I expect," Latisha thought, not really caring where Alan Clayton was at that moment. All she could think about was Bren Hunter and the fact that she would be seeing him in two days. "His brother-in-law—you know, the one who owns the house in Rye—promised to keep him away from Sarah for the rest of their holiday, and that much is all I know."

"Well, let's hope he succeeded," Josette drawled,

horrified at the events during Latisha's short stay on the British Virgin Islands. "You've been back five days and she hasn't called yet. Not even to check on how the ceremony for Daddy went. I rather expected her to be there."

"I think it's best if we allow Sarah to get on with her life in her own way," Latisha suggested, while reaching for a glass of fresh orange juice on the breakfast table. "By the way, she wants us to charter the yacht in a few weeks, so she may fly into Florida, and you'll see her then."

"Miss Lady of Leisure," Josette said jokingly, wiping her hands on the denim overalls she was wearing. "When Daddy died, she got the lion's share of his money. You and I only got property and a share in the yacht."

Latisha swallowed at the reminder. "Let's leave it at that. You didn't contest the will and neither did I. And Mum had no say. Sarah was his wife before he died."

"I expect so," Josette said, returning to the kitchen sink to pick up a handful of freshly cleaned plant pots and transferring them to the breakfast table. "So . . ." she paused. "I hope you poked this Alan in the eye and yanked his ear."

"Actually, I grabbed his crotch," Latisha admitted, chuckling. "And threatened him. You know, there wasn't an ounce of remorse in the man whatsoever. In fact, I struggled to see the humanity in him."

"Men like him don't have souls," Josette declared. "They just take, take, take, and never give."

Latisha nodded "That's precisely it. He was just his usual boastful self, full of his own ego. I don't think he saw me as anything real with feelings at all."

"I wonder how many others there have been," Josette mused out loud.

"Probably hundreds," Latisha said, sadly. "And do you know what really gets to me?" She paused. "He never said he was sorry."

"An apology would probably make him choke," Josette said scornfully.

"It's like . . . he's so full of contempt for women or something," Latisha went on, confused. "You have to wonder why he's like that, don't you think?"

"Probably neglected as a child, who knows?" Josette drawled. "I see it in school when I'm teaching sometimes, boys acting cruelly toward girls in class. There's one boy in particular who likes to tug at the braids of a certain girl, and enjoys watching her cry. It's troubling for me as a teacher. They should bring the Lord's prayer back into schools. That's what I'm campaigning for." She paused again. "You said the brother-in-law is a congressman?"

"Bren Augustus Hunter," Latisha pronounced.

Josette looked at her sister's face under the baseball cap crowning her head. Latisha was dressed in a simple pair of denim shorts with a white short-sleeve T-shirt under a fringed vest. As sisters, they looked alike, but it was clear that Latisha was definitely changing.

"Your eyes just sparkled," Josette teased, chuckling. "I saw."

"They didn't," Latisha replied, returning a smile. "Okay . . . maybe."

Josette gave her a smug look. "Do tell."

"He's invited me to Washington for two days," Latisha revealed, "and I've decided to go. He's arranged a car to pick me up at the airport and I'm to meet him at the Willard Intercontinental Hotel."

Josette leaned forward and placed her hands over the back of a chair. "For what?"

"To see the sights, have a good time. Get to know him." Latisha exhaled. "He likes me and wants to get to know me a little better, but . . ."

Josette panicked. "What is it?"

Latisha shrugged. "I don't know. He's Veronica's brother. She's Alan's wife. And there's also a woman named Vanessa Harper."

"Is she a threat?"

"I don't know. Maybe."

"Did you ask him about her?"

"Yes. And he said she isn't."

"Do you think he's lying?"

"Hard to say," Latisha admitted. "Call me cynical, but that is what politicians are best at."

"But we are talking about a congressman," Josette reminded her. "He would have to keep his nose clean if he wants to move on up, so I should imagine he's being truthful."

Latisha sighed, sipping more orange juice. "I hope so, because I do like him and there's a definite spark between us that's making me excited about seeing him again. I gave him your telephone number, in case he needs to reach me to change any arrangements. I hope you don't mind."

"Mind?" Josette exclaimed. "Why didn't you give him your cell number? How did he reach you to make the arrangements in the first place?"

"He gave me a number to call him in Washington," Latisha said. "So I used your phone when I arrived here in Florida. I'm sorry, I didn't think."

Josette looked directly at her. "Then start thinking. This time, you be careful. You don't want to be embroiled in another wild fling. Being horny is one thing. Taking your time's quite another."

"I don't think Bren Hunter's like that," Latisha returned, thinking back to when they had talked and the things he had told her. "He seems sincere."

"All men want sex, eventually," Josette cautioned. "What you need to be certain of is that he romances you first and fulfills your needs outside the bedroom before you get to the bedroom. If ever you feel uncertain, don't do anything. And if he thinks you're worth it, he'll wait."

Both women were silent for a moment. When Latisha finally spoke, it was with admiration for her sister. "How did you come to be so wise?" she asked, even though Josette was four years younger.

"Learning from my experiences, or rather my mistakes, has taught me a thing or two," Josette confessed. "Before I met Steadman, of course."

"Talking about experiences," Latisha said. "You'd never guess who made his way into my cabin on the *Caribbean Rose*. Linford Mills."

"What?" Josette gasped, deciding to pull away the chair she had been resting her hands on. "Daddy's old friend? The . . . governor?"

Latisha nodded. "Yes. He was naked in my bed."

Josette burst out laughing. "What kind of business vacation were you on? The man's a relic from the last century. If he's still going around the block, he should be using a walking stick by now, surely."

Latisha started giggling at her sister's funny expression. She placed her hand over her mouth to stifle further bouts of giggles. "I showed him the door, of course." She chuckled.

"Of course," Josette agreed.

"And that's when he started telling me that Congressman Hunter would not be taking someone like me seriously."

"Ah, he's jealous," Josette said, with a wave of her hand. "You don't want to pay attention to that. Men like Linford Mills resent losing their youth and try to plant the seeds of insecurity in women they feel they can control."

"More pearls of your infinite wisdom?" Latisha said admiringly.

"Either that or I'm getting old in my young age." She glanced at her watch. "Dear, I've got a lot to do today. Pot these plants and make an early lunch for Steadman. He's on a long shift at the hospital today."

Latisha glanced at her own watch. "I've got to run," she realized, on seeing the time, 9:33 A.M. "I'd like to pick up a few things for this trip to Washington before I forget. By the way, did you like the painting?"

"I love it," Josette enthused. "I've always wanted a Boscoe Holder piece since I saw one of his exhibitions in London in the late nineties."

"Good." Latisha nodded. "Now about me. Maybe I need a new evening dress."

"That's the spirit." Josette chuckled. "You go and buy yourself a nice dress and some shoes, because in four days' time, Cinderella is gonna be on her way to the ball."

As Latisha approached the Willard Intercontinental Hotel's front desk, the clerk, a weary-looking elderly Turkish man, notified her that a man was waiting to see her in the Round Robin Bar. Latisha placed her two small suicases on the floor, signed the register, and took her electronic key before entering the bar. Beautifully styled furniture, silk drapes, and expensive carpeting lent a plush ambiance to the place.

The hotel was traditional but offered high-end luxury and sophistication. A notice on the front desk indicated that it had undergone a recent multimillion-dollar renovation that had completely restored the mosaics, the marble, and the majestic columns to their former beaux arts decor. Nothing had been spared and the hotel had all the amenities expected by the business or leisure traveler who wanted to spend time in the nation's capital.

Latisha looked around at the beautiful hotel. For one terrible moment, she imagined that Alan Clayton had tracked her down to wreak vengeance on her for having told Lady Sarah about his playboy antics. But it was Bren Hunter who was seated at the bar, discussing the state of Eastern Europe over a glass of imported beer with the bartender.

Bren was dressed in a dark blue suit and a pale blue shirt buttoned to his neck, with a loose tie in place. He looked amazing with his freshly trimmed haircut, looking every bit the congressman winding down after a long day. His briefcase was resting on the bar, next to his half-empty glass, when Latisha gingerly approached from behind and placed her hands over his eyes.

"Guess," she said, chuckling, feeling the tug on her heartstrings.

"Queen Latifah," Bren declared.

"Close." Latisha laughed, removing her hands. "Halfway there. You were right about the queen bit."

Bren turned on his stool and faced the woman standing before him. Without a second thought, he put both hands around her waist, reacquainting himself with every feature on her face. Her makeup was nearly gone after the long trip, but still enhanced the texture of her brown complexion. Latisha wore her hair down, though two clips held stray ends in place at the crown to keep them from falling in her face. The blue suit she wore seemed a touch dated and warm for the evening, he decided, but it in no way swayed Bren from thinking he was still looking at the most adorable creature he had ever held in his arms.

"And how was Her Royal Highness's trip?" he asked, planting a kiss against the side of her neck.

"Fine," Latisha said, not quite believing that she was now in Washington, D.C. "The limousine ride from the airport was lovely. Thank you. I was just about to go to my room."

Bren's eyes glanced sideways to her two suitcases on the floor. "I think the queen needs an escort and help with her luggage."

"Of course," Latisha said, adding, "The desk

clerk said the guest bill had already been taken care of."

"I told you I'd take care of it," Bren assured her, leaning forward slightly. "So you can freshen up and meet me down here for dinner."

"Sounds cool." Latisha smiled, checking the time. "It's nearly 7:00. How about I meet you, say . . . 7:30?"

"Sounds good," Bren agreed, pulling her toward him for a brief hug before jumping from the stool and lifting both her suitcases. "Let's go and find your room."

"Hey," the bartender alerted, pointing at Bren's document case. "Don't forget this one."

Bren looked round. "I'm always doing that."

"Leaving state secrets in a public place is an offense," the bartender joked.

Latisha reached over and picked up the case. "I'll carry it," she told Bren. "Which way?"

He led the way and Latisha followed, hardly able to contain her excitement.

There was one thing Latisha quickly learned about Washington. It is a city full of memorials. The Boy Scouts Memorial, the Freedman's Memorial, the James Garfield, Ulyesees S. Grant, and Jefferson Memorials. The Korean War Memorial, the Vietnam Veterans and Vietnam Women's Memorials, and the National Law Enforcement Officers Memorial.

It was during her visit to the Franklin Delano Roosevelt Memorial that Latisha found Bren Hunter's watchful gaze on her. She responded with mild flirting, fluttering her eyelids ever so slightly as a smile tugged at his lips. The way Bren explained each site instantly tightened the muscles of her stomach. Perhaps it was the way his gray slacks fit his long legs, emphasizing their powerful muscles. Or the way his blue silk shirt, with its rolled-up sleeves and open collar, clung to his broad-shouldered torso. Latisha couldn't say, all she knew was that everything that was female inside her recognized a perfect male specimen with a purely primal shiver.

"What are you thinking?" he asked, taking a closer look at Latisha and adoring the way she appeared in the embroidered blue tunic, jeans, and the comfortable leather sandals that she was wearing, which were just what she needed to tackle walking about on a hot summer's day in July.

Latisha responded with a question of her own. "How many more memorials are we going to see?"

Bren chuckled. "Just three more to go. The Navy Memorial, the Second Division Memorial, and the Lincoln Memorial."

"And that's it?"

"Well, there are two monuments," Bren said, having planned to take Latisha along with him to take a look. "The Peace Monument and the Washington Monument."

Latisha glanced at her watch. It read 3:32 P.M. "After we see those, can we get something to eat?"

"Of course," Bren said. "Whatever you want."

Latisha smiled at him.

She had enjoyed their evening the night before. Bren had been the perfect host. She had met him in the bar and followed his lead to the restaurant. The food was marvelous, and the company even better. Bren had discussed everything with her, from politics, to world events, to whether kangaroos really do jump as opposed to hop. She laughed at his sense of humor while he enjoyed his reflection in her lustful gaze.

Latisha was aware that Bren had calculated how much she liked him. It took very little guessing to see that his admiration of her was growing, too. She in turn began to talk about her childhood, her upbringing in Britain, her father's work, and how his traveling around the world with her and Josette when they were younger had given them a well-rounded knowledge of the African diaspora.

That had prompted Bren to expound on the topic of his visit to Africa. He recalled his despair at seeing the suffering, the war, the torn lives and deprivation. Her eyes had widened seeing how impassioned he seemed about making a difference. He had the power to do many things, she realized, as he explained what he was going to do in his role as a member of Congress.

"We have to control the weapons," he insisted. "We need to legislate who America provides its arms to." And from there the topic was opened to precisely how he would advise the president.

To Latisha, a British subject under the rule of the monarchy, she could only sit and listen to Bren's analysis of the situation. Bren offered insight into the multibillion-dollar inner workings of the Pentagon, the bunker mentality at the top, the cover-ups of weapon failures, and the devious games of the movers and shakers.

He made her realize the question of whether arms were needed and how it fit into a global strategy. And that few member of Congress had a sure enough grasp of what was really going on. Latisha soon realized, when their dinner was over, that Bren seemed destined to open a Pandora's box that most military commanders, congressmen, and even policymakers would want to avoid.

When Bren finally walked her to her room at the end of evening, with a promise that they would spend the following day touring Washington, she was more than excited to see him again. His good night kiss was confirmation of his promise to show her a good time, and Latisha had gone to bed dazzled and happy. He had stayed in his apartment, which was not far from the hotel, arriving to pick her up at 10:30 that next morning.

Her smile widened as Bren took hold of her hand and led the way to the west end of the Mall to take a look at yet another of Washington's landmarks. There was a natural and decidedly alluring way in which his fingers laced through her own. Latisha liked it. More than liked it. The spark she felt was deeper than anything she had ever felt before. As she walked along beside him, a dark cloud lifted from her head and she became aware of her sensuality once more.

It was 4:14 P.M. when they had concluded the last round of sightseeing. Exhausted, Bren decided it would be easier if they picked up some take-out food and brought it back to his apartment. Latisha readily agreed. Less than a half hour later, they were in a taxi. Latisha was excited. She would finally see the place where Bren spent his time.

This was home when he wasn't in Brooklyn or Rye. It was the heart of American politics. She imagined him waking up in the morning, showering, and dressing in one of his expensive suits. Rye, and Brooklyn for that matter, was another place altogether. It was where she imagined he would relax. Sit in front of the fire, kick off his shoes, watch his children run around the house, if he chose to have any. It was a place she loved.

"Bren," Latisha said curiously. "Have you ever imagined yourself with children?"

"Of course," Bren said, as though it should have been plainly obvious. "Three, maybe four, or seven," he elaborated.

Latisha chuckled. "With how many wives?" she joked.

Bren cut a furtive glance at her. "You don't think you're up to the task?"

"Oh, I'm fit," she responded, rising to the bait. "Well-rounded hips."

Ben nodded. "That I agree with. And I wonder what else."

"A fine body to outline and define," she proclaimed with a chuckle, enjoying the flirtatiousness.

"With a single red rose," Bren told her, licking his lips in fascination. "Only something soft and silky, like petals, should touch your skin before I do."

"Hmm." Latisha marveled at how romantic that sounded. "And when you do?"

"When?" Bren drawled at her assumption.

Latisha pulled back. "Unless—"

"I do," Bren cut in. "With my lips and everything I own, when the time is right."

She smiled at his chivalrous nature to wait. "And then?"

"You'll never be the same again," he promised. "And that's a guarantee."

Heady thoughts were on Latisha's mind when the taxi pulled up to the sidewalk outside a modern glass and steel apartment building. They walked through a glazed-glass and brass-plated entrance into a lobby area where a concierge was at his station, watching his portable TV set while seated behind security monitors. He smiled, recognizing Bren, before pressing the elevator button. Instead Bren and Latisha chose the stairway that led up to the second floor, where he placed a key into the door of his apartment. They entered facing a cream-colored hallway that Latisha decided looked surprisingly small, before Bren took her farther inside into an expansive living room.

It was simply designed with flashes of accent color. The walls were a pale shade of blue. There was very little furniture, all unusually designed. One dark blue sofa. A plain white coffee table. A palm tree situated close to a bookshelf. The floor, paint-washed in a pale shade of ivory, had no rug. Two windows revealed a view of Washington, D.C. The street below echoed with the sounds of the city that filtered through an open window. Latisha relaxed immediately.

"I'll get us some plates," Bren offered, walking straight through an opening that led directly into a small kitchen.

Latisha followed him and immediately spotted

an odd-looking item on one of the workbenches. It was made of polished aluminum and she couldn't quite decide if it was an imitation of a bird or a plane. Up close, the object looked like a cross between a spider and a moon rocket. She picked it up and turned it around in her hands, staring at it, bemused, before Bren saw her bewilderment.

"It's a Juicy Salif," he informed her casually.

"What does it do?" Latisha asked.

"That's what it's called," Bren continued, while taking two plates from a shelf and transferring the take-out food they had bought to serving plates. "It's a lemon squeezer. It was created by French designer Philippe Starck."

Latisha stared at it. "Have you used it?"

"Nobody uses a Starck lemon squeezer." Bren laughed. "They just have them to confirm a certain status."

"You mean you bought this to validate your status as a congressman?" Latisha asked in sheer amazement. When Bren nodded, she ventured, "How much did it cost?"

"Four hundred dollars."

"You paid four hundred dollars for a lemon squeezer you can't use!" she choked out, half laughing.

"It's a Philippe Starck," Bren repeated with a bigger chuckle. "People buy him for his high-end design sensibilities. I have a Miss Sissi lamp in the living room. It's very bourgeois."

Latisha shook her head, surprised by the Bren Augustus Hunter she was fast discovering. Who was this man who had such power and knowledge that she was quickly becoming swept away

by his world? She placed the squeezer back on
the bench and took the plate Bren offered her.
The Chinese food looked appetizing.

"Drink?"

"What do you have?"

Bren opened the refrigerator. "Grape juice,
pineapple juice, tomato juice. Cola?"

"I'll have a glass of grape juice," Latisha said.

"You go and sit down and I'll bring it in," Bren
said, reaching up to the shelf for a tall glass.

Latisha retraced her steps back into the living
room and took a seat. Placing the plate on her
lap, she glanced across the room. Only then did
she see the picture frame on the bookshelf of a
much younger image of Veronica. Latisha's heart
quickly stopped as she recalled the anguish and
despair she had last seen on her face. She had
not liked to see someone so distraught over love.
When Bren arrived to hand over her drink, she
could not help but inquire about Veronica.

"How's your sister?" she breathed, finding herself unable to call her by name.

"Veronica's fine." Bren hesitated. He tossed
Latisha an uncertain glance before returning to
the kitchen for his own food. When he returned,
his expression had deepened with curiosity. "Why
do you ask?" he finally asked, taking a seat next
to Latisha, close enough for her to turn into a
seething mass of nerves.

"I was worried about her," Latisha admitted.
After a moment's pause, she added, "I've been
wanting to ask . . . after I left, did you keep Alan
away from—"

"Yes," Bren interrupted, on a flat note. "I
threatened to tell Veronica everything if he left

the hotel under any circumstances. He didn't want to risk upsetting her. He saw the state she was in and behaved."

Latisha sighed. "Good. That's great."

"What did you tell Lady Sarah?" Bren asked suddenly, unsure.

"The truth," Latisha confessed. "I didn't mean to. She saw me off at the airport and I saw how unhappy she looked at not having heard from Alan before I left, and I couldn't leave her looking that way. She needed to know."

Bren nodded sadly. "She handled it okay?"

Latisha nodded, recalling the glimmer of something dark in Lady Sarah's eyes. "I think so. She was quiet, mostly. Alan had bought her a ring, but apparently it was her money that paid for it."

"Oh no," Bren seethed, glancing across at Latisha. "This happened in Tortola?"

Latisha nodded.

Bren cursed beneath his breath before he spoke. "I don't want you to worry about anything with regards to Alan Clayton," he revealed on a firmer note. "I'm taking care of everything."

"What are you going to do?" Latisha asked, aware of the threatening tone in Bren's voice.

"Never mind," he related, shrugging off the matter. "I'm handling it."

Latisha swallowed a large gulp of juice from her glass, aware of her heart beating against her ribs. She imagined things getting badly out of hand. She could see the scene unfolding. Bren and Alan being in a fight. Bren being charged for criminal assault because Alan was the weaker of the two. Then the whole mess ending up in the newspaper for everyone to gossip about. The ultimate kick would be the impact on Bren's flourishing political career.

"Just be careful," she cautioned.

Bren saw that her mood had changed and he gave her a wide smile. "Eat up," he encouraged. His brooding eyes took on a provocative glint and Latisha obeyed.

Chapter Ten

Latisha traced her fingertip along the curve of her eyebrow and blinked. She turned sideways and found herself nestled comfortably into the crook of Bren's shoulder. They had eaten and slept right there on the sofa, exhausted from the day's sightseeing. She raised her head and looked at Bren. He was lost in his own dream. Latisha wondered whether she was a part of what was causing his eyelids to flicker, certain she was the object of his fantasy.

She raised her hand and touched Bren's right cheek. Beneath her smooth fingers, she felt the rough stubble of hair and the trickle of excitement that ran along her fingers. Latisha gasped at how free she felt to be able to touch Bren Hunter with such abandon and rapture.

Then to her amazement, his eyes opened and Bren gazed at her. "Hey," he said, startled. "What's going on?"

"It's me." Latisha chuckled, springing away from him. "We fell asleep."

"Did we?" His words were uttered lightly as Bren pulled himself up into a sitting position, rousing himself into consciousness. "What time is it?"

"Time for me to return to the hotel," Latisha said, just as lightly. "It's dark outside."

Bren consulted his watch. "It's 11:30." He blinked. "Surely we have time for a coffee and then I'll take you back?"

Latisha nodded. "That's sounds okay."

Bren rose to his feet and stretched his limbs. "How do you take it?"

"Black. Two sugars."

He walked slowly into the small kitchen while Latisha reshuffled herself into a more comfortable position. She still felt tired, even though the short nap had revitalized her. The remote control was on the coffee table and she reached over and picked it up. Pressing the switch to activate the television, she began to flip through the channels until she settled on an old MGM musical with a chorus line and songs that were now dated.

When Bren returned, Latisha was thoroughly engrossed in the story of a young actress trying to make the cover of a New York magazine. She was giggling at the fifties-style clothes, the overdone makeup that emphasized eyebrows and red lips, the hats men wore in those days, and the vernacular that bordered on polite chitchat, yet always seemed to begin with the word *why*. Bren looked at her, curious, as he placed the coffees on the table nearby and switched on the Philippe Starck lamp. The soft rays of light bounced against the walls of the room, lending an intimate ambiance to the surroundings.

"Good movie?"

"Why, yes, Mr. Hunter." Latisha chuckled. "Have you noticed how the American language has changed in movies? You wouldn't hear Angela Bassett or Nia Long talk like Doris Day, would you?"

Bren chuckled. "No."

"I'd love to see a modern-day black musical," she went on. "And I'll be in the chorus line."

"You sing?" Bren inquired, sitting next to her as he offered her a mug of coffee.

"It was once an ambition of mine," Latisha admitted, forlornly. "Only I wasn't committed enough. I had no focus."

"What sort of singing did you do?" Bren probed, wanting to know more.

"Session work, background vocals, that sort of stuff," she answered. "I enjoyed it, but in England it's very difficult for black singers to be recognized by the recording industry, and I didn't see myself as . . . someone with a voice like Mariah Carey."

"Is it easier in America to get noticed?" Bren asked, somewhat surprised.

"I think so," Latisha admitted. "There are more black producers, more record labels, much more support. And of course the chance of living the American dream."

"The American dream," Bren repeated, exhaling loudly. "We've come a long way since Civil Rights," he proclaimed. "Today, we have Condoleezza Rice and Colin Powell now advising the president. Someone like me has grown up to become a member of Congress, with dreams of my own. The world is shifting and changing all the time."

Latisha's eyes widened in sheer admiration. Bren was truly fascinating. She still couldn't believe she was sitting in his apartment. Under the most amazing of circumstances, they had met again. There was a deep, tangible connection with each other that neither of them could ignore. The flicker, the spark, that initial infatuation was still there, simmering, smoldering beneath a soaring heat destined to rage.

She could feel the heat of that furnace in the pit of her stomach. It was fueled by hot coffee, which she sipped slowly for fear that any evidence of the burning fire within her would betray itself in the expression on her face. Latisha struggled to keep her gaze fixed, nodding occasionally to Bren's conversation about his hopes for America. But she knew she had failed to convince him that she was truly listening the moment he stopped talking.

Her drifting, wandering gaze on his lips captured Bren's attention seconds after he'd taken his last sip of coffee. His eyes sparkled knowingly as he removed the mug from Latisha's hand and placed both items on the table. Moving closer, he touched her lips. It was a simple gesture with his right index finger, but the soft caress sent a tingling sensation through Latisha's nervous system.

Bren arched his eyebrow. "I think I'm causing another tremor on that Richter scale of yours," he uttered assuredly.

Latisha chose not to lie. "I think you are," she confessed brazenly.

Bren leaned forward. "I shall have to accommodate you with a kiss," he told her, "but first . . ." He reached into his trousers pocket and took out a small burgundy-colored box. Opening it, Bren took out a pendant and placed it in the palm of Latisha's hand. It winked at her in the light. ". . . I wanted to find the perfect time to give you this."

It was weighty. An opal stone set among a cluster of tiny rubies. Latisha's hand shook as her tear-glazed eyes simply stared at it. Dumbstruck, she was hardly aware of Bren brushing the back of her hair to one side to fasten the clasp of the necklace around her neck. The gold chain she had failed to see attached to the stone nestled lightly against her skin and the pendant lay heavy and cold above the low cut of her embroidered tunic.

Latisha felt as limp as a rag doll when Bren gently tipped her chin and she felt herself flop into him. His mouth sealed hers with skillful familiarity until she could barely breathe, and when she tried to catch her breath, he sweetly nipped her lower lip just hard enough to remind her that he had not yet finished the mindless taking of her lips.

Latisha's body—mind, heart, and spirit—relished every second. As though he sensed her helpless supplication, Bren's lips softened. The nip became a soft nibble so persuasive that her lips parted and allowed his tongue in. Bren traced a promise inside her mouth, with a flick and a swirl against hers to torment her with his desire. It was meant to show her what his kind of intimacy was all about.

Her body quivered at his skillful ease. Latisha was awakened to the flash of heat that worked its way to her lower abdomen where it dissolved into pure liquid yearning. She was drugged. Taken completely over with the overwhelming magni-

tude of Bren's unadulterated passion. And then
his lips were gone and he left her startled for a
few brief seconds before she felt them warm and
wet against her neck.

He moved his way down to the pendant against
her heaving breasts, then dropped several more
kisses right there at the divide of her bosom before working his way back up to her neck.
Latisha's throat exerted a deep moan moments
before Bren nursed a kiss there. She was shaking
with excitement, not wanting to rush anything,
yet feeling she needed more and soon.

Bren was aware of Latisha's desire for more of
him. His fingers slipped under her blue tunic
and began to caress the softness of her velvety
skin. Running his fingers down the side of her
body tickled and he enjoyed the way she giggled
into his mouth. Retaking her lips, he deepened
his kiss until he felt her body weaken beneath his
fingers. His hands rose upward to her breasts, but
he chose not to delve further, just simply outline
the curve and shape of her lacy bra.

In the far recesses of Latisha's mind, a voice
silently begged that Bren would boldly strip every
layer of silk and lace until she could feel his fingers brush gently against each nipple. But in
reality, Bren's teasing touch used the soft fabric
as a barrier between torment and ecstasy. He did
not want to take liberties. He had no desire to
take Latisha Fenshaw swiftly and without honor.
Bren wanted the slow pace. The slow burn. He
wanted time for Latisha to drip with yearning for
him to fill her need.

Another tremor beneath his fingers caused
him to plunge his tongue into her mouth with

fervent longing. His body reacted, too. It protested against his decision to take things slow. His limbs were not happy that the buildup of excitement was to go unfulfilled. His heart rate tripled with the burning ache of his manhood. Bren's body jerked with suffering and longing. A jolt of pain riddled his senses. But his mind was steadfast. He knew when and where he wanted things to happen and he would wait. It would be soon.

He lifted his lips and held the soft gaze in Latisha's copper-colored eyes. They smiled at him. His heart melted at how sweet she looked. "Linford Mills was right. You do have lovely eyes," he told her.

Latisha gazed at him. "Linford told you that?"

"Yes." Bren nodded, pressing another brief kiss against her lips.

Latisha heaved a deep, satisfied breath at how good it felt to be so close to Bren, but she blinked nervously and Bren noted it. "What's the matter?"

Latisha shrugged. "I know Linford's your friend. I just happen not to like him very much, that's all."

"He's an interesting man," Bren related. "He's always inaugurating one Caribbean service or another and enjoys glad-handing politicians. I think he likes the ego boost."

Latisha shrugged, refusing to conjure up the image in her mind of when she had found Linford Mills in her cabin. Instead, she placed her hand on the pendant against her chest and was amazed at the sudden emotional rush that shook her spirit. "This is beautiful," she told Bren, shifting the subject to a much more important matter. His gift to her proved that she was indeed someone special to him. "Now I have you close to me."

"You do," Bren declared softly, moments before he pinned Latisha against the arm of the sofa to retake her lips in a kiss so gentle that Bren felt an emotional rush, too.

The last few kisses were gently planted at Latisha's nape when Bren heard the knock at his front door. He grimaced and his brows rose as he reluctantly sat upright. He consulted his watch for a second time. He was startled to find an hour and a half had passed so quickly. His eyes sliced a ravenous glance at Latisha. She looked heavenly nested in his sofa; he was loath that she should ever move from her position.

"Is there someone at your door?" she questioned, unsure if she had heard a knock, too.

"I'm not expecting anyone," Bren returned, standing to his feet with his eyes still fixed on the glorious woman who was keeping him company. "I'd better go see who it is."

Latisha nodded as he left the room. She heard his muffled footsteps in the hallway and the front door open. A female voice rang out like an echo, causing her to immediately reposition herself and fix her hair with a quick shuffle. Seconds later, Latisha sensed more footsteps before Bren reentered the room. Her face dropped the moment she saw the woman standing at Bren's side.

The newcomer looked sensational in a yellow Chanel suit. And she had hair. Masses of it, microweaved in cascades of swirls and curls around her shoulders leading all the way down her back.

Tall and leggy, groomed and highly maintained, with classic heels, expensive earrings, and swinging a Louis Vuitton shoulder bag with mild gaiety, the woman had model looks and all the merits to suit. A tiny nose, perfect red lips, and a complexion of wild golden honey. Latisha was numbed.

"I'd like you to meet Vanessa Harper, chief operating officer of the Democratic National Committee," Bren introduced, watching as Vanessa boldly walked over and offered a firm handshake to Latisha, who had remained seated. "She's just popped by to drop off some papers."

Vanessa's eyes homed in and connected, and Latisha did not fail to see the sting. "Hello," she murmured.

"How nice to make the acquaintance," Vanessa acknowledged before returning her attention to Bren. "I had no idea you were entertaining tonight," she said, disappointed. "I saw the light beneath the door and thought I'd knock."

"Latisha Fenshaw's from England," Bren elaborated, throwing a wink across the room at her. "She's a trustee on the board of two organizations as well as a representative to several charities that were all set up by her late father, Sir Joshua Fenshaw, before he died," he expanded. "We were . . . getting to know each other a little better before you arrived."

Vanessa's mouth tightened. "Then let me not disturb you," she retorted, deftly reaching into her shoulder bag and removing two folders. "I just wanted to leave these amendments for you." She deposited them into his hand. "We can talk over what you want to do at the office tomorrow. I can make a breakfast meeting."

"Actually . . . I'm taking the day off tomorrow," Bren reported with a smile. "I'm playing tourist guide to an English lady." He sliced a cheeky gaze at Latisha. "I can do it the day after, say 8.00 A.M.?"

Vanessa was unperturbed. "Perhaps I can come over tomorrow evening. We can discuss the important factors over a bottle of wine."

Bren's gaze shifted immediately to Vanessa. "I'll be otherwise engaged tomorrow night," he told her firmly. "The earliest I have is an 8.00 A.M. on Thursday."

"If you say so," Vanessa conceded, shooting a fiery glance at him. "There are a few other agendas I need to confirm with you, but they can wait." Her attention now directed on Latisha, she added, "Politics is a very dangerous game, Miss Fenshaw. The congressman has to be very careful with whom he associates himself, and it's my job to steer the way clear for him to do his duty. That means no scavengers wanting to drain, suck, or sap his energies. Those are best kept for the office he serves."

"Stop embarrassing the girl." Bren chuckled, nudging Vanessa by the waistline toward the door. "I'm sure Miss Fenshaw will adhere to everything you say and I appreciate you stopping by."

It was only when Latisha heard the front door close did she feel able to breathe again. When Bren returned, she was almost riddled with guilt. "You shouldn't be neglecting your work for me," she exclaimed remorsefully.

Bren laughed, walking over to the sofa and

pulling Latisha to her feet. "I'm not. I'll be back in New York later this week, so pay Vanessa no mind. She likes the fact that I'm the son of a man who was once one of the highest-ranking officers in our state and, in his day, the only black attorney general in the country. My father's position, especially when he became a senator, was the gossip in my neighborhood when I was a boy. Vanessa's nostalgic about all that. She's just making sure I live up to my expectations, that's all."

Latisha nodded as Bren hugged her and planted another kiss against her lips. But she remained uncertain about exactly how she would cope with his political life when he kissed her good night outside the Willard Intercontinental Hotel and waved as the taxi returned him home. As Latisha closed the door to her room, her uncertainty grew. She debated what would be expected of her as the woman in the congressman's life.

And more importantly, Latisha thought, as she hopped into bed and closed the cleanly pressed sheets around herself, would Vanessa Harper tolerate the situation? It was the most pressing question on her mind as she drifted into a restless sleep.

The hotel room was flooded with bright early morning light when Latisha awoke. She opened her eyes with a quiver of excitement, notably aware that she would be spending her second and last day in Washington, D.C., with Bren before her return to England.

Jumping from her bed, she rushed over to the

window and drew open the curtains to take a look across the city. The sky was clear, indicative of another warm day, and a quick glance at the digital clock beside the bed told her she had enough time to shower, change, and have breakfast before Bren's 10:30 arrival. She would have to prepare herself for another round of sightseeing, as this was what he had in mind, as well as a visit to the White House, which she was much looking forward to.

At 10:15, Latisha was leaving the restaurant when she spotted Bren. He was fifteen minutes early, but she was not alarmed as Bren lived close to the hotel and was far more likely to arrive sooner than later. She crossed the lobby and caught up with him just when he was about to enter an elevator car to take him to her floor. Latisha smiled as she tapped him on the back and watched him turn around to face her.

As he did so, she immediately caught the anguished expression on his face. "What's the matter?" Latisha panicked, troubled that Bren also seemed restless.

"Veronica's in the hospital," he said. "They're keeping her in for a few days. It seems she's had an argument with Alan."

"What about?" Latisha asked, curious whether Alan had made any disclosures about his activities.

"It seems she's seen an announcement in the local newspaper that he is to be married to Lady Sarah Fenshaw," Bren informed her.

Latisha gasped. "What?"

"Someone planted that story," Bren said, seething. "I don't know what evil satisfaction they gained from it, other than to see Veronica more distressed." Bren glanced at the elevator car, which had arrived. "Can we talk in your room?"

Latisha nodded, though she felt sick as she silently followed Bren into the car, and kept quiet until they were within the confines of her hotel room. Once there, she seated herself on the edge of the bed while Bren paced angrily across the floor, his annoyance growing with every passing moment until Latisha began to wonder whether they would enjoy the day with everything hanging over them.

"Alan swears he knows nothing about it," Bren related, furiously. "God, if he was here right now, I'd . . ." His gaze moved to Latisha. He could see she seemed troubled. "What is it?" he demanded to know.

"I think Sarah is a woman deeply scorned and is out for revenge," she revealed, sadly. "I saw the look in her eyes when I told her about Alan at the airport. I should've told you I suspected something."

"You mean *she* did this?" Bren exclaimed.

Latisha nodded. "I can't imagine who else it could be. She must be here in the United States."

"The silly woman," Bren derided angrily. "She's just upped the ante on how quickly I go for Alan's throat. This could just topple Veronica into another suicide attempt."

Latisha grew alarmed. "Suicide!"

Bren stopped pacing the floor and ran an exasperated hand across his forehead, not realizing he had let the distressing secret slip. "Yes," he said gravely. "She found out about one of Alan's infidelities a year ago and tried to take her life in

March. It was Alan's sisters who nursed her back to health. They found her in time."

Latisha gulped. "Alan's sisters. Hermonie and Muriel?"

"You know them?" Bren asked, amazed.

"Know them!" Latisha felt her stomach turn over, nauseated. "Alan introduced them to me at his mother's house. They all knew he was playing me for a fool and kept quiet about it. I met Alan in May last year. It would've been . . . two months after her attempted suicide."

"That woman . . . Constance Clayton . . . she'll stop at nothing until she destroys my sister." Bren scowled harshly. "She and her daughters must've decided you were a better prospect. Constance never wanted her son to marry Veronica. In her eyes, her darling Alan was far too good for my sister."

Latisha quickly recalled her first meeting with Veronica. *The acid test was his mama, and now that I've proved to her I'm keeping my man I have nothing to worry about.* "Poor girl," she sympathized immediately. "She's not in the hospital because—"

Bren shook his head. "No, it was Alan who called me. He said she got distressed over seeing the announcement in the newspaper and he decided to take her to the hospital because she looked ill. Her blood pressure is high, that's why they're keeping her in."

"I'll have to call my sister and find out if she's seen Sarah before she does anything more stupid," Latisha suggested on a melancholy note. "This is turning out to be a nightmare."

Bren was at her feet in an instant. "I'm sorry. I'm being insensitive, talking about Veronica and her husband like this when today should be about us."

Latisha had tears in her eyes. She mindlessly held on to the pendant Bren had given her the night before, her mouth dry and her throat tight. "He's always going to be there, between us, isn't he?"

"No," Bren insisted.

With him on his knees in front of her—in an open-necked white shirt, where she could see tantalizing glimpses of nutmeg-brown skin and dark body hair, and even smell the musky scent of his aftershave—she was not convinced. Latisha began to measure her options.

Think of the complications, she told herself, as her gaze dropped to Bren's compelling pewter-colored eyes. *Think of Alan—the lies! Veronica—sick! Lady Sarah—vengeful!* Think what she could be risking here, her heart even suggested as Bren's eyes flickered in a downward path over a body he couldn't wait to touch. First with rose petals and then with the practiced movement of his fingers.

Latisha had dressed simply in a gypsy-style denim skirt and a white T-shirt, with white sandals on her feet that complemented her hazelnut-brown complexion. With her glossy black hair pinned up around her oval face to keep her neck cool and her makeup minimal, she did not realize how appealing she seemed to Bren at that moment. Maybe it was the pendant around her neck, proclaiming his ownership, or the uncertain glistening of tears welling up in her eyes, Bren was unsure.

He braced his hands on either side of Latisha, aware that his very action provoked a tingle of excitement within her. Latisha's breath caught until she finally spoke. "I don't want him to spoil anything for us."

"He won't," Bren assured her, the very suggestion causing something violent to rise up within him as he put one hand behind her neck and pulled Latisha gently toward him. "I promise." He didn't want to hear Alan's name from her trembling lips and he was going to make damned sure that wasn't going to happen, either.

Taking her face in the palm of his hands, using one thumb to graze her lips, Bren raised his head and kissed her. Tentative at first, and then he delved deeper, taking her in slow mouthfuls. The blessed heat of her reaction traveled like lightning to the very core of his soul. Bren caught Latisha's moan in his mouth and threw a little whimper of his own back into hers, telling her exactly how he was feeling.

Latisha's mind pivoted into a tailspin. How could she possibly resist a man on his knees? *I can handle this,* she tried telling herself. Bren invited her closer. She sank into him without hesitation, lifting her hands to fold around his neck, while he allowed his own to slide downward. She loved the taste of him. He was like black grapes and honey, tangy and fluid, and she wanted more.

His tongue delved in; she accepted it readily. She kissed him with every heartfelt emotion that coursed through her body. Latisha swooned and was lost. All her mind seemed capable of registering were the hot lips attached to her own, sweeping her into a cocoon of such wondrous joy that every limb wept at how sweet it felt to be in Bren's arms. Such was her euphoria that Latisha hadn't realized she had leaned forward with too much haste to capture more of what was on offer.

Within seconds, her body weight toppled over onto Bren and they both found themselves collapsing onto the floor in a bout of fevered laughter. On his back, Bren held on tight to Latisha, enjoying the way his fingers began to familiarize themselves with the shape of her buttocks. And then he rolled her over on to her side, and leaned above her on his left elbow, staring deeply into her enchanting eyes.

"You're so beautiful, do you know that?" he told her.

Latisha smiled up at him, charting every measure of his square face. Bren's firmly shaped cheekbones and long, straight patrician nose. His nutmeg-colored complexion and dark Afro. His voice, still so deep, smooth, and silky that the very sound of it seemed forever etched in her mind, was unforgettable.

"Tell me more often and I'll believe it," Latisha joked.

"Don't you think so yourself?" Bren asked, worried.

"It's not what I see that counts," Latisha mused. "I'm content with how I look. It's what you see that matters."

"I see many things," Bren admitted in a lustful note, running a finger from her throat down to where the pendant nestled against her breasts, where the telling dictates of her heart were all but a giveaway of how she felt. "And I want to see more."

"All in good time." Latisha chuckled, putting a halt to his wandering hands.

Bren took the hint. He smiled, pulling himself up, fighting down the amazing urge to spend more time with Latisha Fenshaw in her hotel room. "C'mon, let me show you the rest of Washington city. We can sort out all the complications later."

They went directly to the White House and viewed it like tourists. Latisha was to learn that it had been designed by James Hoban, an Irishman who was the winner of a design competition in 1792 to construct the president's residence. Bren went on to explain how the British troops advanced on Washington in 1814 and burned the house before it was rebuilt.

She learned about Dolley Madison, who had cut out of its frame a portrait of George Washington for safekeeping during the war before its return to the house. That Jimmy Carter's daughter had once had a tree house on the west side of the south lawn. That it was believed the ghost of President Lincoln lurked among the corridors, and that the president's desk, which had been made from oak timber from a British navy ship that had been trapped in Arctic ice, was now back in the Oval Office in the West Wing.

It was all historical stuff, much of which Latisha found interesting, but what was more fascinating to her was being with Congressman Bren Hunter. She was aware of how her need for him was growing with every passing hour, how she wanted nothing more than for them to return to her hotel room and spend the entire day there learning more about each other. Her thoughts fascinated her, for Latisha had not indulged in such fantasies before. Perhaps it was the slow burn, she wondered, waiting for an opportune time to be with Bren.

Latisha did not care what the reason was. All she knew was that she could not bear to return to England.

Latisha sighed as they stepped out into the golden sunlight, the visitors' tour having reached a close. She tried to smile, but felt it slip from her lips.

Bren took a hold of her hand. "You're thinking about when you leave tomorrow, aren't you?" he surmised quickly.

Latisha nodded.

They departed from the small crowd on the White House tour. The streets were busy. In the height of the late July summer, Washington, D.C., was alive with people taking in the sights and the hustle and bustle of such a large city. Caught in the whirl of activity, Latisha could hardly think straight.

"I'm just getting to know you and—"

"You'll be back soon," Bren enthused. "Only this time, you'll be dating the right man, not someone who'll be yanking your chain."

Latisha tried to smile. She wanted to believe it. Wanted to trust that everything that had happened in the three short weeks of being in Tortola, Florida, and then Washington was fate's way of giving her some direction about where her life was going. No matter how bizarre, how incredible some of the paths had been, Latisha felt certain there was a message there somewhere. Somehow, she was destined to see this man again.

Her only problem was, did she have enough faith to accept this certainty?

"You're very sure of a lot of things," she told Bren. She looked behind her at the White House, now several blocks away. "Like living there one day."

Bren chuckled. "In ten years, maybe. When America's ready to accept a black president."

"And me as the First Lady?" Latisha wanted to laugh at how ludicrous it all sounded.

"Hey," Bren urged, "if an actor and his actress wife can make it, anyone can. They just have to hold on to the dream long enough."

Latisha had to smile, she couldn't help herself. "Yeah. I forget you Americans love to have dreams. Well, I'm an English gal. We tend to be more conservative."

"You'll be back," Bren assured her, lacing his fingers through hers. "Didn't you tell me in Rye that you spoke at a charity in New York?"

"The Jamaican Cancer Care," Latisha confirmed, recalling the last time she had been there. It was the day after Valentine's, when she had also arranged to see Alan. "Another one of my father's endless charities that is now one of my responsibilities. In fact, I'm scheduled to make another visit in four weeks."

"You see?" Bren chirped. "Progress already."

Latisha's mood perked up. "So it is."

"We should have dinner tonight at the hotel," Bren said, easily. "I'd like to—" He was cut short by the ringing of his cell phone. Bren paused, letting go of Latisha's hand before answering it. Latisha noted the grimace on his face as he recognized the caller. "Vanessa, hi."

She was unable to detect what it was Vanessa Harper actually wanted, but Latisha was not fooled. The call was a clear sign that the chief operating officer of the Democratic National Committee was staking her claim. It was also a sign that Vanessa was not only charting Bren's whereabouts, but was sending a warning that she would not let the congressman so easily fall in love. And if Latisha knew anything about women, she would say that Vanessa Harper had just made her first move.

Bren, she noted, seemed annoyed when he closed his cell. He used words that registered in Latisha's mind as simple endearments that would pass between friends. Nothing to be unduly alarmed about, but she was curious nonetheless. Why couldn't Vanessa have waited until her meeting with Bren in the morning?

"Everything okay?" she inquired.

Bren blinked. "Yes. Everything's fine." He nodded, retaking a hold of her hand. "What was I saying?"

"We were talking about dinner at the hotel," Latisha reminded him, annoyed that he had chosen not to explain anything to her.

Bren nodded again. "Right. Eight o'clock would suit me fine. But not at the hotel. Let me take you somewhere out on the town."

"That sounds even better," Latisha agreed, unable to shake the niggling feeling in the pit of her stomach that Bren was hiding something. "I can wear my new dress."

"Hmm, sounds interesting," Bren joked. "Will it reveal anything?"

"Just my shapely curves," Latisha told him, attempting to lighten the mood, "and cleavage."

Bren chuckled before planting a kiss on her right cheek. "I look forward to seeing you in that."

Latisha suddenly did not feel so convinced, but kept her smile fixed. "I look forward to seeing you dressed to suitably impress, too." But the fear she heard in her voice found an echo in her heart. Try as she might, Latisha could not shake the unmistakable feeling that Vanessa Harper remained a threat, whether Bren was aware of it or not.

"I intend to," he promised.

We'll see, Latisha thought suspiciously as they took a turn and began a leisurely stroll along Pennsylvania Avenue back toward the hotel.

When Bren returned to his apartment to change for his evening date with Latisha, he got a call from Chico Maccola. The voice at the other end of the phone sounded rancorous, as though he had just tasted his first ounce of blood. Bren sat down on the sofa in his living room, listening intently to information that, in addition to what he had been through that day, shook his senses.

"I've found something," Maccola triumphed, like a schoolboy who had just earned a good grade. "It seems our friend is broke."

"Broke!" Bren was dumbfounded. "What's he been doing for money?"

"Good question," Maccola proclaimed, intent on making the discovery sometime soon. "The bugs are in the house and we're listening."

"Thank God Veronica isn't there," Bren said, absently.

"What was that?" Maccola asked, uncertain he had heard correctly.

"She's in the hospital," Bren explained, running a tired hand across his forehead. "High blood pressure."

"Oh no," Maccola exclaimed, worried. "Is she all right?"

"She's fine."

"Which hospital?"

"Beth Israel Deaconess Medical Center."

"Okay."

"Keep me posted on what else you find," Bren told the private detective. "Let's hope those creepy crawlies you've planted do their job."

"Don't you worry, Mr. Hunter," Maccola said with a measure of determination. "The house is infested and we're picking everything up nice and clear. Sooner or later, our man is gonna make a slip and I'll be right there to get it on tape."

Chapter Eleven

In a Carolina Herrera beaded cocktail dress, Manolo Blahnik lace shoes, and embroidered wrap, her hair swept up in a chignon and her makeup applied with the utmost precision, Latisha Fenshaw felt beautifully elegant knowing that she would meet the approval of any congressman.

She was certain Bren Hunter would find her irresistible, so Latisha told herself as she began to add the finishing touches to her appearance by spraying on a dash of Versace perfume for added effect. The perfume was invigorating as she surveyed her handiwork in the mirror of the hotel's bathroom, impressed with the way she had changed her ordinary daytime look to one of opulent chic and stately sophistication.

Her hazelnut-brown complexion was positively glowing beneath the golden shimmering sheen of her dress, which reflected her glamorous new image. Low cut, revealing ample cleavage—enough to arouse any man's libido—but in a tastefully modest way. She liked it. The dangling earrings were longer than what she usually wore, but intricately designed to enhance her look. Her red lipstick was not her usual shade either. What it said about her was this was a woman who was daring, delicious, and dangerous.

I love it, Latisha thought as she left the bathroom, walking carefully since she was unaccustomed to prancing around in four-inch high heels. Bren was tall and would appreciate her lips being a tad closer to his own. She had thought about buying the shoes in Florida. And this would be their last night together before she returned to the ordinariness of her own life back in England.

Latisha wanted Bren to remember her this way, a woman whose appearance conveyed wealth, education, and background to match the likes of Vanessa Harper. She felt herself flinch at the very thought of the other woman. Latisha still recalled, with a touch of envy, Vanessa standing in Bren's apartment in a Chanel suit.

On her own salary—a combination of modest earnings split between two trusteeships and charities that were still more pet projects of her late father than anything she had personally contributed to—she could not afford the kind of high-maintenance wardrobe and pampering that Vanessa Harper no doubt could.

The last time she hosted one of her father's black-tie affairs on the *Caribbean Rose,* she told Lady Sarah that the dress she had been wearing was on loan from a well-known designer, who demanded its return as soon as she was back in the United States. But in truth, she had purchased it from a secondhand dress shop when she was last in New York City. She could not match the likes of Vanessa Harper, whose political life provided money, success, and the sort of haute couture that was de rigueur among her social set.

With that in mind, Latisha felt a sudden pang of apprehension about her budding relationship with Bren. Was he the man for her? Was she indeed the woman for him? It was a concern still on her mind as she departed her hotel room to meet him in the lobby, as arranged. She imagined the restaurant would be lavish, and hoped they would both enjoy it, but as Latisha entered the elevator, her nerves were on edge.

This time, she was pondering Bren's mood. The day's events had been traumatic. He had learned that Veronica was in the hospital and she had discovered that Veronica had attempted suicide last year. It was not the kind of news they needed while spending two days together in Washington, D.C. Then there was the problem of Lady Sarah. Latisha had not been able to reach her. She had called her sister in Florida, who had admitted that she had not seen their stepmother either. Somewhat troubling, it had to mean Lady Sarah was holed up in Boston somewhere.

The situation worried Latisha.

Lady Sarah Fenshaw was a woman of understated beauty. She had been surprised at her father's choice in such a younger, more frivolous woman to her more conservative mother. The wedding, on the tropical shores of Antigua, was a wonderful memory from their short marriage. No one had expected Sir Joshua Fenshaw to die. He was in his early fifties. And Lady Sarah had held her head high at the funeral, notwithstanding the presence of Sir Joshua's first wife, her mother.

So, why would she now be behaving in such a wild way? Latisha thought about it as the elevator car descended. She suspected Alan Clayton's guise had triggered something. He had, it seemed, messed with the wrong woman.

Latisha was at a loss as to what Lady Sarah would try next, after having planted a wedding announcement in Boston's local newspaper. Latisha was certain Lady Sarah was behind it. That certainty was still with her as she made her way toward the lobby.

The moment she saw Bren Hunter, Latisha's mood lifted. She instantly forgot all the thorny problems that they faced as the distance between them gradually diminished until she found herself standing face-to-face with the man she had first seen in Rye. He had looked powerful then, but more so now. He was not dressed in a tuxedo, as she had suspected, but decked out in a tailored Brooks Brothers two-button suit. Polished Cole Haan Santoni master-crafted black calfskin hand-stitched shoes were on his feet, and his overall appearance was magnificently accented with a Paul Smith shirt and tie. Latisha was instantly aware that Bren was the most handsome man in the hotel.

The pewter-colored eyes brightened. His mouth broke into a smile and Latisha felt her heart skip a beat. Congressman Bren Augustus Hunter was hers for the evening, and Latisha was overwhelmed. But she regained her composure with speed, taking a breath to gird herself to be cool and calm. It would be too much to fall apart now, she told herself, reminding herself that she was leaving the next day. Tonight, she would enjoy herself and remember this night forever.

"Hello, beautiful," Bren greeted, instantly dipping his head to brush a kiss against her cheek.

"Hello, handsome," Latisha replied, before seeing the single red rose Bren was handing her. She chuckled. "A little romance?"

"Until later," Bren promised.

Latisha felt her blood frizzle at the suggestion as she followed Bren out of the hotel and into the street. To her surprise, a black stretch limousine was waiting for them both. Latisha's heart was thumping wildly as the driver, standing by an open door, urged her inside. Bren followed and soon they were both seated. The car entered traffic, traveling at cruise speed so its passengers could enjoy the early evening milieu of Washington, D.C., through the tinted windows.

"This is wonderful," Latisha enthused, watchful as the varying numbers of people on the wide landscaped sidewalks, the tall buildings, distant monuments, shops, restaurants, the J. Edgar Hoover Building, and the White House itself came into view.

Bren noted how happy Latisha seemed. "I thought you'd enjoy another look at the city," he said mildly. "When it's dark and when the lights are on, that's when power looks really magical."

Latisha gazed at Bren, knowing she was seeing true power personified. Not in the same way as the head of state, or even monarchy, but as an achiever. Bren was a political fighter, a legislator, and an adviser to the president, someone who believed in human rights and that privilege, class, or birthright did not make you a superior person. As every aspect of his character became familiar, Latisha realized something deeply meaningful. She was falling in love with Bren Hunter.

It was three hours later, while she was feeling full, lazy, and half seduced by a mixture of candlelight, a bottle of red wine, a round of aperitifs, a three-course meal, and Bren's conversation, that Latisha began to size up the extraordinary day. She was also aware of her growing reluctance to return to England. She tried to tell herself it would be easy, if only Bren did not make her laugh with enough wisecracks to keep her in stitches. If only he weren't so damned handsome, in a patrician sort of way, with that overriding confidence, strength, and will to succeed—her first thoughts when they first met in Rye.

"You know," Bren said, leaning back in his chair, warming his cup of coffee with his large, sensual hands, his eyes smoldering, "I think it's time we got cosy someplace else."

Latisha arched her eyebrows, then glanced at her watch. It read 10:14 P.M. "Maybe you're right," she agreed, aware of the delicious pounding sensation in the space that separated her heart from her stomach.

La Colline, the French restaurant where they were seated, located on Capitol Hill, catered to heavy-hitting lobbyists and lawmakers, and the cuisine had been a model of excellence. With a meal of house-smoked salmon and ravioli stuffed with mixed wild mushrooms sparked by a zesty tomato sauce, Latisha was more than aware that her stomach was full. So she knew the tremors flittering to and fro inside had little to do with the food she had eaten and more to do with her feelings for Bren.

The city lights were just as Bren told her they would be when they finally departed, before entering into the night. Bright, illuminating, and almost transcendent was how they appeared. Latisha found herself leaning against Bren's strong, muscled frame as they rested comfortably in the limousine on the journey to his apartment for a nightcap. She suspected that this would be her last occasion to be close to him. Latisha could not see a time when they'd ever meet again. But she kept her thoughts to herself. She did not want to spoil the evening, or break the mood.

She held Bren's hand and laced her fingers through his, savoring the moment, marveling at how her heart melted as he slowly raised his head and looked down into her face. And then her eyes closed as his lips took hers. Latisha sank into him without hesitation, lifting one arm to fold around his neck, while Bren used his free hand to slide slowly downward. Along her back, past the hectic pulse of her heartbeats that quivered along her spine, downward until his hand settled against the curving form of her hip.

And through it all, their mouths kept a vigil with each other. Warm and soothing, hot and deep. The seduction was on. Latisha knew they had only one place to go, and she was fully on her way there. Everything her sister had told her flew into the night with each passing kiss. *You don't want to be embroiled in another meaningless, mad, wild fling of unrequited passion* skipped on by like a bird in flight. *If ever you feel uncertain, don't do anything* hovered briefly, then dissipated. Latisha was certain. She had never felt more certain of anything in her life. When the limousine pulled up outside Bren's apartment, she was hot, racy, and ready to go. . . .

They understood each other, recognized the deeply tangible feelings erupting, and fell like two doves onto Bren's bed. Legs entwined, arms embracing, their mouths locked, sealing a new kind of passion.

A tiny explosion of delight vibrated through Latisha's body as her world disappeared. And then Bren was planting kisses all over. On the rapid pulse beating at her inner wrist. On each line in her palm. On the tips of her fingernails, where further exquisite feelings were lingering indecisively, causing her to drop the single red rose Bren had given her onto the fine white cotton sheets beneath her shaking limbs. And then his lips were back on hers, nipping her mouth carefully . . . slowly . . . seductively in tantalizing caresses of pure, liquid fire.

Latisha slowly released the buttons on Bren's shirt and clutched at his naked shoulders, taking delight in how strong his body felt beneath those very fingers he had kissed. Suddenly, she whispered words she had never uttered to any man before while in full heat.

"I'm going to tie you up with my hosiery, gag you with my knickers, and layer you with fresh cream so I can savor every part of your body until you beg for mercy."

Bren felt as if he had been fired off like a rocket. "Oh yeah, girl," he murmured, seconds before he jumped up from the bed, ripped off his jacket, and threw it down onto the floor. Returning to the bed, he comfortably lay on his back and cupped Latisha's head between his hands, bringing her face down to his. He allowed her to bury her tongue inside his mouth. Bren drew it in like a predator feasting on its prey, voraciously. He enjoyed the way Latisha tasted him, too. They wriggled against each other, wildly, impatiently. They were out of control.

Then Bren felt his stomach muscles contract. He looked into Latisha's eyes and disturbingly saw Alan Clayton's eyes gazing back at him. He touched the insides of her silky thighs, sensing the Lycra of her hosiery, but felt the treachery ravage his heart that Alan's fingers had touched the same spot, too. Bren closed his eyes and saw the terrible truth stamp itself on the inside of his eyelids. He had been too blinded, too swept up with his desire for Latisha to pay attention to the niggling, trapped jealousy in his mind. How could he make love to a woman who had already been taken by his brother-in-law?

Bren rolled over onto his stomach. "Darling," he said, stalling, seeming unable to curtail his desirous emotions amid the churning feelings in his stomach. "About Alan . . ."

Latisha heard the bitter suspicion in Bren's voice and understood immediately. "I didn't, not with Alan." She came clean in a hoarse sound of sexual impatience.

"What?" Bren raised his head and glanced across at her. In the beaded cocktail dress Latisha was wearing, where her cleavage beckoned to be squeezed and adored, Bren found it hard to keep his hands off her. It was sheer will, and his respecting her right to be heard, that kept him at bay.

"I went through eleven months of frustration," Latisha went on. "Months of torture. Weeks of wondering when I was going to see him next. Days of going mad with fantasies of when we were going to be together. And when I did see Alan, finally," she scoffed in derision, "he had an excuse for that, too. He was either too tired or had a lot on his mind. Or there was a ball game he needed to catch on the TV. We shared a bed," she admitted, uncertain whether Bren had chosen to believe her, "but the only thing Alan and I did was sleep in it. Alan never made love to me."

Surprise brought Bren's eyes to hers. "He failed you?" he asked incredulously, the shocked expression on his face almost comical.

"Every time," Latisha concluded. "It's not something a girl likes to brag about, either. That the man she had been devoting much of her attention to was unable to fulfill a certain area of her life. I couldn't even tell my sister." She paused. "That's what I meant when I told you in Rye that I never did understand what he wanted from me."

"Not sex," Bren finished, having remembered the curious statement. "He'd obviously taken care of that somewhere else."

"His wife, probably," Latisha surmised, relieved that the truth was finally out. "I was just company, I guess. Someone to talk to. Look at. Remind him he could still catch the eye of another woman. Who knows?"

Bren's amorous intentions grew quickly. "You must be—"

"Needing you very badly," Latisha confessed, her breathing becoming shallow at the mere thought of being kissed again.

"I'm going to make up for everything you've missed," Bren promised, pulling her toward him, where he instantly began to kiss life back into her. And then his hand was on the rose, outlining the soft curves of Latisha's brown flesh, enjoying the way she giggled as the red petals tickled her senses. "No part of you is going to be overlooked," he told her. "Whatever you've been lacking, I'm going to give it to you. I know what you need."

Latisha heard Bren's declaration and closed her eyes. . . .

He worshiped her as if she were bare on an altar. Undressed, Latisha looked almost heavenly to Bren. As he gazed admiringly at her, he considered himself the savior of all her desires. His heart pumped when he heard her release a sharp gasp as he pulled a nipple into his mouth and began to pulse his tongue against it. She wriggled and her stomach released a basketful of flutters. But Bren was only beginning his feast of being with such a glorious woman. He honored the full roundness of her breasts, praised her shapely hips, graced the soft outlines of her thighs, and then delved inward to pay full homage to the secret of her fire.

Then his lips were back on hers, giving glory

to every corner of her mouth. Latisha's hand shot out and found a tightly muscled shoulder. She gripped. She felt the warmth of his living naked flesh, the hardness of Bren rubbing and caressing her thigh, the slight prickle of chest hair against her breasts. All of it sent a pleasurable, whimpering sigh from her mouth to his. Bren's long brown fingers skimmed along her neck, leaving a trail of hot fire in their wake, before his tongue left her mouth and began to lick the sweltering flames only he seemed capable of lighting. And then those very fingers were stroking her cheek, taking delight in her soft, smooth hazenut-colored complexion, while he adored the darkening desire in her eyes.

Bren was alive with a new burst of energy he had never experienced before. A fresh drive that erupted full force the moment he felt Latisha steal downward to stroke his power source. The feel of her fingers as she measured the length of him had his chest expanding on a fierce intake of air that knocked him sideways. And then she was pushing him over onto his back, while she moistened her softly pulsing mouth. Bren's eyes flickered in heightened anticipation, unable to predict what Latisha was going to do next. When the tip of her tongue began to drop a string of kisses, first on one nipple and then the other, making their way downward to his groin, where she planted further kisses on that very power source, he was lost. No man with blood in his body could resist the feeling of being in heaven.

Latisha's mind was in total disbelief that she could control Congressman Bren Hunter so easily. He was in total surrender to her. She could feel each response, every tremor and ripple of his flesh beneath her fingers. Beneath her seductive kisses. His breath was tight, his eyes were glazed, and his heart was pounding against his rib cage as she twisted and deliciously pulled at the curls of hair on his chest, providing sweet pain and pleasure.

And then he was reaching for her like a snake about to strike, unable to dampen the rising tension coursing through his body. He rolled Latisha over. She gazed up into his pewter-colored eyes and his heart almost leaped at the joy he saw there. She knew he was taking over the moment he reached for her right hand and deliberately drew it downward between their two bodies onto his manhood.

"I love the way you touch me," he whispered, his voice so mild and full of yearning that Latisha felt a jerking tear at the back of one eye.

"Then let me—"

"No," Bren commanded, overruling any heartfelt gestures of her wanting to please him further. "It's my turn."

He began a new kind of worship. Bren idolized everything he saw. His heart pumped ever more madly as Latisha squealed while he devoured and glorified the most sensitive area of her soul. Her fingers fumbled in his hair as she felt sensation after sensation rush through her, as she felt the tightness of Bren's hair, as he tormented her with every flick and lap of his tongue until she could curtail her excitement no more.

"Bren . . . please . . ." she groaned.

He raised his head. "Please what?" he murmured, before retaking his position between her legs.

He squeezed her bottom with his fingers, bowed down to the apex of her sex, and treating her like a goddess, devoured her with such fervent need that Latisha felt uncertain she would survive the experience. Such pleasure was truly heavenly. Her soul rocked, her body convulsed, and her fingers dug into the flesh above Bren's shoulders. And then a cheeky finger stole an inch of her, sliding into the sweet luxury of her haven. Latisha went nova. Her body lurched forward, her head turned from side to side against the softness of Bren's pillows, and her legs writhed in the struggle to be free of such delicious delight

She begged. "Bren . . . please."

With lustful impatience, Bren pushed himself up onto his knees and laughed softly. "I'll just go get a condom," he whispered, stroking a seductive finger between her legs, triumphing in the whimper that Latisha threw back at him in response.

He was at a chest of drawers in a flash, fishing inside for what they both needed. Latisha watched without moving from her position as Bren ripped open the packet and applied the latex. When he rejoined her and they were lying side by side, everything changed. The whole room became charged with serious intent. Totally uninhibited, they began the sacred pledge to each other. This time the ceremony of seduction was fraught with teasing and determination to reach full satisfaction.

Instinctively, Latisha welcomed Bren as he settled his lean hips between her clinging thighs. She kept her gaze fixed on his darkened eyes as he ventured to take her. Her legs were wrapped around his body and her arms clung to his back. Their eyes locked, communicating without words, for words were not needed at a time like this. They were in their own nirvana.

She tried to wriggle her hips. His hands took hold of her buttocks to hold her still. She arched against him. He throbbed inside her. Her breath was short. His was shallow. She closed her eyes. He thrust deeper. Her body trembled. The tremor pushed him to swell more. He squeezed her bottom as she groaned. She screamed as an orgasm shot right through her. Bren choked his against her ear. She felt him fill the condom. . . .

Latisha sensed someone standing at the bottom of the bed. The figure was hovering beneath a veneer of powder and lipstick, tapping a disapproving forefinger against pursed lips. Still quite sleepy, she considered the image to be a figment of her imagination and cuddled up closer to the warm body lying next to her. Sensing her near him, Bren turned and faced her. Their tired eyes locked. A bolt of sensual pleasure was transmitted between them and that was when they heard the cough. Someone had carefully cleared her throat. They both looked toward the bottom of the bed.

"Vanessa," Bren gasped. He sat up immediately. "How did you get in here?"

"With the key you gave me, of course." Vanessa swallowed, her gaze traveling sideways, bypassing Latisha altogether, to the broken lamp shade lying on the floor. "Oh dear," she chided, on a more direct tone. "That's not worth fixing. I only paid ninety dollars for it."

Lamp shade. Latisha blinked, rousing herself awake. Further pieces of last night began to fall into place. She and Bren had worked most of the night on each other. They began the ceremony time and time again until there were no more condoms. Amidst it all, she had knocked over the lamp shade while performing a more acrobatic position. After all, she had told Bren she was fit. He had simply wanted her to prove it. At the cost, to him, of what now appeared to be a gift presented to him by Vanessa Harper.

"What are you doing here?" Bren insisted, pulling the top layer of white bedding around himself, preparatory to getting out of bed.

"I'm here for our eight o'clock meeting, remember?" Vanessa sounded out with a smirk spread wildly across her face.

"At the office," Bren bellowed, flashing a quick glance at the bedside clock, which read a different time entirely. "It's only 7:15 A.M.," he blasted, annoyed.

The witch, Latisha told herself, fully comprehending Vanessa's intentions and deciding the woman was not going to get away with it. "As you can see," she intervened, proud of the cool detachment in her voice, "the congressman was otherwise engaged before your rude intrusion. We'd both like you to leave."

Vanessa stared at Bren, horrified at the instruction passed to her by someone she considered to be nothing close to her own value or worth. "You're not going to have her talk to me like that, are you, Bren?" She appealed for clarification, but did not receive it.

Bren rose to his feet, his nakedness hidden beneath the bedding around his waist in the manner of a man embarrassed by the turn of events. "I'd like the key to my apartment," he remarked, holding his hand out for it, his tone clearly disappointed.

Vanessa flinched. "You gave me this key to commemorate our being together," she whimpered, saddened at his asking for its return. "You see, Miss Fenshaw"—she diverted her attention to Latisha with a steely voice—"the congressman and I are lovers."

It was Latisha's turn to be horrified. She looked at Bren. "What's going on?"

Vanessa's voice was like acid. "Don't be so naive," she derided, pinching an invisible piece of lint from her tailored lilac-colored Stella McCartney–designed suit. "This is Washington, D.C. Favors are passed and given all the time here, even the ones of a more delicate persuasion. What did you think you were in, the romance of a lifetime?" She seemed hell-bent on waging a vendetta. "Girlfriend, there's no such thing."

Latisha was lost for words.

"I'm sorry, Bren," Vanessa continued, suddenly fixing him with a withering stare. "But my nature does not stretch to three in a bed. You will have to deal with one of the interns for that sort of perversity."

Perhaps if she hadn't been naked in Bren's bed, Latisha might have dealt with the situation differently. But she was made instantly vulnerable. Weakened by everything she had heard. Humiliated that there was a more sinister agenda beneath the skilled seduction she had undergone the night before. Suddenly, Washington seemed a foreign place, even though its Capitol dome, White House lawn, and monuments were sites she had seen or visited throughout her two days there. Thankfully, that afternoon, she would be going home, back to England where she belonged.

She sat up, pulling the second layer of sheet from the bed and wrapping it around herself. "I don't know what's going on, but—"

"A compromise, my dear," Vanessa interrupted scornfully. "We all have to live by them, even you. He may be yours now, but tomorrow he'll be mine again."

"The only thing a compromise gets you in life is something you didn't want in the first place," Latisha lashed out. "I'd like to get dressed now and get the hell out of here."

"You stay right there," Bren ordered, as he glared at Vanessa with impatient eyes. "I don't know what little game you're playing here," he spat out at her, "but it stops right now." And as if to prove the point, he marched over to where Vanessa was standing, looking immaculate and serene in lilac-colored high-heeled shoes, with her long mane suitably spread around her delicately molded shoulders, and promptly yanked his key out of her hand.

"Bren, tell her," Vanessa challenged, unable to match his strength as he prized the tiny metal key from between her fingers. "Put this poor girl out of her misery."

"I did," Bren admitted. "Last night."

"Bren," Vanessa whimpered again, wounded. "Tell her how we made love in that very bed on the night you got elected to Congress as a member of the House of Representatives," she insisted. "Tell her how I bought you that lamp shade when you asked me to move into this apartment and warm your bed while you were away in Africa. I kept the cinders burning because you wanted it that way."

Latisha's blood ran cold. "I've heard enough."

"You've heard nothing yet," Vanessa objected. "Bren needs me and I need him."

As she gazed at Bren, Latisha wondered whether Vanessa was right. She finally saw what she hadn't seen before. Bren, a person full of idealism and energy, but who would soon come to discover that he only possessed a tiny fragment of power. In time, he would be driven to expand on that fragment, make new alliances, join more groups, get appointed to more committees, make connections with the press, find a wider circle of friends in his administration of the same caste as Vanessa Harper. Then he would be caught up in turning the Washington wheel of internal politics, Congress versus the president, be consumed by his constituency work, driven by his career and developing the kind of clout needed to command in the ultimate power game.

Latisha asked herself, did she really want to be a part of this fever? Was federal power preferable to, say, the financial muscle of New York or Los Angeles? Was the commercial might of Houston, Chicago, Pittsburgh, and Detroit any better? Would she be more content with someone who worked in Silicon Valley outside San

Francisco, who was at the leading edge of high-tech and electronics and who would have no interest in status or influence, rules and conventions, tribal rivalries and personal animosities of the type she was now facing?

It was clear to her now that most politicians were destined to fraternize with colleagues from within their own party. How else would any back-slapping take place? Every relationship, whether it be political, business, or personal, was probably tainted with the calculus of power, too. Bren Hunter needed Vanessa Harper and Vanessa needed him, just as she said, to advance both their dreams inside the beltway of what was considered the political community of Washington. Who was Latisha to stand in the way of democracy lived the American way?

"Bren, she's right," Latisha conceded, her heart pumping in denial of what she was saying. "Vanessa can help you."

"What?" Bren growled, so bedazzled he felt his legs almost give way. "She," he protested, while pointing at Vanessa, knowing full well she was telling the truth in a custom-designed way to suit only her, "was simply looking after my apartment while I was away. It's nothing like what you think."

"Bren . . ." Latisha was too shaken to continue.

"Perk up, dear," Vanessa encouraged on a dry note, when seeing how speechless and dismayed Latisha had become. "You're leaving today. The congressman needed a little light relief before his hectic schedule commences, and you were it. Just chalk up your experience to the game and let go."

"The game?" Latisha was mortified. She looked

at Bren and felt as though she was going through another déjà vu. Was this another Alan Clayton all over again? Convinced she saw a phony smile devoid of any soul behind it and an empty expression on Bren's face, she felt herself crumble. "You deserve a twenty-one-gun salute," she croaked unhappily. "You're very good at conveying broad intention, and I can't believe I fell for being messed around all over again. I just want to get out of here before I misinterpret anything more. I'm in way over my head." And she could see it, too. All the sprawling complexities leaping at her from all directions.

"That's it," Bren raged on a murderous note, his eyes raking Vanessa with true contempt. "Latisha, stay there," he demanded for a second time. "Vanessa, I'm showing you to the damned door."

He took a hold of her arm and Vanessa resisted. "Don't do this, Bren."

"Just move," he cursed, roughly pulling her along.

Latisha felt nothing except a numbness when the bedroom door swished closed. All she could think about was how wonderful she had felt awaking in Bren's arms that morning. She had been at his side, floating on a sea of sedation. Now she was under yet another rainstorm of lies and deceit; she hardly knew how to weather it. Their lovemaking had been so spiritual, so moving, tears behind her eyes threatened to pour as her loins moved in remembrance of it. Bren had given her as much as he had taken, but now, while she jumped from his bed and began to slip into her underwear, Latisha felt as though he had stripped her to nothing.

A tug of emotion washed over her as she pulled

on her dress, scolding herself for entering into such a problematic affair. It had been fraught with complications from day one, from the moment Alan Clayton left her life. There was Bren's being related to Alan. Her having met Alan's wife, Bren's sister. Then there was Lady Sarah, her stepmother, inadvertently caught up in an affair with Alan. And then there was Bren, who lived in two worlds—his hometown, and the special world of the capital, totally unconnected with the realism of what was going on. But she had the power to stop it all. And that was exactly what she planned to do.

Pulling on her shoes and grabbing her handbag, Latisha opened the bedroom door, bracing herself for a nuclear showdown. But she found Bren on his own, moments after he had slammed the front door shut, shunning Vanessa into her own abandonment. His stricken eyes were on Latisha in an instant. She was standing at the foot of his living room, tall and proud, with the beads of her dress glowing against the hazelnut brown of her skin tone.

He pulled the sheet from around his feet to prevent himself from falling as he walked toward her. "Latisha," he said calmly. "Let me explain."

"No, Bren," Latisha implored, unable to deal with the run of emotions causing riot in her soul. "Whatever happened in your life before you met me are things I cannot change, be jealous of, or even complain about. Because they were before we got together."

"Of course," Bren agreed, nodding his understanding of her.

"But," Latisha said on a more solemn note, "you have an unfortunate carelessness about who you give your keys to, and in one way or another I seem to have been wrapped up in the consequences of that."

Bren was silenced. "I don't want to lose you."

"Like I said," Latisha told him. "You can't change the past."

"Look, I haven't deceived you," Bren said, wishing to dear God he had told Latisha the truth when they had talked while sipping coffee at Sebastian's Hotel in Tortola. That Washington could be a lonely place, but had the ability to swallow people in.

"You need to get back to your life," Latisha concluded, shaken by the torment of her heart breaking into pieces. But she kept her composure, barely. "And I need to get back to mine. We told each other something like this once before. I think I'm also going to postpone my visit to the Jamaican Cancer Care in four weeks," she added, knowing Bren might use the opportunity to try and see her in New York. "Let's forget we ever met."

"Latisha!" Bren's voice was choked. "Don't do this."

"I'll check out of the Willard Intercontinental and make my own way to the airport," she told him shakily. Seeing the tears in Bren's eyes, Latisha knew she would not be able to hold out any longer. She hurried toward the door, knowing full well he would be unable to follow her since Bren was not dressed. "Good-bye."

"Latisha!"

She opened the door and closed it just as quickly, shutting off the echo of her own name. It was the last thing Latisha remembered as she left the apartment.

Chapter Twelve

Sitting at his desk, late in the day, staring at the papers in front of him, Bren saw nothing. His eyes were clouded with images of Latisha. He had no interest in what the political world was arguing about. If a war was impending it had no meaning to Bren. For he had his own worries that were closer to his heart, waiting to set off an explosion of their own. And only Latisha Fenshaw could press that button. Only she possessed the power to end his emotional fallout right now.

Let's forget we ever met. That's what she had said. But he could not forget. How was he going to square things with Latisha when it was clear to her that Vanessa Harper had once been his woman, had once slept in his bed? He cursed silently to himself. It was not a conversation he was looking forward to. Latisha might end up in a state worse than when she had left him.

He had tried to reach her. Had ignored his important breakfast appointment with Vanessa and instead rushed over to the Willard Intercontinental in a taxi. But the reception desk was to tell him that she had checked out minutes after arriving there. So he had rushed to the airport, but had been unable to find her. It occurred to him that she had probably changed her flight schedule, to be certain he would not find her.

She was that smart. What self-respecting woman would want to deal with an argument right there at the airport about another woman anyway? Though his and Vanessa's relationship had been over a long time ago—three years to be exact—he did not doubt that Latisha had been embarrassed to learn the story from Vanessa herself. He should have told her sooner, from the moment he had introduced them both. No, earlier than that, he told himself again. He should have told her the moment they shared a conversation about his work while seated at the bar at the Sebastian Hotel in Tortola.

She would be back in England by now. He frowned, glancing at the wall clock in his office. It was well over a week since he had last seen her. He wondered if she was thinking about him. Whether she was considering how special their lovemaking had been. But was it special enough for him to win her back? That was what Bren wanted to know. The torturous question forced him to swing his chair around and stare outside his office window. The bleakness of an early evening in August stared back at him.

His body ached. It was the ache of a man who had fallen in love. The solemn fact was something Bren had known for many days now. From his first setting eyes on Latisha again on the *Caribbean Rose* the evening of her cocktail party in the British Virgin Islands. Saying good-bye had been harder than he had anticipated. The future he believed he wanted now played like an old movie in his head. For without Latisha in the supporting role, there could be no happy ending. She was the kind of woman he imagined next to him for the rest of his life.

His work, his flourishing career, everything he deemed challenging or conquerable, no longer seemed important enough to hold the strings of his life together. He felt he had lost his competitive edge. Even his Senate ambitions seemed less appealing. Instead, everything was tied up in complicated knots of convoluted proportions. His mind was still in turmoil when the telephone on his desk rang, for the umpteenth time that day.

Bren swung his chair around, picked up the phone, and recognized the familiar voice. "I'm done for today," Lucy informed him. "I've booked you on a first-class flight into New York."

"What time?"

"The 8:22 P.M.," Lucy revealed. "You pick up your boarding pass and ticket at the airport, and should be in New York by 9:00 P.M. I've booked a driver there to take you home."

"Okay," Bren acknowledged.

"I've also listed all your meetings for next week in your New York diary," Lucy continued with a professional tone. "Your most pressing engagement is with your political adviser, Bobby Fischer, who also told me to remind you to bring a copy of the report the secretary general on the United Nations Organization Mission to Africa gave you."

Bren nodded. "Yes."

"I'll leave your memos on my desk, next to your diary, for you to take with you," she added. "They are stacked in date and time order."

"Thank you."

"I'm off now," Lucy continued, "but I have a Mr. Chico Maccola on line one. Do you want to take the call?"

"Put him through, Lucy," Bren instructed, "and have a good weekend. Good night."

"Good night, sir."

The line clicked and Chico spoke quickly, relating details as to his suspicions about Alan Clayton's money source. Bren listened intently, not paying much attention at first, as it took him a few good seconds to refocus his mind from Latisha to the subject of his brother-in-law. But as Chico spoke more concisely, revealing more information, Bren sat upright in his chair.

"Where are you?"

"I'm in a restaurant on M Street," Maccola said. "Just saw the wife of a senator I know."

"You're in town?"

"Got in today to work on a lead. I was hoping we could hook up."

"Come on over," Bren ordered sternly. "Now."

An hour later, Chico Maccola walked coolly into Congressman Hunter's Washington office. Bren had already downed a drink from his oak cabinet to steady himself and divert his mind from thinking about Latisha. He watched from behind his desk as Chico, impeccably dressed in an expensive dark suit, with a beret crowning his head and his ponytail on display, removed his signature shades and formed a pleasing grin on his face.

"Go ahead, real slow," Bren demanded when

they'd settled down over martinis. "From the top."

As Chico Maccola began to detail his findings, they took on ever more toxic proportions the moment the private detective produced paperwork obtained from Veronica's home, and Bren's discomfort and uneasiness grew. "You got this from inside the house?" he asked.

"We took the opportunity of going in while your sister was in the hospital," Maccola answered apologetically. "Alan visited her at Beth Israel Deconess Medical Center, then took a flight into New York. We didn't figure he would be coming back that day, so we went in."

Bren tried to pick his way through the jumble of French wording, but nothing could really prepare him to take in what Alan Clayton could possibly be doing with cargo-loading documents specifying shipments from the harbor of Gustavia on the small island of Saint Barthélemy in Guadeloupe to the Democratic Republic of the Congo in Africa. It all suggested trafficking of some nature.

"Do you think he's up to something illegal?" he asked, uncertain what it all meant, knowing that the Congo region was involved in a civil war.

"Whatever it is, it ain't good," Maccola insisted. "I'm gonna have to get the rest of it translated by one of my people."

"Wait a minute," Bren said, stalling. "I found a blank receipt for an offshore bank account at my house in Rye. I checked out the bank while I was in the Caribbean. It exists. Now if you're saying Alan is broke, he may be getting money from abroad."

"Like a loan?" Maccola suggested.

"Or maybe he used that phony deed he concocted to raise some funds on it."

"Deed?" Maccola was lost. "What deed?"

"Didn't I tell you?" Bren snapped, hardly believing he had overlooked such a hard piece of evidence. He quickly filled Chico in on the details.

"We need that back," Chico insisted firmly. "With that, we can get him on all sorts of charges. Fraud. Forgery. The works. Do you still have it?"

There was only one person who had it, and Bren didn't want to think of her right now. "Yes, I can get it," he suggested in a shallow breath.

"Good." Maccola paused. "Maybe there's a connection to something."

"Maybe." Bren heard the hesitation. He knew it was not like Chico Maccola to pause midsentence. "Is there anything else?"

"I think I'll leave these . . . with you," Maccola said, clumsily handing over the shipping documents to Bren, his brows frowning when two sheets from the bundle slipped from his fingers and onto Bren's desk.

There it was again. Another pause. Bren took the papers and schooled his eyes. "And?"

Maccola turned pale, then he reddened, then wiped his brow. "Nothing."

Bren was not convinced. "Still working on that case with the governor and his mistress?"

"Which governor?" Maccola said evasively.

"What about that case with the Speaker of the House and the gossip columnist, what's her name?"

Maccola opened his mouth, then censored himself.

"Anything you want to tell me about you coming into Washington today?" Bren pressed.

"Listen, Bren." Maccola's voice quavered. He rubbed his jaw and gave in. "There's something you should know about Veronica and me. I think the baby she's carrying is mine."

Bren was still laughing when he left JFK Airport in the hired limousine Lucy had arranged, which was taking him on the way to Rye. In no time at all, Chico Maccola and his sister had become a couple. Bren did not seem to think it appeared the least bit odd that Veronica and Chico were both now supposedly as inseparable as two lovebirds. He was not sorry that Maccola had been so candid with him either. In fact, he felt nothing but relief.

After Veronica's suicide attempt the year before, and her progressive recovery, she had met Chico while on a visit to learn more about her brother's work at his office in New York. Chico had just begun working for Bren on the case investigating his brother-in-law in an effort to locate the woman with whom Alan had been having an affair. What Bren was to learn now was that the private detective had taken his sister out to lunch that day. They had struck up a friendship that slowly blossomed into something more. Throughout Alan's infidelities, Veronica had sought comfort in Chico Maccola.

Maccola was to explain that Veronica had tried to keep him at bay, but it had become increasingly harder for them both. She was determined that her near-three-year marriage to Alan Clayton would work, more out of spite for Constance Clayton than any real love for her husband. Somehow, she had managed to stop things before they got too far, but her defenses had become shaky when she suspected Alan of having forged another relationship outside their marriage.

Maccola had never pressed Veronica to take things further, even after he discussed the number of women Alan was seeing. Bren had paid him to ward off the women by whatever means, and he had done so while accepting Veronica's steadfast determination to keep to her wedding vows. No matter how much he wanted her, he had always remained self-controlled. But one night, Veronica found herself wanting Chico to lose his professional ethics and restraint. Her resistance had vanished and Maccola, unable to fight his attraction, gave in.

But it was Veronica's guilt that had ended their short-lived affair. She had gone back to Alan, discovering shortly afterward that she was pregnant. Maccola was to tell Bren that Veronica had led Alan to believe that the baby was his, but that her husband could not possibly be the father. That her trip with Alan to the British Virgin Islands had opened her eyes to the fact that Alan did not love her, that she now wanted to leave him, and that she had come to see her unborn child as justifiable revenge and a gift for all the heartache she had suffered.

She told Maccola how much she had wanted to be with him during her vacation in the

Caribbean. Chico promised he would look after her. He was returning to Boston to collect Veronica's things and planned to take her to live at his home in Brooklyn. She could later sell her florist shop and move her business to New York. "Never underestimate the power of love," Maccola said, dazzled by how much his life had changed.

Bren's chuckle caught the attention of the driver, who gazed through his rearview mirror and saw a tired but relaxed congressman. He recognized Bren Hunter's face. On occasion, he had driven VIPs around the city—politicians, singers, and movie stars, as long as their pictures appeared in the newspaper or on TV. He smiled and acknowledged his passenger before training his eyes back on the road.

Bren noticed the stare, the flicker of recognition in the driver's eyes, and threw him a polite smile before gazing through the passenger window, his thoughts distracted not by the passing traffic, but by an image of Latisha Fenshaw. Every facet of her face suddenly came sharply into view. Her glossy black hair, the oval shape of her face, the slender figure and copper-colored eyes. Her kissable pink lips and the sculptured line and detail of her hazelnut-brown body that had trembled and rocked beneath the strong power of his own.

He moved uncomfortably and pushed his briefcase to the far corner of his seat in frustration. Every inch of his loins protested, wanting to be with Latisha again. He could not put his finger on exactly what it was about her, why he could not let this obsession go. Even while his treacherous thoughts had goaded him with provocative images of her being with Alan, he could not let her go.

And when he had discovered the truth, that Alan had never seen her eyes when she was in the throes of passion, he wanted her more. That sweet privilege had become his for the taking and he had taken it like a man dying of thirst. Latisha quenched every part of his hot, arid body with such bountiful desire that he was left questioning why he had never felt so satisfied in his life before. Now she was gone. He was in a desert, and hated it. His body felt parched, his lips felt dry, and his mind was filled with a mirage of Latisha.

Bren shifted again, feeling the need to explain himself, yet scoffing at the very notion of his need to do so. Latisha Fenshaw was being fussy, he told himself staunchly. His affair with Vanessa Harper was over. She should not be punishing them both for his past. He had never delved into her sexual peccadilloes in quite the same way. If he had wanted to, he could've accused her about Alan. He could've behaved in the same jealous way and held her accountable for contributing to the breakup of his sister's marriage. Granted, Latisha was not responsible, but he had never made her feel guilty for being a small cog in the wheel.

Yes, if he ever saw Latisha Fenshaw again, he would tell her precisely that. He would outline exactly what his relationship with Vanessa Harper consisted of. He would instruct Latisha that she should not judge a man for his past mistakes, but based on how she had been treated by him. And he had treated her like a princess. When they made love, he had graced and honored every measure of her body and soul.

Bren fidgeted with his hands while shuffling in his seat a third time. *If I see her again,* he corrected, knowing that Latisha was going to cancel her trip to New York for her father's charity. But he needed to recover the deed he had allowed her to hold on to for safekeeping and wondered how. He had no address for Latisha in England. He could contact George and Nancy Wright in Tortola and have them pass on a message on his behalf. Or he could try to locate Lady Sarah Fenshaw on the *Caribbean Rose*; that is, if she had returned from her tricks in Boston.

Bren connected one problem neatly with another while the limousine sped along. Given the circumstances—Vanessa's bitchiness, Alan's betrayal, Veronica's pregnancy, and Lady Sarah's vendetta—he realized it was amazing he had gotten so close to Latisha at all. A fiercely private person, Bren could not understand why he had allowed his personal affairs to become so complicated.

All his life, in particular during his nearly four years in Congress, his political ambitions had come before anything else: his personal life, his friends, romance, or family life. Since meeting Latisha, he now had the urge to run away from it all to find comfort in her arms. In his mind, only she could fix the emotional mess he was in. The same mess that had dogged his consciousness every hour, every minute, and every second of the day, from his waking to his restless attempts to sleep at night.

He was still in a quandary when the limo began

to pull in to Rye. Bren immediately relegated every troubling thought to the back of his mind, resolving to enjoy his weekend in the quiet hamlet he loved. His time in Rye was nothing like being at his Washington apartment or his apartment in Brooklyn Heights. At the house he had spent years renovating, Bren was able to find a peace that touched his soul. He was looking forward to spending more time there. To really relax and find some perspective to put his life back on track.

But as the limo turned the corner and began to make the short journey toward his house, Bren caught the solitary police car stationed on his driveway, with its lights on and two men standing there, awaiting his arrival. He instantly became alarmed, dread filling his head. Something had happened, he surmised quickly, thinking the worst. He thought perhaps burglars had broken into his home. That a neighbor had been shot. Or maybe it was bad news about a family member. Worse still, a government problem or a threat to national security.

As the limo slowed, Bren pushed open the car door and jumped out onto the sidewalk. He quickly dug into his right jacket pocket and palmed the driver with a fifty-dollar tip, before waving the car away. Hurriedly, he approached the first plainclothed officer who was standing in front of his double garage and took out his congressional identification card. Flashing it to the stocky man in his late twenties and the second officer, Bren demanded to know what was going on.

"Congressman Hunter?" the stocky man greeted him, walking forward and identifying himself as

Detective McKinley and his partner as Detective Gates.

"Yes," Bren acknowledged.

"There's been an incident today involving an automobile registered in your name," Detective McKinley explained, getting right down to business. "Do you own a blue Bentley, sir?"

"What?" Bren asked, but more than aware that the eyes of his neighbors were no doubt trained on him behind their twitching curtains.

"A blue Bentley with Washington plates?" He read from the top of his head the exact registration.

"Yes," Bren affirmed, knowing that the last place he had left his car was inside his garage.

"Your Bentley was involved in a collision with another car on the FDR in Manhattan, sir," Detective Gates noted for the record.

Bren sighed, folding his arms against his chest in disbelief. He stared at both officers, who were standing within inches of each other, looking tired and haggard for a Friday evening. "I think there's been some mistake," he said. "I know where I left my car. If it were stolen, you guys would've been the first to know."

"Sir," McKinley persisted. "We traced the registration. It's your car."

Bren pressed his lips into a hard line, refusing to take in the situation, but deciding to play along with the two officers. "Was there anyone hurt?"

"Just the passenger, sir," McKinley told him.
Bren blinked. "Who?"

"She had no identification on her person,"

Gates went on to explain. "We were hoping you would be able to identify her."

Bren's brows rose. "Me?"

Detective McKinley eyed him curiously. "We noticed you returned to your home in a limousine, sir," he pronounced with a suggestive lilt in his tone. "Can I ask where you were at approximately 5:30 today?"

"At my office in Washington, D.C.," Bren revealed, annoyed. "I left there on the 8:22 evening flight and have just arrived to find you guys waiting outside my house."

Detective Gates rocked back and forth on his heels. "I'm sorry we had to ask, sir," he said sheepishly. "It's just that we have been unable to find the driver."

"He wasn't in the car?" Bren blasted. The obvious truth that his car may have been stolen was beginning to filter into his brain.

"The driver was not on the scene when medics arrived," Detective McKinley confirmed. "We believe he would be the person who stole your car, sir."

"Look," Bren cursed, reaching into his left jacket pocket for his house keys. "I'm certain there's been some mistake." He immediately walked over toward the garage doors, manually unlocking them and pulling the heavy metal up and over his head, to find a complete void. It was not what he expected. "Before I left for Washington on Monday morning, I left my car in here."

"And you're certain about that?" Gates persisted.

"Of course I'm sure," Bren declared, furious. "I

hardly use the damn thing. I had a notion about selling it before Christmas. It burns too much gas."

"Do you have any idea who may have taken your car, sir?" Detective Gates questioned sternly.

Bren saw red. "Alan Clayton," he seethed.

"And who may he be, sir?" Detective Gates pressed.

"My brother-in-law," Bren shot back, before another pang of panic shot through him. "The woman," he said. "She could be my sister. He's married to my sister, Veronica Clayton. She was at a hospital in Boston, but I haven't checked in the last twenty-four hours. This woman, is she—"

"Alive?" McKinley said. "Yes, sir. She'll live."

"Where is she?"

"We had her at the precinct for a good while after the accident," Detective Gates informed him lamely. "She did nothing but drink coffee and claim that she was suffering from a bad case of amnesia."

"You're kidding me," Bren gasped. "Does she have any broken bones?"

"Nope," McKinley said. "Not a scratch on her. Just a slight bump on the forehead."

"So where is she now?" Bren dared to inquire, not certain if he wanted to know the answer.

A female voice suddenly interrupted Detective McKinley as he was about to speak. "Officer," she exclaimed on a hurtful note while poking her head out of the police car window, "when are you going to let me out of here?"

Bren's body stood rigid. "Sarah?" he shrieked.

"You know this woman?" Detective Gates breathed.

"She's Lady Sarah Fenshaw," Bren proclaimed in a dry tone. "The widow of the cricket legend, Sir Joshua Fenshaw."

"Wow," Detective Gates enthused instantly. "I loved that guy."

Detective McKinley stuck to business. "Maybe you can get her to tell us who was driving the car," he insisted firmly. "And there's something else you should know," he added on a more solemn note. "She was high on something when we found her. She's one unhappy lady."

"I'll get her inside the house," Bren swallowed, disliking the added responsibility he was taking on, which he knew would mar his weekend. "She has a stepdaughter I can get hold of in Florida," he told them, suddenly recalling that Latisha had given him her sister's number. "I'll give her a call."

"You do that, sir," McKinley instructed. "Your car's been towed. We'll call tomorrow with the details and to check whether this . . . Lady Sarah . . . is ready to regain her memory."

"Sure," Bren acknowledged, following the officers toward the police car, where Detective Gates proceeded to open the back door and help Lady Sarah out.

"Ma'am, your husband was a great guy," Gates said, taking a careful hold of her arm. "Great with a bat, a fly guy with the ball. One helluva guy."

Bren was surprised to find Lady Sarah looking a touch thinner than when he had last seen her, even more so when he found her handcuffed. "Was that really necessary?" he reproved, watching Gates release the restraint.

"Just doing my job, sir," came his reply.

The moment Lady Sarah was free, she fell straight into Bren's arms and wept. While the police officers drove away, with Gates echoing his sad sentiments like a true sympathetic but loyal fan, Bren led her to the house and settled Sarah down for the night in one of the guest bedrooms. Only then did he pick up the telephone. He knew the news would reach Latisha eventually. He prayed that on her hearing it, she would seize the opportunity and come right over. He dialed the number and waited patiently. When he heard the welcoming "hello," he introduced himself to Josette Fenshaw.

"It's about your stepmother," he said, calmly explaining events. "She needs help."

Chapter Thirteen

She had gotten on her high horse and galloped away. Latisha arrived in England courageous and a woman refusing to allow another woman, or man, to reduce her to the role of victim. But a week later, while she was in her bath staring blankly as a mountain of white bubbles burst softly against her brown skin, Latisha had become a pathetic heap. The impact of finally leaving Bren Hunter was beginning to take its toll.

She had become a woman lost. It was not just the loss of his smile, his very presence, the things about his character that she had liked about him. It was also the tangible loss of hope. Of gaining the true love she thought she had found in this man. Bren Hunter had been, to her, the man of her dreams, her hope for a future. She had fancifully imagined—dared to believe—that he would be the man for her. But it was not to be. How could anything be possible when her life was, once again, full of deceit?

The very thought of Vanessa Harper's existence suddenly erupted in Latisha's mind, tormenting her. A supremely confident woman had emerged when her defenses toward Bren

were weak. They had spent a wonderful day in
Washington, D.C. He had given her a special present to remember him by. Her hand reached for
it. She held the pendant between her fingers,
having refused to take it off before taking a dip
in her bath.

Latisha's eyes filled with tears. Once upon a
time, she had felt quite special to Bren Hunter.
In Washington, he had again succeeded in making her feel special. But all good things come to
an end. In two short days, Bren's past was in her
face. And it came in the form of a pair of shapely
legs, a body to die for, a brown face that shone
beautiful against a mane of long hair, and a head
full of political intelligence much higher than
her own. Vanessa had all the qualities to bring
any man to her feet. And with the position she
held within the Democratic Party, Latisha felt she
couldn't compete.

How could she when Vanessa Harper and Bren
Hunter had a lot in common? They both lived
for American politics. They were players who understood the inner workings of power, the
constant campaigning, the political influence,
the corridors that led from the White House to
the Pentagon and back to Capitol Hill, and the
risks involved in playing the game. These were
things Latisha listed in her head. She reminded
herself that she wasn't a part of that world.

There was no hope, Latisha thought, while
sinking farther into the water, thankful that it was
warm enough to soothe her troubled mind. Suddenly, she did not see herself as someone who
could attach herself to a powerful man such as

Congressman Hunter. He was someone who had won public recognition.

Latisha kicked the water and felt a thousand bubbles burst between her toes when she saw herself as someone unsuitable for him. *Why didn't I listen to Josette?* her mind screamed. Her sister had warned her not to rush into another fling. It was not as if she hadn't been told. And that made Latisha feel worse. *American men are dangerous,* she thought harshly, before quickly amending that one thought when she reminded herself that Alan had been born in Guadeloupe.

A single tear rolled down her cheek when she instantly considered the last six months of her life. Alan was the worst thing that could have happened to her, and Bren had been the best. The two extremes felt hard for her to bear, that two men could have been so different. Alan was the lowest of the low and Bren was the highest of the high. And in such a short time knowing Bren, she was chagrined to find herself falling in love.

The truth made Latisha's limbs shake. *How could I have been so stupid?* she scolded herself. She went over in her head why any relationship with Bren Hunter could not work. The list was formidable. *At least I got out in time,* Latisha contemplated sadly, finally raising herself out of the warm water and attempting to lighten her mood, knowing she was expected at her mother's house in less than an hour for dinner.

Twenty minutes later, Latisha turned her back on her mirror, having changed into a patterned black and beige tunic and matching skirt, with soft cream-colored sandals on her feet. She walked the length of her bedroom to the door and made her way downward to the lower floor of her apartment, stepping over a cluster of bags still situated by the front door. They held the small remnants of items she had bought in Tortola, which she had not emptied since returning home.

Latisha felt a sudden pang of emptiness at the reminder of having left Bren Hunter there. She was soon to realize that her short-lived romance with the congressman seemed more about her leaving than staying. Before Tortola, she had left him behind in New York. And now she had left him in Washington. *What am I running away from?* Latisha thought, as she slammed the front door behind her and ventured to her car.

The waning early August sun was failing to poke its way through a dark cloud as she slowly cruised along the streets of London in her BMW convertible sports car. Though she had the hood up, she kept a window open to allow a whispering breeze to slightly ruffle the carefully coifed style of her hair. Latisha knew how fussy her mother could be, so besides clipping the loose strands of hair, allowing a few stray ends to fall around her earlobes, she kept her makeup simple. She tried to cover the frown lines on her face that lately her mother seemed to always notice.

Latisha did not want to explain events of the past few months to anyone. It had been enough talking about her life with Lady Sarah and Josette. They were far away, which was probably why it had felt easier. But her mother, Lady Marlene Fenshaw, lived close by. The only time they did not converse was when Latisha was working abroad with her father's charities overseas.

It was the second time since she had arrived back in England that Latisha was going over to her mother's for dinner. The first time, she had not felt the loneliness of losing Bren. She had figured she did the right thing. Catching a later plane out of Washington to avoid a scene at the airport had worked. She had made her escape without any drama. But now Latisha was in another struggle. She had found it hard to sleep the night before, even harder when she awoke that morning. If only she could get Bren out of her mind. If only she could forget she had ever met him, as she had told Bren to forget her. But Latisha could not.

When she arrived outside her mother's home, her mind was already debating whether to enter. She knew a number of other family members would be there, which was often the case when her mother served dinner late on Saturday afternoon. Latisha had no stomach for talking or for eating. For that part of her body was still churning with lovesick feelings and a desire to be in Bren Hunter's bed again.

Latisha blinked away her lustful thoughts and left her car to walk up the pathway toward a double-fronted stone house in Regents Park. Her late father had provided for her mother well. Lady Marlene Fenshaw had no reasons for complaint, for the house she lived in and the standard she had become accustomed to were settled by her father before he married Sarah, and modestly covered by his estate after he died, with a private pension fund.

Latisha was to remember her father the moment she walked through the back door and straight into the hardened chest of her cousin Bertram. Her father's nephew, the spitting image of Sir Joshua Fenshaw, was standing in her mother's kitchen helping himself to more carrots and broccoli from the stove. Though Bertram was her uncle's son, he was not as slim as his father.

Bertram was stocky, just like her own father had been, with chubby cheeks, heavy dark brows, and a broad-lipped smile. Sir Joshua's nose had been slightly bigger, his complexion darker, and his piercing eyes more alert. Latisha grimaced when Bertram, immediately on noting her entrance, put his plate down and wrapped his big, rough arms around her. The bear hug lifted her clean off the floor before he planted her back there.

"Hey, cousin," he greeted, loud and smiling. "You still don't weigh a thing."

"Hello, Bertram," Latisha said, forcing a smile. "How are you?"

"Me?" Bertram queried, shrugging his shoulders as though slightly offended. "I'm good. Couldn't be better now that I got my diet going on."

Latisha gave him the once-over with her eyes and realized her cousin seemed to have gained another twenty pounds beneath the oversized shirt he was wearing. "That's great." She nodded, tapping his tummy, thinking it was time her cousin took an active interest in sports. "You keep that up."

"Yeah, I'm on target," he bragged. "A few more pounds off and I'll be trim by Christmas."

"Great." Latisha nodded again, aware that her

cousin had already lost the battle. "Where's Mum?"

"She's upstairs on the phone with someone," her cousin explained, nodding his head toward the dining room. "Mom and Dad are in there, eating dinner. And how are you? Your mom tells me you just got back from overseas."

"Last week," Latisha clarified. "The Caribbean, then I stopped off in Florida to see Josette."

"Little sis okay?"

"Yeah, Josette's doing fine there," Latisha continued, resenting the small talk. She wanted nothing more than to go home and wallow in her own self-pity. "She likes the school and the weather. I'm missing her already."

"She still with her man?" Bertram probed curiously.

Latisha nodded.

"He still got his job?"

"Steadman's still working at the hospital," Latisha clarified, aware of the impending question on Bertram's lips.

"You got yourself a man yet?" He laughed.

There it was. Latisha cringed at the sarcasm in Bertram's voice and refused to admit defeat. "Actually, I met a congressman while I was out there," she said, proudly, picturing Bren's square face, nutmeg-brown complexion, and dark mysterious eyes.

"A what?" Bertram gasped in shook.

"Congressman Bren Augustus Hunter of the tenth congressional district in Brooklyn. He has offices in New York and Washington, D.C., and may run for president one day."

Bertram was silenced. When he spoke, his

voice was awed. "You got yourself an uptown guy with big ideas?"

"Yep."

"Then you be careful with him if you want that guy to keep his big ideas," her cousin warned astutely. "If he marries you, he'll be less likely to hit that top spot he wants."

"Is this another one of your wild philosophies?" Latisha sighed, recalling Bertram's conversation at a family wedding the year before. He told her his theory about the male genes and how women were more evolved than their male counterparts. She was at a loss as to what her cousin was going to say next.

"It's proven science," Bertram insisted, "I'm just looking out for you."

Latisha placed her bag on top of her mother's kitchen workbench and glared at her cousin, crossing her arms beneath her breasts. "What's proven science?"

"Married men are less likely to make their mark on society," Bertram proclaimed, suspiciously. "A man gets wed and that's it for him. He loses his competitive edge, that urge that drives him to excel."

"And . . . this is . . . tied up with the male ambition evolved over millions of years?" Latisha laughed in disbelief.

"Right," Bertram affirmed, refusing to succumb to the sarcasm in her tone. "Genius stems from man's evolved psychological mechanism, which compels him to be switched on. He then becomes highly successful. But that mechanism turns itself off when he gets married and has children."

Latisha closed her eyes for a few brief seconds.

"So let me get this straight," she said before opening her eyes. "Given your philosophy about men and the male genes, I'm to understand that if Congressman Hunter and I were to be married, he would lose his drive to become president of the United States?"

"It's proven science," Bertram repeated.

It was the first time, all day, that Latisha actually heard herself laugh. "You know something?" she began. "Your views contradict everything I've been through with Congressman Hunter these past few weeks. Like the science that a man is set to mate at the first given opportunity. It's not true."

"He waited for a romantic moment?" Bertram asked, amazed.

Latisha tapped her cousin on the shoulder. "You really need to stop reading too many books and get out more," she advised. "Get yourself a girlfriend." Latisha picked up her bag, preparing to leaving the kitchen.

Bertram stalled her. "Wait a minute. This guy . . . he really likes you. You gonna see him again, right?"

Latisha turned on her heels and faced her cousin. "Actually, no. I'm not."

"Why not?" her cousin demanded in a soft tone.

"Right now, I'm afraid he's going to break my heart," Latisha confessed. "And I don't have the courage for a long-distance relationship." With that answer, she left her mother's kitchen and entered the dining room.

Her aunt and uncle welcomed her. She exchange pleasantries and then found her gaze on a third person seated at the table. Latisha recognized everything about him all too well: his café-au-lait complexion, a testament to his multiethnic roots, his silver, wiry Afro hair, the flabby body wreathed in fat, and his blue-brown eyes that now seemed more shifty and unpredictable than when she had last looked at them.

He was not supposed to be there. She had left him back in Tortola, after ejecting him from her bedroom for his ill manners and lurid conduct. Now here he was, in her mother's home, sinking his teeth into her mother's food. Latisha's body stood rigid. She was struck at Linford Mills's audacity. Surely the man could not have followed her to England. But the more she began to question his motives, the more certain Latisha became that this man was in her mother's home for a reason.

Dressed casually in a pair of oversized jeans and an open-necked blue-and-green-striped shirt, Linford wasted no time in throwing a possessive glance at Latisha from where he was seated. His appearance was less that of a governor and more someone who had just returned from a gathering with friends. At least, that was how it seemed to Latisha as she watched Linford mingle with her aunt and uncle as though he had known them for years.

She returned his leering glance with a pensive stare, deciding she would keep her manner calm and her voice equally so. She did not want to arouse suspicion among the members of her family that she found his presence there in any way distressing. When Bertram suddenly rejoined them from the kitchen, Latisha immediately shook the rigidness from her body and affected a notable smile.

"I didn't know we were having company," she mentioned as Bertram came through the door. "It feels almost like yesterday when I last saw the governor on the *Caribbean Rose*."

Linford chuckled. "I told you we should stop meeting like this. People will talk."

Latisha tried to find a quick way of getting right to the point, but didn't feel quite ready to make that jump. Instead, she waited a breath, then replied, "What brings you to my mother's home?"

"Latisha," her aunt chastised. "That's no way to speak to someone important like the governor. It was kind of him to pop by and see your mother."

"I thought it'd been a while since I've seen her," Linford said casually. "The last time was at your father's funeral. Lady Marlene told me I was welcome to visit anytime, and here I am."

"And what brings you to England?" she rephrased, glad to be getting to the point, finally.

"Oh . . . just some business at the House of Parliament," he said lightly. "Nothing for you to worry your little head about."

Latisha hated the patronizing way in which he spoke and felt the simmering of something ugly brewing in the depths of her stomach. She did not like this man. She loathed his being within a foot of her. And as she watched her cousin Bertram take the seat next to him at the table, her eyes were ever more wary as to the true purpose of Linford Mills's visit.

"Are you going to join us for dinner?" her uncle suddenly interjected.

Latisha, still rooted to where she was standing, had no intention of doing so. "I think I'll go upstairs and see my mother first."

"There's just one thing," Linford said, stalling, when he noted Latisha having found her feet quick enough to move around the furniture toward the door that led to the stairway. "I believe Congressman Hunter may have left some papers with you." He saw the blank expression on Latisha's face and continued. "He asked if I could collect them for him. I'm to meet him in Washington next week for golf. He needs them quite urgently."

So that's why you're here, Latisha contemplated wryly. *Bren sent you.* Her heart skipped at the very notion that she could use Linford Mills as a confidant to relay any message back to Bren. Hell, she didn't trust the man and she had no idea what papers he was referring to. She stared at Linford for a beat, annoyed at Bren for selecting such an unscrupulous character to mend the barrier that had grown between them, and with a straight face, spoke quite innocently.

"I don't know what you're talking about." Then with her head held high with pride, she reached the door, held her hand on the doorknob, and politely excused herself upstairs to her mother's bedroom.

Latisha found her mother sitting on the bed, absorbed in animated conversation on the telephone. The oval-faced woman, whose unwrinkled hazelnut-brown complexion, shortstyled hair, pink lips, and mascara-clad eyes made her look younger than her actual years, threw a smile across the room at her daughter before talking into the mouthpiece.

"Your sister's here," she said excitedly. "I'll put her on."

"Josette's on the phone?" Latisha questioned, quickly rushing across the bedroom to sit on the bed. She decided that after she had heard what her sister had to say, she would drop the bombshell about Linford Mills's arrival there. "I didn't know."

"She called the house to talk to you," her mother explained, handing over the phone. "I didn't know you were here either. I'll be downstairs."

"Okay," Latisha acknowledged, taking the handset. While her mother left, she spoke into the mouthpiece. "Josette?"

"You're never gonna believe who just called me," Josette's spirited voice bellowed down the line immediately.

"Who?" Latisha shrugged, expecting to hear the name of some famous gospel singer who was going to lend their celebrity to her sister's campaign for restoring prayer in public schools.

"The man you gave my number to," Josette reminded her. "Congressman Bren Hunter."

Latisha nearly dropped the phone. "Bren?"

"Now, I know I never liked her and only respected her for our father's sake," Josette started, "but I'd never wish her any harm."

"What?" Latisha asked, totally lost.

"Sarah," her sister confirmed. "That's why your guy called. I thought it was because he was trying to reach you thinking you had returned here, but he says Sarah's staying as a guest at his home in

Rye and that she's suffered some sort of breakdown."

Latisha held her breath, finding everything she'd just heard difficult to take in. When she finally spoke, her voice was trembling. "When . . . when did he call?"

"A few hours ago," Josette drawled, "It's really early in the morning here. I took the details down and told him I'll call you."

"How did he find her?" Latisha asked, the first of what felt like a thousand questions.

"I don't know," Josette said, snorting. "Sarah's always been a little scatterbrained for me to handle and I don't want to be the one to go up to New York to get her either. I'm not close to her like you are. Now I know you just got back home a week ago, but I've got too much work to do and—"

"I'll go," Latisha interrupted, aware this was more her responsibility than Josette's.

"I'm sorry," her sister apologized. "I hope she's okay when you get there."

Latisha sighed. "Did Bren say anything else?"

"Oh yeah," Josette recalled. "He says if I could get the message to you, could he also have the document he gave you in April?"

"I don't understand," Latisha answered, absently racking her brain for what Bren could possibly be referring to and why he would send Linford Mills to get it. Then it suddenly dawned on her. It would be the falsified deed to his house that Alan Clayton had given her. "Oh yes," she gushed. "I have it." She was about to tell Josette that she would pass the document to Linford, when a thought struck her. " Is he . . . is Bren expecting me?"

"I told him you were back in England, but that after I'd passed the message on I imagined you'd be right over," Josette said. "He shouldn't be troubled with our stepmother like that. It's time Sarah sorted herself out."

"Of course," Latisha agreed, deciding she would not tell Josette about Linford Mills after all. Something was most definitely wrong and she needed to go back downstairs and discover exactly what.

"I'm assuming things with you and this guy are still ticking over nicely?" Josette pried.

"Sure," Latisha lied, fixing her brain on what her sister was saying. "We're doing fine."

"Good." Josette's voice lifted. "Then this is a great opportunity for you to see him again."

"I know," Latisha said, with a sigh. "I'd better get off the line and try to arrange a flight. Did you tell Mum?"

"No," her sister said. "I would prefer we keep Sarah's business out of Mom's hair. Call me when you get into New York."

"I will."

The phone clicked dead and Latisha exhaled a large breath. Just when she thought things couldn't get any worse, they had. Fate seemed destined to put her right back into Bren Hunter's territory. With Lady Sarah now in a state, she could hardly ignore the situation. There was no choice but to face the person whose image had paraded around in her dreams. Only one thing troubled Latisha. Should she be relieved at seeing Congressman Bren Hunter again or should she be petrified with fear?

Not sure which, she left her mother's bedroom

and rushed downstairs. The idea was to confront Linford Mills on the matter of Bren's deed. But when Latisha reentered the dining room, she was not to find hide nor hair of the governor anywhere.

"Where's Mr. Mills?" she asked her mother, startled at his having disappeared.

"You were rude to the man, so he's gone," her aunt said, rebuffing her.

Latisha arched her brows and thought about the earliest flight she could take back to New York City.

Lady Sarah awoke with a start. She knew exactly where she was, remembered exactly what had happened the night before, and within seconds was out of the warm bed she found herself lying in. Feeling relieved that she was still dressed in her clothes, she shot through the solid pine door in an instant, without a second glance.

She found Bren Hunter seated downstairs in his living room, watching the early breakfast news on the television. He hopped to his feet the moment he heard her rushing in like a hen on two legs, flapping her wings in a flurry, and eager to heckle him about the events of the night before. Bren ordered that she be seated, refusing to listen until he had planted a cup of fresh Colombian coffee in her hands. Only when he had done so did Lady Sarah begin her tale.

"You're in danger," she warned on a hot breath, taking a large gulp of coffee. "Alan knows you've been having him followed."

Bren shook his head, though he leaned forward in his chair to place both hands against his open knees. "What are you talking about?" he asked Sarah slowly.

"There isn't time," Sarah insisted, like a true conspirator. "He's involved with people in your government. I found out by complete accident. That's why he tried to kill me on the FDR last night."

Bren blinked, hard. "Sarah, is this some kind of joke?"

"Come on, would I make this up?" Sarah said, annoyed. Seeing Bren's blank expression, she moved on, intensely serious. "Listen, I had an affair with your brother-in-law in Tortola. I found out later from my stepdaughter that he was married. I wanted vengeance, so I followed Alan to Boston for a showdown."

"You put a wedding announcement in the newspaper," Bren added, his face twisting as he recalled how the news had troubled his sister.

"I did that to find him," Sarah insisted. "I had no idea where he lived, where he worked. I only remembered something Latisha said about Boston."

"And?"

"I paid someone at the newspaper to pass on my mobile number," Sarah went on. "I stayed at a hotel until Alan phoned. We argued about the ring."

"The ring?"

"I was beside myself," Sarah said, reeling, with a telling little quiver that had nothing to do with her anger or fury. "I paid ten thousand dollars for it in Tortola. Alan led me to believe he was buying it as a present for me and that he would give me back the money when he took me with him to the

States. But he was lying. The ring was a fake. I found out when I tried to take it back after being told everything about him having a wife. The shop refused to accept it. When I took it to another jeweler to try and sell it, they told me why. I realized Alan used me to get ten thousand dollars."

"Through a bogus jeweler?" Bren exclaimed, failing to disguise his disbelief at what Sarah was saying.

"It's all true," Sarah insisted.

Bren shook his head. "My brother-in-law is a lot of things, none of them good, but this story you're telling me . . ."

"It's some sort of setup he's got going on down there in the Caribbean," Sarah persisted, unsure of all the details. "All I wanted was my money. Alan told me it was in a bank in New York and that he would give it back as long as I didn't tell his wife or you about what he had done. So I agreed."

"Why New York?" Bren queried. "Why not Boston?"

"I don't know." Sarah shook her head, deciding to sip more coffee to calm her nerves. "I just agreed to meet him there. Outside Grand Central Station."

Bren's brows rose. "Then what happened?"

"He picked me up in a car and I honestly thought we were going to the bank," Sarah revealed. "Then while he was driving, he started to talk about the arms trail he was running from the United States through the Caribbean and into Africa. He actually bragged about the people who were in his pocket. Public officials in office."

"He came clean, just like that?" Bren asked, doubtful.

Sarah stared at him firmly. "He told me because I'm not supposed to be alive," she said in a deathly tone. "Don't you get it? He had no intention of returning me my money."

Bren's hands rose to his face in disbelief. Alan didn't know how to throw a fist, let alone try to kill somebody. The man was a full-fledged gigolo. Bren stared at Sarah. He could see that she had no difficulty in squaring vengeance with conscience, but he imagined Lady Sarah had never expected to find herself in the United States, relating that she was in danger. "Did Alan say who was part of his operation?" he asked, rubbing at his cheeks, almost as though feeling the blood drain from them.

"There's Governor Linford Mills," she said nonchalantly.

"Governor Mills!" Bren berated. "Come on. You're going too far now."

"A Senator Stockton and Congressman Izenberg," Sarah persisted. "And there was another guy, I didn't get his name. I think there may be more."

Bren swallowed, his body shaking with anger. Detective McKinley had said Sarah was found high on something. He wondered if he had been close to the truth. "You discovered all this last night?"

Lady Sarah nodded. "Alan mentioned your name. He was asking me whether I thought you knew anything."

"Nothing like this," Bren revealed on a caustic note, imagining his brother-in-law was more frightened of being thumped than trafficking guns. "I hired a private detective to watch him and to keep Alan's affairs away from his wife. My sister is a vulnerable woman and I didn't want her to do anything . . . stupid. The private detective's job was to ward off the mistresses. If Alan thinks I know something, why hasn't he made a move?"

"I don't know," Sarah returned harshly. She realized Bren was not taking her seriously. "C'mon, you must've realized that corruption exists in all governments. This can't be new to you."

"Be careful what you're saying," Bren warned.

"Alan's outside the system," Sarah said. "So how come he knows so much? Maybe he's taking orders."

Bren's brows narrowed. He was rather hoping he was among a new breed of politicians. That he, and others like him, exercised influence that would far outweigh the old breed of political insiders playing by their own rules. It was all about who was in the center of the maze and who was not. For among all the yardsticks Washington was measured by, access was primary. This was something Bren was aware of and so he knew Lady Sarah had a point.

"I don't know how many people Alan knows," Bren finally admitted. There was always another circle within a circle to penetrate. A couple of minutes with a key player in a corridor, a committee room, or on the damn street was sometimes all it took.

"There must be someone you can trust who'll believe my story," Sarah offered. "I don't know about the police. I think Alan's people may have got some of them in their back pocket, too. I'm afraid he's going to find me."

Bren racked his brain. "The only person I've called who knows you're here is your stepdaughter."

Lady Sarah's eyebrows arched. "Latisha?"

Bren felt a jolt of lustful adrenaline shoot through his system at the potent mention of her name. "Actually, I called Josette."

"That means Latisha will be coming over," Sarah remarked nervously. "I don't want her caught up in any trouble. You need to call somebody before she gets here."

Bren remained wary of the gravity of the situation, a part of him unconvinced that his brother-in-law would have such power and access within his slithering, boneless, and conniving body. "What makes you think Alan was trying to kill you?"

"I got into the car in Manhattan," Sarah persisted, imploring Bren to believe her. "I was in it five minutes tops when he injected a needle into my leg."

"Did you see the needle?" Bren challenged.

"No," Sarah conceded. "But I felt it."

"You felt it."

"It hurt," she retorted, peeved at the congressman's cynical tone. "I knew if I didn't start to fight or do something, I would probably pass out and wind up dead somewhere."

"So you, what . . . tried to take control of my car?" Bren guessed.

"I didn't know what I was doing," Sarah admitted, still frightened from what she had gone through. "I just kept lashing out and the next thing I remembered was Alan hitting another car. We slammed right into it. When I awoke, paramedics were all over the place, Alan was gone, and two police officers arrested me."

"And that's when you gave them my name?" Bren exclaimed.

"I'm trying to protect you," Sarah insisted, objecting to the way Bren was digesting the news. "I know it all sounds like something . . . out of a movie, but it's true. Besides, you were the only person I knew in New York. There must be someone you can call."

"And what do I tell them?" Bren countered, unsure he wanted to level any accusations. "I've met Congressman Izenberg. And Linford is actually a close friend. I play golf with the man. I can't start naming names without evidence."

"Then you, Latisha, and I are all treading on thin ice," Sarah warned, her tone becoming highly pitched.

"What's Latisha got to do with anything you're telling me?" Bren demanded, aware that his heart had suddenly lurched forward in his rib cage. He pictured Latisha's adorable face, the kiss he had left on her lips, and frowned at Sarah.

"That was something else Alan talked about," Sarah informed him wryly. "You and Latisha. He's paranoid about what you both know. Like I said, I don't want my stepdaughter involved in any trouble. So you call someone, now."

Bren thought for three brief seconds about the cargo-loading papers Chico Maccola had found at his sister's house. He began to ponder the theory whether Alan was really involved in something. Whatever it was, he cared enough about Latisha to investigate Sarah's story. "I hope you're right about this," he breathed, standing to his feet, aware that if he were in any way to cast suspicion on another member of Congress without indisputable evidence of guilt, he could be hanged, drawn, and quartered. "I'll just go get my document case."

Only then did Bren become shockingly stunned. A quick replay of the events of last night unfolded in his mind like a lightning bolt. Bren was struck with the full force of it when he realized what he had left behind in the limousine. His briefcase, holding important printed matter of a sensitive nature, and which he had intended to show Bobby Fischer, his political adviser, was probably now in the hands of a total stranger. He swore a profanity.

Lady Sarah was on instant alert. "What is it? What's the matter?"

"I'm in big trouble," Bren said, quickly making large strides toward the telephone, his brain thumping wildly at how easily the contents of his briefcase could confirm with everything Sarah had told him. "And I don't know how to get out of it."

Chapter Fourteen

Latisha was dismayed to find herself right back at the place where she had begun her first adventure with Bren Hunter. She had canceled her appearance at the forty-second Jamaica's Year of Independence Ball, a celebration sponsored by her U.K. trust—which included a cabaret, Caribbean cuisine, and a raffle—to return to the quiet hamlet of Rye.

On her phoning the house from the airport, Bren, in a troubled voice, had made a simple request that she talk to no one and take the limousine he had arranged right away. Latisha had no idea what to make of it. Was Lady Sarah really that ill? She had thought this throughout the entire flight. And why hadn't Bren sounded pleased to hear from her? This had added to her fear all the more.

And now here she was, right outside Congressman Bren Hunter's door. Latisha looked around at the green trees, the cut lawns, and the trimmed hedges. The road, as usual, seemed quiet, though she was almost convinced there were more cars parked than was customary for just after midday. Suddenly, a brief moment of turbulence shook her body. She was to remember the other times she had been at this house, her first visit after the Fourth of July. She had, of course, been there by invitation of the wrong person. Graham Jefferson was to quickly become someone named Alan Clayton, and behind his handsome facade was a man attempting to make her his mistress.

Latisha's body shook again at the mere thought of her stepmother having suffered a similar debauchery by the same man. That fate could be so cruel as to strike them both. Had she herself become intimately involved with Alan as did Sarah and his wife, she might have been doubting her own sanity right now. For when a woman gives her love to a man who refuses to return it, everything she is easily falls apart.

And this was why, on her journey to the United States, Latisha had decided to keep a wide berth from Bren Hunter. She was to collect Lady Sarah, thank the congressman for his hospitality in looking after her stepmother, then leave. There was to be no room for reconciliation or for addressing their feelings for one another. She did not even want to think about any ifs, buts, or maybes. That was the plan. With this resolve firmly implanted on her mind, Latisha knocked on the door of the converted horse barn.

Enough time passed for her to admire the copper glass awnings above her head before the door was answered by a Caucasian-looking man Latisha did not recognize. There was only one thing she knew for sure. He looked official. From his double-breasted gray suit, polished black shoes, white shirt, and dark blue tie, to the sweeping cut of his brown hair. His piercing brown eyes gave his approval of her general appearance with the swift appraisal of a man trying to catch the eye of a woman. And then he spoke sharply.

"Latisha Fenshaw?"

She nodded. "Yes."

"I'm Bob Fischer," he said, widening the door to allow her in. "The congressman has been expecting you. He's about to air a five-minute news segment."

"Oh," Latisha answered, bewildered, stepping over the threshold.

She became alarmed the moment her small suitcase was immediately taken from her. The plainclothed security personnel at the front door kept a straight face while instructing her to pass over her handbag and to keep up with Bob. Latisha obeyed on seeing the handgun in his holster and followed Bob's lead, quickly throwing a glance along the hallway, until she made it into the main living room. On reaching there, she stared aghast.

The first thing that met her gaze was a mobile TV camera facing someone seated in a chair. Only his feet were visible to her—black socks, black leather shoes, black tailored trousers—for the room where she had loved to sit by the open fire was full of people. Cable wires leading to two large lights threaded beneath her feet on the hard wooden wide-plank barn floor. At either side of the large open windows, and particularly by the door that led out to the garden that overlooked Long Island Sound, were four more security personnel wearing earpieces, their long arms folded against the front of their bodies like soldiers awaiting command.

For all intents and purposes, the furniture that

would normally circle the main fireplace had
been pushed to the far side of the room to accommodate the cluster of people who were
talking quickly among one another, passing orders to and fro as though their lives depended on
it. Latisha knew immediately that they were
members of a news team the moment she caught
the familiar face of a well-dressed woman clutch-
ing a cushioned microphone with the word NEWS
emblazoned on it. She was being made a fuss
over off camera by a stylist, and Latisha soon realized that the woman was Maria DeMoss, a news
anchor from a well-known channel.

"Wait right here," Bob ordered quietly, leaving
her stationed nearby while he went over to the
person seated in the chair.

While Bob walked straight into the cluster and
leaned forward in front of the TV camera,
Latisha tried to look over his head to see whom
Bob was whispering to. When she failed to get a
glimpse, her eyes gazed upward toward the ceiling beams where she began to familiarize herself
with her surroundings, before she dropped her
gaze. Her copper-brown eyes immediately fell on
the face in front of the camera.

Bren Hunter stared directly at her. Latisha felt
her heart thump right into her rib cage the moment his eyes lit up on finding her there. And
then his face slowly broke into a brief smile. The
sincerity of it reached across the room and
touched something tangible in Latisha's soul.
Every steadfast resolution that she had made earlier in her head, that she could so easily walk
away and leave this man, quickly flew from
Latisha's mind. Instead, she found herself staring

at the one person who had so suddenly made her life seem much brighter again.

The stylist still hovering around him, Bren's square-jawed face shone like a midnight star. His nutmeg-brown skin looked smooth and silky, his firmly shaped cheekbones and straight patrician nose were primped for the camera, and his short dark Afro had been shaved and neatly trimmed around the sides of his face to give him telegenic appeal. Latisha was in heaven.

While she watched Bren's kissable lips being dabbed with a gloss to add color for the benefit of the camera, her own eyes returned the sparkle displayed on his own. And then he winked, greeting her, and a frizzle of heat rocked her body. The cheeky gesture was all it took to have Latisha's mind spinning with renewed feelings of hope. Before she knew it, she instinctively wet her lips and threw Bren a heartfelt smile of her own.

She could see, even with the distance between them, that he acknowledged it. The taut, invisible wire of their affection stretched between them and tugged in a manner Latisha knew she could not ignore. *I'm in love,* a tiny voice in her head told her truthfully. *This must be what it's like. This wondrous, light-headed, sexy, and deep emotion that makes it feel almost impossible to breathe.* Latisha felt herself gasp at how real it felt.

Bren had not taken his eyes off her, but instead had chosen to absorb every facet of her face. He liked everything he saw: the hazelnut brown of Latisha's complexion that complemented his own, her oval-shaped face and the glossy black hair swept around in cascading curls that reminded him of his attraction to her. The slender figure beneath the knee-high sixties-style pale blue plastic coat she was wearing, where her sculptured legs were a sight to behold in dark blue high-heeled shoes. And those eyes. He could never get tired of looking into those copper-colored eyes where he knew he lost himself time and time again.

He felt the tug of that imperceptible wire that closed the distance between them. It pulled at his loins, dug into his flesh, and pressed hard against a certain part of his anatomy that did not fail to respond to the sight of his fancy. *God, you're beautiful,* he thought of Latisha, as his gaze continued to chart her standing in his living room. *This must be what it's like to want something so badly, and then find it right there for the taking. It feels almost impossible to breathe.*

"We're counting down," Bob's voice broke in.

Bren snapped his gaze away and refocused. "What?"

"One minute," Bob warned.

Bren nodded. He looked across the room and found Latisha distracted by the arrival of Lady Sarah from upstairs. She had remained in New York, staying in one of his guest rooms awaiting Latisha's arrival. Judging by the animated way in which Lady Sarah was talking, he imagined that for the third time in as many days, she was probably explaining, yet again, the entire events of the last three days, only this time to Latisha.

Bren had known that when his document case surfaced, connections between the trafficking of arms and the report given to him by the secretary general on the United Nations Organization Mission to Africa would set off explosive headlines to fever pitch. It was imperative, as a member of the Democratic Party, that he be ready to take on the media, and a quick call to Bobby Fischer was all it took. Timing was crucial.

The election year and the presidential campaign had already raised the issue about appropriations under the Arms Export Control Act with an emphasis on the supply of weapons to Third World countries. Bobby Fischer saw Bren's opportunity to raise awareness before the election of a new president. He was strongly advised to make a strategic move on behalf of the Democrats.

When the stylist applied the last finishing touches for his appearance in front of the TV camera—a pin depicting the flag of the United States on the left lapel of his suit—the countdown began. Bren cast a quick flash at Latisha. She was seating herself in a chair Bob had indicated, her face drawn and seemingly pale at having digested what Lady Sarah had told her. He had no time to console her. As he stared back at the camera, a red light glared right at him. Five . . . three . . . one.

"I'm Marie DeMoss at CNN, and today I'm live with Congressman Bren Hunter, a representative of the Democratic Party, and whose remarkable admission three days ago sheds new light on the crucial issue of the Arms Export Control Act and set off an astonishing chain of events that has led to the resignation of two members of Congress and left others fighting for their political lives.'"

She turned toward Bren. The camera was on him. "Congressman, you must've been surprised when your briefcase was found in Central Park.

Do you believe it was deliberately stolen so that its contents would bring Alan Clayton to the public's attention, forcing him to implicate members of Congress in illegal arms trading?"

"If the case hadn't emerged, doubtless there would've been a cover-up with endless speculation as to how large parts of Africa acquired their weapons," Bren declared.

"So you are suggesting government involvement?"

"A select committee will determine whether that was the case."

"Sir." Maria DeMoss spoke concisely for the benefit of the TV audience. "The president at his press conference today has made it clear that his administration did not know about the two Republicans who are denying their involvement. Are you convinced a select committee will flush out the ringleaders?"

"I can't speak on behalf of the president," Bren said, "but I think answers will be found following a full investigation."

"The astonishing twist in this affair is that Alan Clayton, who is said to be a minor player and not a credible source, is in fact your brother-in-law," Maria DeMoss remarked, amazed. "Surely there could be an implication that you are also involved?"

"I'm not," Bren stated emphatically. "I have done nothing to breach my duty to my country or the office I serve."

"But the relevant evidence implicating Alan Clayton was found in your briefcase," DeMoss accused. "Along with an official eyes-only report of a sensitive nature. Can you explain how you came to be in possession of either paper?"

"They were part of a fact-finding mission," Bren explained, "which I have been unable to use since both documents were sold to the media and printed in newspapers across America. I can only hope the outcome opens a public debate about how members of our government operate, manufacture, and control our weapons."

"Sir, it has been suggested that this is a deliberate ploy by your party to undermine the presidential reelection campaign," Maria said on a contentious note. "Any truth in that?"

"No," Bren said simply.

"Are you planning to defend your brother-in-law?"

"That's a matter for the state attorney general," Bren replied. "Alan is in custody and has promised to name names. Whatever statement he chooses to make will have nothing to do with me."

"His disclosure could mean we see more resignations?"

"That would be interesting," Bren remarked.

"One last question," Maria said, suspiciously. "Do you have any idea who stole your briefcase?"

"I have no proof," Bren insisted, on a final note.

"Congressman Bren Hunter, thank you." The news anchor turned and faced the camera. "We will be keeping a close eye on this story as it unfolds. This is Maria DeMoss for CNN News."

"Okay, everybody," a voice bellowed out. "That's a wrap."

Bren immediately pulled the tiny microphone

from his lapel and jumped up from the chair. He glanced across at Latisha and caught the fearful look in her eyes before he returned his attention to Maria DeMoss. The moment he saw the camera move away from her face, he was right over at her side. Bren tapped her on the shoulder and watched her swirl round to stare at him without a care in the world.

"Did you have to be that up front?" he demanded, harshly.

"This is hot news," Maria responded, shaking her head as though she truly did not understand Bren's wounded feelings. "We tell it as it is."

"To suggest that I could be involved?" Bren railed.

"You wanted to absolve your guilt, didn't you?" Maria proclaimed.

"Yes."

"So what's the problem?"

"I didn't think it would be like this," Bren said, annoyed. "You throwing suspicion on me to rebut it."

Maria shrugged. "Welcome to the real world. If you want to make it in politics, you'd better get used to it." And with that answer, Maria DeMoss turned to her crew and started calling the shots. "C'mon, guys. Let's go."

In what seemed like no time at all, the crew had packed up their camera, lights, cable wiring, makeup, amplifiers, and other equipment and left without a trace. Only the security personnel remained and Bob was already dismissing them, three for reassignments to other duties. While he did so, Bren slowly strolled over to Latisha.

She was still seated next to Lady Sarah, who

had also been entranced throughout Bren's entire live interview. On crossing the room, Bren stood over both women like a mountain displaying a few fallen rocks and dug both hands into his trouser pockets. Latisha could see how vulnerable Bren appeared as his gaze caught her own. In the time it had taken her to watch his interview, Lady Sarah had told her the final details about the entire explosive affair that had put Bren in his current position.

Latisha rose to her feet and knew that Bren needed a hug. He needed something deeply consoling to soothe the ravages of what he had gone through. And that was the first thing she did, put her arms around Bren's shoulders and pulled him close. She felt the rigidness of his body, the hardened muscles beneath his shirt and jacket, and moved closer. Only when those muscles began to relax and Latisha sensed that Bren had moved his hands out of his pockets and around her waist did she know he was truly with her.

There was an odd feeling of relief a few hours later when Bobby Fischer finally left with the last of the security personnel. The furniture had been put back into place, Lady Sarah had returned to her guest room for the night, and Latisha found herself sitting on the Navajo rug in front of the large fireplace, where Bren had built an open fire before handing her a glass of red wine.

It was from the same bottle they had been drinking earlier at the dinner table in the kitchen, where Lady Sarah had rustled up a hot meal for the three of them. Bren had tried to explain to Latisha everything that had happened after her return to England. Though she had been confused by all the details, there were still pockets of intrigue that had her asking more questions, all of which required answers.

"I know Alan's a gigolo, and a shifty one at that," she said, her brows narrowing. "And I always imagined he was up to something by the way he always dealt with me, but an international arms dealer, whose favorite trick was to get involved with wealthy single women to take as much money from them as possible to finance his illegal operations, is not what I figured."

"With help from a sophisticated network of people," Bren added, taking a seat next to Latisha on the rug in front of the fire.

His eyes said he was glad she was with him. Latisha was wearing a white cotton tunic with embroidery detail on the sleeves and neck line. The short pale blue skirt beneath was pleated at both sides and though he may not have been able to see her legs under the table, Bren was fully appraising them now.

Their slender sculptured shape glistened in burnished shades of copper and gold tones in front of the fire. Her eyes were lost in the flames, but Latisha's senses were fully aware of Bren seated next to her. His very closeness was like having a million tiny sparks of fire crackling over her skin, just like the flames licking against the wooden logs, burning them to cinders.

"These women must have given him money," she said.

"Did you give Alan any money?" Bren asked.

"No," Latisha shrieked, disgusted at the mere suggestion. "I don't earn as much as you think. All I own is my apartment in London, which my father paid for, and a third share of the *Caribbean Rose*. Besides, my Mum always told me never to trust a man who asks to borrow money."

"Good mother." Bren nodded his approval. "Lady Sarah lost ten thousand dollars, but I've promised to reimburse her."

"You have?" Latisha shuddered.

"I accept full responsibility," Bren told her chivalrously. "If I had done something about him sooner, she would never have suffered."

Latisha was quiet long enough to take a sip from her glass. "What will happen to Alan?" she asked a moment later.

"Since his name became public, seventeen women have come forward lodging formal complaints. He's alleged to have convinced some of them to part with money, jewelry, and even property. If the Justice Department doesn't get him for his involvement in this scandal, arms trafficking from Guadeloupe, they're sure to get him for fraud."

"I've brought the phony deed he's forged on the house," Latisha said, taking another sip from her glass. "It's in my suitcase. Did you know, Linford Mills came to see me at my mother's house in England to get it?"

"What?" Bren gasped, alarmed.

"He told me you had sent him," Latisha explained, confused. "I went to talk with Josette on the phone and when I came back, Linford was gone."

"What would he want with . . ." Bren paused.

"Sarah named him as one of Alan's accomplices. He and Alan must've spoken about it."

"And Linford may have realized a paper trail could be linked to him," Latisha summarized astutely. "Alan must've told him that he gave me the deed and Linford tried to recover it."

"I'm going to make sure the whole matter gets investigated," Bren stated confidently, making himself comfortable by kicking off his shoes. "They must've tried to raise money with it and I want the full weight of the law to come down on them both. If anything, it'll hasten the divorce between Alan and my sister."

"Veronica's leaving him?" Latisha gasped, amazed.

"She's already packed her bags," Bren disclosed, hardening his lips. "Apparently, the baby she's carrying isn't Alan's. It belongs to someone else, and she's moving in with the guy."

"Really," Latisha drawled, not the least bit surprised. She had long suspected something was not right in Tortola when Veronica was at her most tearful. "I'm gonna cook him up good," she had threatened. Bren's sister had pounced in the manner of a woman carrying more than an unborn child, but also a hefty secret. The remark had shaken her then, but the truth did not do so now. She repeated Veronica's own sentiments. "Like the old song goes, 'who's making love to your old lady while you were out making love?'"

Bren detected her tone, but carefully chose not to comment on it. Instead, he asked casually, "Is your wine okay?"

Latisha looked at the dark red liquid in her glass. She could not imagine why Bren was asking her this now, when she had sampled the wine earlier over dinner. Nonetheless, she felt the cool, lingering taste on her tongue of ripe blackberry and red grapes, with a hint of spice and pepper. She shrugged. "It's weighty with fruit. From your cellar, I suspect?"

Bren nodded, resting on his bottom and stretching out his legs. He roasted his toes comfortably in front of the fire while he spoke. "A vintage from the Rhone Valley in France. It's produced in a small region called the Cotes du Ventoux, east of Gigondas in southern Rhone."

The information held no meaning to Latisha, but she smiled and took another sip, nodding her approval. Another sip and she glanced at Bren. His expression told her immediately that he was struggling with something else on his mind and did not know quite how to communicate whatever it was to her. She imagined the congressman was not usually so tongue-tied, and it was not so unlike how she felt at that moment. Feeling unsettled and nervous, Latisha glanced up at the ceiling.

Bren's brooding gaze followed. "When I first bought this place, it was a mess," he breathed. "There were termites in the walls and trees growing in the gutters. I did a complete renovation, keeping it as barnlike as possible."

"You've done a wonderful job with it," Latisha admitted. "I liked this house the moment I first came here." She flinched at the sudden reminder. A sigh and another sip from her glass and Latisha decided it was time she spoke frankly to bring matters out into the open. "Where were you then?"

Ben frowned. "In Africa. Unaware of what was happening."

"And Halloween?"

"Back in Washington."

"The second of January, when I visited again?"

"In Boston, at my parents' home—with Veronica," Bren hastened to add. "Alan told us he had to work. We didn't suspect a thing."

"And the day after Valentine's?" Latisha probed further.

Bren had long decided that if they were going to talk, he was going to get everything off his chest, once and for all. "I spent it in Washington with Vanessa," he replied with honesty.

Latisha inhaled deeply, not expecting such a blunt answer. "Were you . . . are you still lovers?" she finally spat out, remaining calm and composed. Though the vintage wine had succeeded in sedating her, her heart was beating with wild anticipation of hearing more troubling news.

"We had learned by then to become adult friends," Bren explained slowly, taking a large sip from his own wineglass to steady his nerves.

"What does that mean . . . adult friends?" Latisha asked, not familiar with such a term and suspicious of it being some form of political double talk.

"Remember when I told you how easy it is for a man in my position to make a mistake and become involved in something he wished he hadn't?" Bren recalled.

"We were at the bar at the Sebastian Hotel in Tortola," Latisha acknowledged, momentarily taking her mind back there.

"I was referring to Vanessa," Bren confirmed.

"We were once childhood friends. She knew my background, my father, and his political success. She was among one of the first people to congratulate me when I was elected. I was no longer my father's son, but someone in my own right."

Latisha listened. That was what she owed them both.

"Vanessa was already part of a survival group in Washington," Bren expanded. "She showed me the ways of the city, introduced me to people, and in that capacity, we became more than colleagues. In that first year . . . I landed on an aircraft carrier, had dinner at the White House, went to see a space shuttle launch. She was good for me."

"And power, of course, is an aphrodisiac," Latisha responded on a jealous note. "She filled your need for an all-consuming power. I'm sure the seasonal changes in the administration provided a fresh crop of networks she no doubt kept you connected to, as long as you remained her man."

Bren flinched at the ring of truth. "That was the problem," he admitted, slowly. "In Washington you have to build coalitions with White House staffers, with people on the Hill, with various movements, and within your own party. Lasting alliances are important to making progress, but there's also the danger of having a special connection with someone, without intending it to go further."

"And Vanessa wanted it to go further," Latisha surmised from her personal confrontation with the woman.

"I ended it three years ago," Bren insisted in

earnest. "We became friends who kept up an alliance because we worked on the same side. My focus moved on to policy issues and my contribution to public service by protecting my constituents in Brooklyn. Vanessa didn't bear a grudge, because in Washington there are no permanent friends and no permanent enemies. A person who may be against you one week needs you the next."

"But she does bear a grudge," Latisha reminded him, still embarrassed by what had happened at Bren's apartment.

"She was just reluctant to concede that I had moved on," Bren corrected.

"And you know that for certain?" Latisha asked, unconvinced.

"I spoke with her only this morning," Bren intoned lightly. "She's helped me with advice on how to surf this political scandal. It's one of the downsides of being a congressman. You don't know what's going to wash over you next."

Latisha felt sick with envy. She stared at Bren, almost disbelieving that he could be so insensitive to her feelings. The heat from his skin wrapped around her like a cocoon, though the idea of his actually kissing her rapidly stiffened Latisha's spine and gave her the strength to resist. "Why are you telling me this?" she demanded, offended at how quickly his confession made her feel insecure.

Bren measured her reaction as one of distrust and immediately attempted to get to the point. "I'm telling you the truth about Vanessa and any intimacy we had is in my past. Whatever my personal future holds, it will never again involve her. And this finding you, then losing you every time we meet." Bren shook his head, while reaching out to touch Latisha's left arm. "I can't go through that again."

The gesture with his hand had Latisha's hormones reminding her that this man's body was too good to be true, especially for a woman who had gone without him for far too long. But her agitated senses registered a breath of caution in that the last few months of knowing Bren had been fraught with one problem or another. She felt ill prepared for any more surprises.

"How am I supposed to believe anything you say," she spat out, "when Sarah told me you'd left your document case in the limousine? It wasn't stolen like the news suggested."

Bren grimaced, wanting nothing more than to stay on the subject of himself and Latisha. "I saw it as an opportunity to take care of Alan for good and took it," he confessed, and readily so. "It was the only way we could all be happy. Getting rid of him."

"You took care of him, like you said you would?" Latisha blinked, hard.

"Just like I promised I would," Bren pronounced.

The breath caught in Latisha's throat. She raised the wineglass to her lips and drained it, no longer in anticipation, but rather in expectation. "This has been quite a day for me."

Bren gazed at her. He drained his own wineglass for courage. "It's not going to be easy being a congressman's wife."

Wife! The one word leaped into the forefront of Latisha's brain and hovered like a predatory bird. She carefully placed her empty wineglass on

the hearth by the fire and tried to think whether
she had heard Bren clearly. Because the last time
Latisha had heard that single, solitary word, she
had been filled with pain and foreboding. Now
there was a certain ring to it, an almost magical
element that enlivened her senses. Even so,
Latisha could not be certain what Bren was implying. She was now a woman who saw things in
the naked light of reality, and so she countered
Bren's statement with a question of her own.

"Are you saying that a congressman and his
wife could become embroiled in controversy at
any given moment?" she asked lightly.

Bren's lips grinned. He knew there was hope.
Latisha had not rejected him and that was all he
needed. "That's the nature of politics," he asserted in a more relaxed tone. "There's never a
dull moment."

"Is that so?" Latisha swallowed, watching Bren
place his own empty glass on the hearth where
the cinders of a dying fire were smoldering red
flickers of heat. He inched closer.

"Latisha." He took a hold of her hand. "Are
you going to give us another chance?"

Latisha felt her heart tremble with uncertainty
at the depth of the question. "Are you asking . . .
that I should want you now and not forever?"

"I'm asking that in time, when you get to know
me, we try and make it last," Bren clarified softly,
throwing her a smile.

Latisha tipped her head to one side, feeling
her heart melt at his captivating smile. "I should
be angry with you for dragging me into this
mess," she murmured, thrown off guard when
Bren began to kiss her neck. "And for a lot of

other things," she added, when every instinct in her body propelled her to give in and accept Bren's strong tug to coax her onto his lap. Latisha's arms looped around his neck. "But somehow, it doesn't seem to matter now."

"And that's good?" Bren reasoned, holding her bottom firmly in both hands.

"The best you're ever gonna get," Latisha told him.

"Let's go upstairs," Bren urged. "I want to see how good this gets."

"Oh, you'll be on your knees," Latisha crooned, running her fingers down Bren's zipper before taking a hold of the tab. "Begging me not to return to England."

"Is that so?" Bren returned, sensing that Latisha had lowered his zipper. The single motion was too much. Holding on tightly to Latisha, Bren rose to his feet while her legs clung tightly around his waist.

"Don't drop me," she squealed.

"You haven't got any Gucci lying around for me to fall over, have you?" Bren joked, recalling the mishap in Tortola.

"No." Latisha laughed, as her mind flew back to the time Bren had tripped over her handbag, landing unceremoniously on the floor.

"In that case," he told her, already carrying Latisha across the living room and into the hallway, "be prepared for the night of your life."

He took the stairs, two at a time, made large strides toward the large double wooden doors at the end of the corridor, and kicked the master bedroom's doors wide open. Latisha held her breath when Bren laid her out onto his bed, spreading her arms and legs like a well-seasoned chicken about to be eaten. And then he was leaning forward, trailing hot, wet kisses from Latisha's throat, down her chest, to the waistband of her skirt.

Latisha enticed Bren with her lips, her teeth, and her tongue, returning each earnest kiss with heartfelt yearning and lust. They both moved to other areas that required a great deal more attention, as each item of clothing became loose and discarded. Their mouths joined and mated moments before Bren set himself between Latisha's parted legs. She was crazy with desire for him. He could see it in her eyes. The amazing sight of her made him dip his head and pull one nipple into his mouth, rolling his tongue around the hardened bud until Latisha was ecstatic with whimpers of pleasure.

"Now, please . . ." Latisha pleaded, circling her warm heated fingers around him. "Get a condom."

From that moment, the pace was rushed to a frenzy. Bren was off the bed and in search of a condom from within the confines of his bedroom while Latisha waited impatiently for his return. The silent communication between them was enough to transmit that they both wanted to make it last as long as possible, but the instant Bren returned his hot, rigid body to Latisha, the battle was lost. . . .

There was a low volume of voices. Latisha awoke to find herself secure in Bren's arms. The dawn of a new day was creeping through the bedroom curtains and she felt comfortable, warm, and happy that everything that had gone wrong in her life had suddenly seemed to have disentangled itself. At last, all was going to be fine, she told herself, and this one thought put a smile on Latisha's face.

She could smell the aroma of fresh coffee in the air and felt her stomach muscles protest for a hot cup. She rolled over, expecting to rouse Bren to open his eyes, and was surprised to find him awake. He was holding the remote control for the portable TV set situated on top of a chest of drawers, and was rapidly switching from one news channel to the other, half listening to the comments made. The cable bulletins, all providing coverage on the upcoming election, were still hot on the trail of the interview he had given the day before.

"Good morning." Latisha's smile widened.

"Sssh," Bren responded, commanding that she be silent. He saw her alarm and leaned his head forward to plant a kiss on her forehead. "I just need to hear this."

Latisha followed his gaze to the TV set. Bren was being accused by some of his colleagues of media hogging, but to those who really knew him, he did not fit the image of a media-hungry black politician. He was described by others as a brainy legislator, quick to master important issues and to make a policy point clear. Latisha listened intently with Bren until the news network ran a commercial break.

It was only then that she spoke. "Has your reputation weathered the storm?"

"It'll blow over soon," Bren told her on a long

sigh. "The presidential reelection campaign will take precedence in a couple of days."

Latisha nodded in agreement. "So," she said smoothly, moving away from the somber subject of the latest political scandal. "This is what it's like to be a congressman, making love all night and awaking to find a beautiful woman in your arms."

Bren's gaze locked on Latisha. "I hope Lady Sarah didn't hear us," he remarked, slightly embarrassed.

"Smells like she's brewed coffee," Latisha told him.

"Now, this is what I call power," Bren teased. "One woman in my bed, another downstairs making breakfast."

Latisha elbowed him. "I don't share my man."

"Good," Bren approved, snuggling his body closer to the warm, velvety flesh he could feel beneath the sheets. "'Cause I don't share my woman. And quite frankly, after last night, you're all that I need." He dipped his head forward and took Latisha's lips in a soft, bruising kiss. They were momentarily lost in each other when the commercial break ended.

"This just in," the news anchor reported. "A man apprehended two days ago and alleged to be involved in a government inquiry into the trafficking of illegal arms is today on the run. Alan Clayton, who is linked—"

"Alan Clayton!" Bren's lips left their pleasure source immediately.

His attention went right back to the TV set. One minute later, the telephone next to his bed instantly rang out, breaking into his concentration level. Bren frowned while reluctantly reaching for the handset, raising it to his left ear, and expecting the caller to be none other than his political adviser, or some other member in his circle of camaraderie about to instruct him on what he should do. He was surprised when he found himself handing the phone over to Latisha instead.

"It's your sister."

"Josette," Latisha gasped, snatching the phone.

"Latisha," Josette roared into the mouthpiece, annoyed. "I've been waiting for you to call me. What's going on?"

"Chaos and pandemonium," Latisha answered, as she half listened to the news on the TV set. She was to hear that Alan Clayton had skipped a four-hundred-thousand-dollar bail, put up by his mother, and he was now a wanted man. But her mind was not on the whereabouts of America's newest fugitive. "Bren's asked me to be his *wife.*" Her last word was spoken on a high crescendo.

"Wow! Congratulations," Josette's voice rejoiced on the other end of the phone. "I can't believe you're going to be a congressman's wife."

"I know," Latisha replied happily, glancing across at Bren. His concentration had shifted from the TV set to the deep sparkle in the color of her eyes. "I'm told there's never a dull moment. And you know something?" Latisha expanded, as news of an ensuing police chase filtered into her head. "I shudder to think what's going to happen next."

The phone was immediately taken from her hand as Bren pulled Latisha against the hardness of his chest and took her lips in another sensual kiss.

Chapter Fifteen

"This is what's going to happen next," the male voice informed them, killing the blissful moment Bren and Latisha were sharing with each other. Alan Clayton watched as their lips abruptly left each other's and almost chuckled when he caught their full attention. "Get dressed, both of you."

Bren stared at his brother-in-law in shock. "You're not going to get away with anything if you pursue this," he warned, moving his hands slowly from around Latisha's body when he detected the loaded gun Alan was holding. "Just turn yourself in and I'll do my level best to try and help you."

"Shut up," Alan snarled. He looked across at Latisha, hidden beneath the sheets. Only her head and the top of her shoulders were revealed to him, with a shower of disheveled black hair pointing in all directions around her startled face. "I still remember the times we spent in that bed."

"Not that we ever did anything while we were in it," Latisha uttered, flinching sickly at the awful reminder.

Alan's eyes flickered a fiery shot of anger. "I have a wife," he hollered back at her, ignoring the slur on his manhood. Sliding his glance across at Bren, he asked, "Where is she?"

"Veronica's here in New York," Bren explained, keeping his voice deliberately calm and almost soothing. "She's getting some rest."

"I thought she was at the hospital for that," Alan remarked, narrowing his brows in suspicion of Bren's answer. "They told me she was discharged last week, and when I went home all her things were gone. She's taken everything. Her clothes, jewelry, money. The florist shop's closed." He held up the gun and kept his eyes fixed. "Where is she?"

"In Brooklyn," Bren elaborated.

"We don't know anyone in Brooklyn," Alan bristled, pondering what it could all mean.

"She's staying at a friend of mine's," Bren expanded further. "He's taking good care of her." Bren suddenly frowned that he had let slip that Veronica was with a man.

"So who is *he* . . . this friend?" Alan demanded hotly.

"Why don't you put the gun down and we can talk about this properly?" Latisha inserted in a bout of bravado.

"Shut up," Alan said. His gaze shifted to Bren. "Who is he?"

Bren shrugged. "He works for me."

"He's a politician like you?" Alan probed. His brows rose in amazement.

"No," Bren exclaimed. "He works for me in an unofficial way."

Those same brows dipped in speculation. Alan began to think. Within seconds, it soon became clear he was beginning to piece together the true meaning of what Bren was suggesting. "What is he . . . FBI . . . CIA?"

"A private investigator," Bren clarified, his voice belying his concern of the situation facing him and Latisha both. "I hired him last year to quietly dismiss each one of your affairs. None of the women let on to us that you were using them for money. I can only imagine that they remained in contact with you and that my investigator didn't do a thorough enough job."

"What's his name?" Alan demanded. His voice was low and troubled.

"I'm afraid I can't tell you that," Bren informed him slowly.

"I want my wife," Alan insisted on a determined note. "Veronica's coming with me. So you're both going to get dressed because we're going for a little drive to go get her."

"Your wife is pregnant," Latisha piped in, nervously. "She's not going to be in any fit state to travel, not after suffering from high blood pressure."

"Didn't I tell you to button it?" Alan snapped at her, growing more agitated by the minute, especially as the TV news report was echoing in the background. "I'm not leaving the States without my wife. I'll get her a doctor when we're over the border in Mexico."

"Mexico," Bren conceded, noting that the telephone handset was still lying on the bed. He had minutes earlier removed it from Latisha's hand long enough to kiss her, aware that she had not concluded the conversation with her sister. As far as he was aware, that had to mean Josette was still on the line and possibly listening in on what was going on. "Listen to me," he said, trying to reason with Alan. "Let me call Bobby Fischer's office. He's my political adviser. He can make suggestions on who we can call to see you through this."

"Let's go and get my wife," Alan persisted.

"Okay," Bren conceded, accepting defeat. "Why don't you and I go into Brooklyn and get Veronica? We don't need to take Latisha."

"Yes, we do," Alan insisted. "She knows too much."

Latisha shook her head in the negative, feeling completely vulnerable while naked beneath the sheets with Bren. That morning she had thought everything were going to be all right; now disaster had struck again. Whatever chase the news was reporting, it could not possibly involve Alan. He was right there in Rye, in Congressman Bren Hunter's bedroom, pointing a gun in their direction. She watched Alan's eyes veer downward, almost in lurid approval of what little flesh he could glimpse of her, when he spotted the telephone handset.

"Alan—" Bren began, hopeful of filtering through to his brother-in-law's troubled mind.

"Who's on the line?" Alan clipped, seeing the handset tipped upright.

"Nobody," Bren and Latisha replied in unison.

"Hang it up," Alan ordered. "Now."

Bren wasted no time putting the handset back into its cradle. He turned to Alan. "What now?"

"You both get dressed," Alan instructed, waving the gun frantically from side to side. He looked at Latisha. "Don't mind me. I've seen it all before."

Latisha felt the red-hot blood of angry frustration pump through her system as she glared at Alan Clayton. But there was no courage left within her to fire back a remark, because she was not clear what he intended to do with the gun. All she knew was that he had tried to kill Lady Sarah, and that thought alone propelled her to wonder exactly where her stepmother was. Had Sarah seen him come into the house, and if so, had Alan harmed her? And if he had not seen Sarah, was she oblivious of what was going on in the master bedroom?

She pondered whether she should risk hinting as to Lady Sarah's whereabouts while gingerly slipping from beneath the sheets and turning her back against Alan to quickly get into her clothes. A quick glance at Bren and Latisha could see that he was uncomfortable with Alan's dominant presence, annoyed at Alan's threatening control, and furious that a handgun was being aimed in his direction.

It wasn't long before they were both dressed in the same clothes they had removed from each other the night before. Alan used the gun to indicate the direction in which he wanted them to go. A walk down the hallway and slowly down the stairs, and Latisha could hear Lady Sarah in the kitchen fixing breakfast. She turned behind and used her eyes to plead with Alan not to hurt her stepmother. He indicated with his free hand that she should remain silent and continue toward the front door.

On the doorstep, Alan quietly closed the door behind him and discreetly used the gun he was holding beneath his jacket to point at the car parked by the sidewalk. "Get in," he ordered harshly, throwing a set of keys over to Bren. "You drive."

Bren took a hold of Latisha's hand and squeezed it tightly. "We'll be all right," he promised her.

Latisha returned Bren a smile. "I hope so," she said in earnest. "I don't want to lose you now that I have you again."

"That's sweet," Alan said sardonically at overhearing them. "I wonder what the real deal is with you two."

"We're in love," Latisha said. "Not that you've any idea what that means."

"Don't make me puke," Alan returned savagely. "Just get in the car."

Latisha saw red. "That's why Veronica left you, isn't it?" she railed. "She got tired of being married to you. A suicide attempt wasn't enough to set her free. Thank goodness she's well rid of you now."

"What is she talking about?" Alan queried harshly.

Bren slammed the passenger door shut to ensure that Latisha did not say another word and to keep her out of harm's way before he dropped the bombshell. "Veronica is going to file for a divorce."

Alan became immobilized with shock. "Veronica would never leave me. What happened last year, that was because of my mother."

"Who made my sister's life hell," Bren said angrily. "She's well rid of the lot of you."

Alan stepped back, alarmed. Latisha glared at him through the passenger-door window and saw the danger erupt from him like a volcano about to explode. "This man she's staying with. Who is he to my wife?"

"Her lover," Bren goaded triumphantly. "And I'll guarantee you this. That baby she's carrying? It's not yours."

"Liar," Alan scorned. "Veronica wouldn't cheat on me."

"She's discovered that you're a loser, Alan," Bren teased further. "You didn't need to shoot your mouth off to Lady Sarah. We've had the house bugged and we know all about the cargo you've been loading from your father's shipping yard in Guadeloupe. Add that to all your mistresses, and the other things you've been getting up to, she'll never come back. In fact, just about your whole life is one big joke."

"Shut up!" Alan yelled, stepping forward. So moved was he by Bren's goading remarks, the handgun he was carrying slipped from the hand he had hidden discreetly beneath his jacket and fell at his feet on the sidewalk.

Bren saw his opportunity and took it. He lunged forward and thumped Alan in the face. Alan bounced against the car, thrown off guard for three seconds, then recovered sufficiently to make an attack on Bren. He pushed his head directly into Bren's stomach and drove him all the way from the sidewalk and onto the drive. While the two men engaged in the throwing of fists, Latisha leaped from the car and picked up the handgun. Still holding it, she ran into the house and alerted Lady Sarah.

"Sarah, call the police," she yelled toward the kitchen, throwing the handgun behind the telephone directories Bren kept at the bottom of the hallway.

"What is it?" Lady Sarah ran out from the kitchen immediately, wiping her wet hands against a cotton towel.

"It's Alan. He got into the house," Latisha informed her. "He's having a fight with Bren outside."

Sarah didn't wait to ask more questions. She was back in the kitchen and on the telephone handset that hung on the wall there, dialing out the relevant numbers. While she did so, Latisha reopened the front door and peeked through. She caught Bren land a right upper cut and felt her heart jump in fear for him. Overhead, she heard the murmur of an engine and allowed her gaze to trail upward, relieved to find a helicopter hovering overhead. It loomed low enough for two security men to jump onto the sidewalk. Latisha watched them instantly endeavor to separate the two men. In no time at all, Alan had been apprehended and handcuffed.

Only when the helicopter disappeared and Latisha saw the flurry of police cars arrive outside the house did she feel it was safe enough to venture outside. Bren welcomed her immediately as she rushed into his arms. Latisha hugged him tightly, then looked up into his face. He had a bruised lip and a swollen eye. But she could feel the strength in his body and knew only a part of his energy had been sapped.

"He's hurt you," she said, almost tearful.

"Not as much as I've hurt him," Bren breathed, casting a murderous glare at Alan while police officers ushered him into the backseat of one of their squad cars. "Where's the gun?"

"It's in the house, behind the directories on the floor."

Bren at once alerted one of the police officers and instructed him where to find it. "You okay?"

"Me?" Latisha sighed, then hung on ever more tightly. "It's you I was worried about. I was so frightened he was going to use that gun."

"Me too," Bren admitted with the slight shiver of his limbs. "Let's go back into the house."

As they walked on ahead, Detective McKinley materialized in front of them from one of the squad cars. "Congressman Hunter," he said sternly. "We're taking your brother-in-law down to the station. Is there anything else you would like to tell me?"

"Like what?" Bren quipped, placing his arms around Latisha's shoulders protectively. "He sneaked into the house and pulled a gun to my face while we were in bed."

McKinley glanced at Latisha. "With the lady?"

"With my fiancée," Bren corrected, looking happily into Latisha's eyes, but his voice was peeved at the detective. "What more do you need to know?"

McKinley backed down instantly. "Nothing. We'll be in touch."

"I want him charged," Bren hollered at the detective while he made his way toward his squad car. "You hear me?"

A number of Bren's neighbors had come out onto the street after hearing the commotion in time to watch the fleet of police cars depart the quiet hamlet of Rye. With his arms still around

Latisha, Bren nodded his head toward a few of them, muttering a nonchalant good morning before taking the step back into the house. He closed the door and almost chuckled at how dangerously comical it must have seemed for his neighbors to witness yet another fracas, and seeing the congressman caught in the middle of it.

"I'm beginning to wonder what they think of me," he told Latisha, mindful that they must have a million different ideas.

Lady Sarah immediately rushed over. "Has Alan gone?"

"The police took him away," Latisha told her, allaying her fears and knowing that her stepmother was far more used to the tranquility of life on the *Caribbean Rose* and not the turmoil of bizarre events that oftentimes emerged in the United States, particularly with someone immersed in politics. Not that she had become accustomed to any of it either.

"Thank the Lord," Sarah said, relaxed. "How did he get in here, through a window?"

"Through a door," Bren revealed, bewildered. "But I had the locks changed, so I don't know how—"

"It's my fault." Sarah blinked, annoyed at herself. "I went to empty the trash out through the back door and pushed the bin around. He must've slipped in without my seeing him."

"That explains it." Latisha sighed. "Gosh, there's never a dull moment."

"Are you both all right?" Sarah questioned, concerned at her lapse of judgment.

"We're both fine," Bren reassured her, slicing a quick glance at Latisha. Her hair was still a mass of uncombed bangs, and her face, devoid of makeup, looked heavenly fresh in the flicker of sunlight streaming through the slip of glass in the front door and into the hallway.

"I've made breakfast." She smiled, on a heavy breath of relief. "And coffee. I know I need a cup. Would you both like some?"

Bren looked down at the adorable woman snuggled against his arm. "Actually," he said on a hoarse note, "I'm gonna need help nursing this eye upstairs."

"Okay, I'll see you two in a little while." Sarah nodded, heading back toward the kitchen.

Latisha smiled as she and Bren went up the stairs. They negotiated their way back to the master bedroom between kisses. On reaching there, the TV set was still reporting, only it was old news. The recent events had not yet hit headlines. Latisha walked over to the set and turned it off. She had no more stomach to listen to what the chattering masses were reporting or discussing. All she wanted was to be back in bed with Bren and to remember how happy she was when she had awoken that morning.

"I'll get some cotton balls and warm water," she told Bren, as he sank onto the bed and began to kick off his shoes.

"No," he said, patting the vacant space next to him for Latisha to join him there. "Your kisses will be enough." He pulled up the sleeve on his shirt and pointed at his elbow.

Latisha grinned and obeyed his instruction. She kissed his grazed elbow. "That feel better?"

"Yes." He pointed at his swollen eye.

Latisha kissed there, too.

He pointed at his bruised lip. She kissed the bottom lip first and then the top lip. Bren groaned, deep in his throat, controlling the urgent need to start again where he had left off before Josette telephoned. Then, as if on cue, the phone was singing out again. Bren moaned, and Latisha reached out and answered it.

"It's Josette," she told Bren before engaging in the conversation. She quickly explained that everything was fine and that she would return a call later. Finally, when Latisha returned her attention to Bren, she was equally eager to get right back into bed.

"Let's start this morning all over again," she breathed, as a tremor of pure reaction shot through her.

"I'm all for that," Bren agreed, as he put his mouth to her throat and secured several kisses there. "Just do me one favor."

"What's that?" Latisha asked, her eyes closed, her heart sinking into the moment.

"Before anything else happens while I'm still a congressman in this great country, lock the door," he ordered, seductively. "And take the damn phone off the hook. . . ."

ABOUT THE AUTHOR

Sonia Icilyn was born in Sheffield, England where she still lives with her daughter in a small village which she describes as "typically British, quiet, and where the old money is." She graduated with a distinction level private secretary's certificate in business and commerce and also has a master's degree in writing. *Significant Other*, her first romance novel, was published in 1993. Since then, she has added six titles to her name. She has been featured in *Black Elegance, Today's Black Woman, Woman 2 Woman, New Nation,* and her work has appeared on the *Ebony* recommended books to read list. Sonia is the founder and organizer of the African Arts and Culture Expo and the British Black Expo in Great Britain. She is also CEO of The Peacock Company. She loves to travel and realistically depicts her characters from the fine tapestry of the African diaspora. *Roses Are Red* was her first title for Arabesque, followed by *Island Romance, Violets Are Blue,* the sequel, *Infatuation, Possession, Smitten* and most recently, *Valentine's Bliss,* a short story in the Arabesque anthology *A Thousand Kisses.* She would love to hear from her readers at:

P. O. Box 438
Sheffield S1 4YX
ENGLAND

Or e-mail her by visiting her Web site at: *www.soniaicilyn.com.*

More Arabesque Romances by
Donna Hill

Arabesque Romances
by *Roberta Gayle*

__**Moonrise**   **$4.99US/$5.99CAN**
    0-7860-0268-9

__**Sunshine and Shadows**   **$4.99US/$5.99CAN**
    0-7860-0136-4

__**Something Old, Something New**   **$4.99US/$6.50CAN**
    1-58314-018-2

__**Mad About You**   **$5.99US/$7.99CAN**
    1-58314-108-1

__**Nothing But the Truth**   **$5.99US/$7.99CAN**
    1-58314-209-6

__**Coming Home**   **$6.99US/$9.99CAN**
    1-58314-282-7

__**The Holiday Wife**   **$6.99US/$9.99CAN**
    1-58314-425-0

Available Wherever Books Are Sold!

Visit our website at **www.BET.com**.